Cop

All rights reserved

The characters and events portrayed in this book are fictitious. Any similarity to real persons, living or dead, is coincidental and not intended by the author.

No part of this book may be reproduced, or stored in a retrieval system, or transmitted in any form or by any means, electronic, mechanical, photocopying, recording, or otherwise, without express written permission of the publisher.

This book mentions various nationalities, races, ethnicities, and countries; various governmental, political, economic, and social systems; and various groups of people and organizations. This book is not meant to insult, stereotype, criminalize, or otherwise offend people of said nationalities; races; ethnicities; countries; governmental, political, economic, and social systems; or people in said groups or organizations. This book is a work of fiction.

ISBN-13: 978-1-955225-00-7

Cover design by: Natalia Junquiera
Printed in the United States of America

STRATOTECH 027

M.T. Lancet

To Anger, the side that drives me to fight

TERMS AND PHRASES

Rex is Jewish, and her story is set over a century into the future; as such, some of the terms used might not be familiar. Here is a reference list of terms used in this story.

ben-zonna—Hebrew for "son of a b***h"

b'hatzlacha—Hebrew for "good luck;" literally, "with success"

chara—Hebrew for "s**t"

dump—trash can

dump-crap—combination of garbage and crap; the equivalent of s**t

goel-nefesh—Hebrew for "nasty," "disgusting"

hawk—a nickname; the equivalent of "dawg"

kelba—Hebrew for "b***h"

khatikhat kharah—Hebrew for "piece of s**t"

khr shvr—Hebrew for "bulls**t"

manyak—Hebrew for "b*****d"

mitnakesh—Hebrew for "assassin"

on the other edge of the blade—on the other hand

precious burning *(insert noun)*—This term is adjectival, used much the same way as "bloody" is today.

screening—movie

slip the cut—to go south, to fail. Term originates from the phrase "make the cut;" if it doesn't make the cut, it "slips the cut."

tohki wanaphika ni—Sioux for "good luck"

zobie—derivative of Hebrew term for "f**k it"

HELL-BENT

Part 1

0.1

She had been hiding from him her whole life. Today was no different. The shadowed opening of the hut, with its drawn-back curtain, felt like a thin layer of clothing over a patch of cold skin. It was no protection from his dark, piercing eyes. Drunk as he was, he would still give her a savage beating if he caught her. Anger rose in her chest, and she fought to keep it from overwhelming her. She shouldn't have to hide. She should be able to face him, to put his face in the dirt. It would be so easy. She imagined the satisfaction flooding through her adrenaline-pumped body as she hurled him to the ground and forced him to stop coming after her. But she couldn't. No one could know what she could do.

Rexala saw his tall form behind a donkey cart, his back to her. As he strode away from her, tossing aside his empty liquor bottle, she knew it was her chance. Blending into the crowd was easy enough. Her simple headdress and loose linen pants were unremarkable among the sea of other covered heads and thickly robed figures. She stumbled along with the bent, slow gait of an old woman to disguise herself from her stepfather's prying eyes. Though her head was down, her eyes were constantly roving, her ears straining for any hint of his distinctive step behind her. She heard nothing but the chatter of vendors selling wares, the bleating of sheep, and the muffled racket from the nearby laser tag arena.

Rex came upon a stained metal tower—the tallest building in the town. As she passed it, she paused, as she always did. Between the tower and its adjacent building was a slim gap that afforded a view of the desert beyond. It stretched away in rippling dunes as far as she could see. Just as she was about to look away, a figure appeared in the gap. It was a desert wolf, lean and graceful, looking toward the town and the city of Jerusalem that rose up beyond it. Rex stared at the animal with envy in her heart. It stood out there, free to go where it liked, with no one to hunt it or capture it. She felt her heart thump in her chest as the wolf seemed to meet her gaze. Then it turned and paced away, out of sight. Releasing a long, dissatisfied breath, Rex set her teeth and resumed the tenuous game of avoiding her stepfather.

Despite her stooped posture, Rex made good time and soon drew up in front of her destination: a low, dark building with a scrubby roof and a heavy plastic door curtain. Slipping past a cart and behind a group of chattering women, she ducked inside.

The familiar black mats lining the walls and floor greeted her, along with the scent of fresh disinfectant. She strode to one wall and pulled off her outer tunic and headdress, revealing a fitted shirt underneath.

"Rexala! Good to see you!" Master Juko's words always seemed more jovial when he spoke Hebrew. He clapped her on the back with a force that rocked her frame, but she was used to it and gave him a smack that lived up to his.

"Good to see you too, Master." She swept her loose dark hair up on her head and secured it with a length of elastic.

Master Juko looked her up and down, then took hold of her arm and inspected the bruise there. "Your stepfather again? Or just a scrape from training?" The last question was one of foolish hope, given with a sad smile.

Rex strode across the mat to a practice bag. "I can't stop him." She struck the bag once with her fist, then once with her knee. "What good is the arts training if I can't even use it?"

Master Juko shook his head sadly. "It is of great pain to me to see one so capable submitting to ill-treatment, but our secret is of the utmost importance. Your father died protecting it."

"Secrets. Always secrets. No one ever knows anything. Only the Alliance knows. Typical." She struck the bag—right-left, right-left—then leapt back, breathing slowly. She circled it like an enemy she wished she could attack, and imagined her stepfather's hulking body in front of her as she drove two savage blows home. "So I just have to wait while that son of a devil gets what he wants. Just take it."

She laughed bitterly and closed in on the bag. Blow after blow, she hammered the rough surface, channeling all her anger and hatred for her stepfather into her fight. She hated feeling helpless to protect some secret. Her father had died serving the United Intercontinental Alliance—the pact that America; along with Israel and Europe; had formed during WWIII. After the Chinese and their allies—simply known as the State—won the war, the Alliance had made it their top priority to keep operations secret so the enemy couldn't get any more advantages than it already had. Now, with unrest growing between the four major State rulers from China, Russia, Iran, and Iraq, it was only a matter of time before a war for dominance broke out. The Alliance had to be prepared to hold fast during the battle and to protect whatever they had left. Rex, having been chosen from birth to enter one of the Alliance's elite special forces divisions, was now bound to the same secrecy her father had been.

That still didn't explain why the Alliance couldn't tell Rex how her father died. If he was dead, the State wouldn't be able to get to him. And if he wasn't. . . Rex shook her head, telling herself that it couldn't be; that he had to be dead. Yet a small part of her wouldn't believe it.

Rex hated the secrets. In a way, she hated the Alliance. Cruel irony had made them choose her to enter their new special forces unit. It was why she'd trained day after day since she was born. It was why she had to let her stepfather abuse her. He could never know what she was capable of.

Despite her anger, she knew she had to make it

into the force. If she was a soldier, the Alliance might finally consider revealing their precious military secrets. It was her only shot at discovering how her father died.

Or *if* he had.

"Your left arm. Keep it a little higher."

Rex smiled wryly at the routine criticism. "I don't give a damn right now."

"You will give a damn when someone's fist breaks through your guard."

"Right." Rex knew he was right. But right now, she didn't want to focus on technique. She wanted to focus on raw rage and see how hard she could pummel the bag she imagined was her stepfather.

***

Going home was the part of the day Rex dreaded most. She had to sneak in the back door of the hut and through the service room to avoid walking in while her stepfather was drinking. She peeked through the crack in the wooden door. He was still out—looking for her.

"Hi, Rexie."

Her mother's soft voice reached her from the kitchen. She always knew when Rex came in, no matter how quiet Rex tried to be. Rex went to her and wrapped her arms around her.

"Hi, Mother."

"You forgot this." Judith slipped a braided leather rope around Rex's neck. Rex touched the coin medallion gratefully. The necklace, handcrafted by her mother, was her most prized possession.

"Thank you."

Judith's worn hands stroked Rex's hair. "How was training today?"

"Better than here."

Judith sighed and turned back to where she had the day's government ration of flour and milk rolled out to make biscuits.

"Anything from the Domestic Violence Initiative?" Rex asked. It was a faint hope. All the charity initiatives were focused on the city, not a fading edge town like Ben-Valta. Her mother's words confirmed her thoughts.

"No, nothing."

She didn't say what they were both thinking—even if someone did take an interest in their family situation, it would be hard to separate them from Rex's stepfather. In ancient Jewish law, if a man died and left a wife and children behind, it was custom for his oldest unmarried brother to take his place as head of the family. After Rex's father died on a secret military mission, Rex's uncle was the only living relative to take his place—though a poor candidate for the position of fatherhood. But if they were separated from him, their livelihood would most likely vanish and they would end up on the streets.

And, despite the terrible situation they currently were in, the streets were even worse.

A knock sounded on the door. Rex tensed on reflex, but she recognized the knock as that of her best —and only—friend, Kani.

"Rex!" Kani stepped in and hugged her, smiling.

Rex tried not to wince as the metal of the other girl's cybernetic arm made contact with a bruise on one of her shoulders.

Rex allowed a smile to touch her face, too. "What did you do today?"

The black girl pulled her human fingers through her many long, tight braids. "I bought hair dye!" She held up a bag. Rex raised her eyebrows.

"How did you manage to get ahold of that?"

"An advertiser from the city square decided to come by! They only had a few samples, but I scraped together enough currency in time to get the last box. Do you want to try some?"

"No, I think I'm set. But I can definitely help you with yours." She had never been one for primping or prettying herself up, but she felt it was her duty as a friend to help Kani feel better about herself. The other girl, who was born without one of her arms, had slim chances of ever being noticed by a young man. In addition, she came from a family that was so poor her parents had starved to death in order to feed her. The kindness of the lady at the garment shop who had given her work was all that had kept Kani from the same fate as her parents. She was a fortunate exception to the widespread tragedy that plagued the lives of the people in Ben-Valta. Between war, disease, and starvation, everyone had lost someone.

"What did you do today?" Kani asked as they sat in front of a polished brass pot—the only mirror in the house.

"School."

Both girls had agreed on the code word "school" for Rex's training. Kani trained once a week at the arts school—Master Juko put on a basic self-defense class to disguise his real work—but Rex couldn't tell her friend that she trained there most of the week. Kani knew she couldn't be given details, so she didn't ask beyond that.

Kani began uncoiling several of her long braids. Rex joined in. Not for the first time, she marveled at the ease with which Kani used her cybernetic fingers. The arm attachment was old and dented in various places, and it squeaked with the other girl's every movement. It was hardly the smooth, high-tech "armor" that some wealthy disabled people could afford. China had triggered the Blackout by destroying all internet satellites—and as a result, all internet-linked technology—then had seized control of any remaining materials that would have allowed the rest of the world to rebuild. Any technological advancements came from them—at the cost of a small fortune. Which meant that people like Kani were left with spare machine parts as excuses for hands. Still, despite her disadvantage, Kani somehow managed to complete almost every task with normalcy.

"I also passed by the laser tag arena on my way back home..." Rex began, then asked, "How much of your hair do you want to dye?"

Kani paused, assessing herself in the mirror. "Just some strands at the front. They call it 'highlights.'"

"Hmm, makes sense." Rex stopped working on a strand further to the back that she had started to unbraid and moved her hands closer to Kani's hairline. "So, Isaiah was there. At the arena, I mean." Isaiah was the boy Kani longed for. The fact that he was rather popular made him an almost certain impossibility.

"Ooh, what did he say? What did he do?"

Rex smiled at her friend's enthusiasm. "He—"

The town alarm bell sounded.

It was a sound Rex hadn't heard in a whole month—not since the armistice with Iraq. But she knew exactly what to do.

"The shelter!" her mother whispered urgently.

They made for the service room, where a trap door led to a bomb shelter for times such as these. Kani went first, then Rex. Rex's mother had taken the first step down the ladder when the knock on the door sounded. She froze.

Rex's heart leapt into her mouth. She didn't want her stepfather locked in a tiny room with them. There was no telling how long they'd be stuck in there. That is, assuming they weren't all found and brought somewhere worse.

The knock sounded again. It wasn't her stepfather. It was quick and firm, not slow and heavy. Rex's mother hurried to the door.

"Don't—" Rex began, but her mother had already cracked the door.

A quick conversation was held between the outsider and her mother. Rex caught only snatches of it. "Attack," "Ishmaks," and "lockdown" told her all she needed to know. For years, the Ishmaks, a radical group of Palestinians, had fought a feud with some of the Israelites. Today was their first attack in a while.

The door opened and two men strode in. One was young and athletic, while the other was covered head to foot in a mask and tactical gear, so it was impossible to make out any details.

"Recruit Zero-Twenty-Seven," the younger one addressed Rex. "My name is Roth. I'm bringing you in for training at the base. Immediately."

Rex eyed the newcomer with distrust. "Why—"

Rex's mother laid a hand on her arm. "This is why you've been training. They're here to recruit you."

"I can't leave now. If the Ishmaks break in, you'll need me." Why did this have to happen now? During every other raid, Rex had been satisfied with the knowledge that if the Ishmaks sacked the town and found them, she would fight to protect her mother from rape, slavery, and death—secret or no secret. If she left now...

The boy—Roth—cut in, addressing Judith.

"We need to get her activated right now."

"Take her outside. We have a guest with us," Rex's mother said.

Kani peeked above the edge of the floor. "Rex?"

"Now," Roth repeated.

"Say goodbye, Rexie. It may be a while. Do whatever they tell you to do." Judith lifted an object from the floor and handed it to Rex. "Here, take your backpack."

Rex gripped the shoulder strap on the pack but refused to put it on. "Mother . . ." *I have to protect you,* she wanted to say. *I can't let them take you.*

Judith touched her hand to Rex's face. Her eyes searched Rex's as if reading the tumult of thoughts behind them. "I know," she whispered. She gathered Rex into her arms and held her tightly, then she pushed her away. "Go. You have to get out of here."

"Kani—" Rex began, but Roth took her by the arm and marched her out the back door.

When they were in the alleyway, Rex wrenched her arm free and turned on the two men. "Don't touch me again," she growled. "And what's the idea? You choose to come now, during a precious burning raid of all times, and you won't even let me say goodbye?"

"It's either go now, or stay around for goodbyes and get killed," Roth said flatly. "Drink this."

He held out a vial of liquid. Rex eyed it suspiciously. Then she remembered her mother's words about compliance. She grabbed the vial and gulped the liquid down. At first, nothing happened.

Then, the most excruciating pain she had ever experienced exploded through her entire body all at once.

Rex thrashed on the ground as waves of pain crashed over her. Her eyes were so heavy that she couldn't force them open, and her ears filled with a pain that shot into her jaw and down her throat on both sides. Every breath was torture, as if her lungs held white-hot coals. She couldn't even hear the screams that were ripped from her own throat.

She would not leave her own house like this. She would not let these two men see her like this.

She willed every muscle in her body to stop moving until her thrashing was reduced to shaking. Her screams became hoarse groans, and she gasped in air, though it burned. Slowly, the pain subsided until it was a dull ache. She stood, still shaking, with her head high.

"Strong and gorgeous. I like this one." Roth gave a wink to his comrade, then tossed Rex a pair of strange-looking boots. "Put those on, quick as you can."

Rex tried to stuff her feet into the boots. They were made of something other than leather, and the fronts opened with a series of clicking noises. Frowning, she placed her feet in, and the front of each boot locked back into place. "Where are we going?"

"You can't know—yet. You'll hate me for this, but, too bad." Roth seized her arm again. A wristlet on his arm expanded rapidly and clicked into place around her wrist like a handcuff.

"I said don't touch—"

Roth twisted his belt buckle and they shot up into the sky, leaving her mother, her best friend, and her entire life in the burning town below.

The world went black.

0.2

Rex woke up in a chair in a dark room. Only a faint sliver of light gleamed through the crack in the door. Next to it, her reflection stared back at her dimly from the glass on the walls.

Wait.

The walls were lined with mirrors.

Straps tightened around her arms as she shifted in the chair. Her stomach spasmed and she groaned.

"What...?"

Electrode cords stretched from her head and chest to a machine mounted on the ceiling. A computer—at least she guessed it was a computer—whirred quietly in the background. Rex stared at the technology. Since the Blackout, most computers had been trashed. Without internet, there wasn't much point in having tech that used the internet as its primary function.

The light flicked on, and she froze upon hearing the whisper of footsteps approaching. An Israeli woman entered the room. She was tall, with black hair pulled back, and had sharp features. Her dark eyes were serious and penetrating. The doctor's blue coat she wore swept behind her to the beat of her boots on the floor. She dragged a rolling chair from the far corner of the room and seated herself on it. With a few taps on the keyboard, the computer whirred louder. The electrodes vibrated against Rex's head.

"Name?" the doctor asked.

"Rexala Bat'Hai."

The doctor nodded. "Good. Don't try to lie while I ask you questions. It won't go well."

Interrogation. Great. But she simply nodded.

"Now, tell me a lie."

Rex was tempted to point out that the doctor had just ordered her not to lie, if only to be difficult, but swallowed the retort. "I love dirty water." There was no beep of protest from the machine, but Rex guessed by the woman's expression that it had detected the falsehood.

"Are you a terrorist?"

Rex frowned. This woman certainly cut to the chase. "No."

As if guessing her thoughts, the doctor remarked. "I'm not going to waste time with irrelevant questions like where you grew up. We already know everything about that."

Rex gritted her teeth. Typical of the Alliance to pry into her personal life.

"Are you or have you ever been affiliated with any terrorist groups?"

"No."

"Have you ever handled, experimented with, ingested, or otherwise interacted with drugs?"

"No."

After a lengthy round of intense questions, the doctor's tone changed. "How much do you know about your father's death?" Her manner was a little too disinterested.

Rex's head shot up. Now this woman was getting personal. "Why?"

The doctor's gaze hardened. "Answer the question."

Rex took a slow, deliberate breath. Something told her she didn't have a choice. "All I know is that he was an officer who died suddenly during the war. He wasn't at the enemy lines." Rex kept her eyes riveted on the doctor's. "That's all the Alliance would tell me."

They stared at each other for a moment. Then the doctor gave a single, decisive nod. She turned back to the keyboard, and the electrodes stopped vibrating. As if of their own will, the wires contracted, pulling slowly back toward their source. Rex tensed as the electrodes detached with a small suctioning noise. She remained wary as the woman pulled something from a case and shut it. Rex felt cold, wet cotton being swiped over the inside bend of her elbow.

"The drug they gave you should be wearing off. It activated your cybernetic implants."

Rex frowned. "Wait . . . implants?"

"You're a cyborg. No one ever told you? You had an operation when you were too young to remember."

"But I don't have any armor." Rex pictured Kani's

"armor"—her prosthetic arm.

"Yours had to stay secret. And the implants aren't armor. Not in the traditional sense."

Rex resisted the urge to search her own body for prosthetics. Instead, she shot her eyes back and forth, searching the unfamiliar room as if it would provide answers. "Where? And what for?"

"In your ears, eyes, and lungs, so you can breathe in the stratosphere. You're lucky. I had to get my implants recently. It's much harder for adults."

"So, those boots and the belt let me fly into the stratosphere? Why?"

The woman's fingers worked quickly as she prepped a needle to draw Rex's blood. "You'll see why soon enough. In any case, the activation drug you drank will probably make you feel nauseated for the next hour. I can give you tea if you need." The needle pricked into Rex's arm. "Look away."

Rex looked away just in time to stop a wave of wooziness. Still, she had to breathe deeply as her stomach gave another small spasm. She hated nausea, and this doctor sticking needles into her arm would only make it worse. "Will the drug make me throw up?" she asked uncertainly.

The woman glanced at her. "Yes." She switched the vial on the needle.

Rex swallowed hard. She hated throwing up, too. "Do you have something I can ... use ..."

The woman reached down and dragged what must have been a dump closer to the side of the table. "Use this. I'll unstrap you in a minute so you can lean over."

"Why do you have me strapped down?" Rex asked.

Something akin to a smile touched the woman's face. "You'll hear eventually." She pressed a piece of dry cotton to Rex's arm and pulled the needle free.

Rex swallowed again and a shiver coursed through her body. "I think I'm going to throw up now," she croaked.

The woman unstrapped her left arm again. The action seemed to take forever. She had just finished when Rex's stomach pulsed and emptied itself over the side of the bed. Luckily it made it in the dump. Rex spat bile and took some deep breaths, brushing long strands of her hair away to keep them from getting soiled. It wasn't as bad as she had thought it would be.

"The drug is mostly out of your body now. You shouldn't throw up again. You'll stay here while I run tests on your blood. I'll come back to finish checking you. Will you be needing that tea?" The woman's stare was so intense that Rex was almost afraid to ask. Almost.

"Yes."

"I'll have someone bring it in." With a quick movement, the woman rose and turned to the door, swinging it closed behind her with a bang. Rex was left alone to wait for her tea.

Someone—or rather something—brought it in only a few minutes later. The robot came on wheels, and it was surprisingly fast. It was a slim cylindrical shape with glowing blue grooves carved into it. An arm with a cupholder on the end offered her a tin mug of steaming tea. Rex eyed the little machine warily. The only robots she had seen were deactivated remains left over from before the war. One that moved around on its own was altogether too unsettling for her. She reached out and snatched the mug. The robot shot back out the door, which closed automatically behind it.

As she raised the mug to her lips with her one free hand, Rex tried to make sense of everything that had happened. How had she gotten here? The boy who picked her up must have brought her after she blacked out from the activation drug. Was she still in Israel? Why did they need to fly in the stratosphere? And what had happened to her mother and Kani? Her chest constricted with the thought. Her mother could be in an Ishmak slave truck somewhere, or already dead. Rex wasn't sure which option would be worse.

Her first order of business was to get unstrapped from the exam table. Setting down her tea, she tugged gently at the band securing her right wrist. She didn't understand how it was fastened. Did it work like handcuffs? Or was there a knot under the railing on the table side? She felt all the way around, searching for a buckle or a knot. Nothing. Gritting her teeth, she yanked at the band and gave a small yelp when electricity shocked her.

The door opened and Rex quickly composed herself, reaching for her tea. This woman kept coming in unexpectedly. Rex didn't like it.

The woman glanced at her with disinterest. "You'll be unstrapped when I'm done with my examination. Open up."

As Rex opened her mouth, the woman shoved the instrument inside and poked it around. Rex sighed and resigned herself to the intrusion. After her dental check-up, reflex test, and a plethora of other invasive procedures, the woman finally unstrapped Rex's other arm. The relief of freedom rushed over her as she stood up.

"Wait." The woman dropped her supplies into a box and put it in a cabinet. "According to regulation, you have to either cut your hair or braid it back every day. Which one do you want?"

Rex hesitated. "I'll braid it." It was Jewish tradition for girls to keep their hair long. There was a scripture verse that said something about long hair being a woman's crowning glory.

The woman nodded. "Someone will show you to the barracks." She pressed a button on the wall.

A few moments later, the doors shot open and a guard dressed in tactical equipment appeared in the doorway. Rex hurried toward him, eager to get out of the exam room.

"Rexala." The woman's voice caused Rex to look back. She smiled. "Welcome to Stratotech."

Rex strode to keep up with the guard, taking everything in. The closed doors and very few windows. The dim, flickering lights. Blueish walls. A shaft of sunlight here and there. She was just beginning to wonder if everywhere was this gloomy when the guard threw open a door and light burst in.

Mouth open, Rex stepped outside into the sun. The wind whipped around her, picking up her hair. She brushed it out of her face, squinting, and felt a layer of something itching her eyes. She blinked rapidly, eyes streaming, and after a moment found that her eyes could take the unusually strong gusts without drying out.

She was standing next to a steel barrier. As the guard began striding away, she craned her head toward the edge, then jumped back with a yelp as her forehead was shocked by some invisible force. She rubbed her head, glaring at the shimmering thing in the air before her. Cautiously, avoiding the invisible wall, she peered just over the steel fence—and her heart stopped.

Below her was nothing but atmosphere and clouds.

"We *live* in the stratosphere?" she exclaimed. For a moment, she stood, taking it in. The gusting wind. The clouds below. The cold, endless blue all around her, as far as she could possibly make out. With a start, she realized that the guard had continued on without her. She turned away and strode quickly to catch up with him.

All around her sat armored military buildings—deep blue steel walls that slanted up to flat roofs. One had multiple levels stacked higher than the other buildings, with one side made entirely of shaded glass that prevented her from seeing the interior. Atop the structure was a tall spike crowned by what looked like a glass platform. As she walked, Rex counted one, two, three . . . four, five buildings in the compound in total. Most of them were grouped together, connected by glass passageways. The guard appeared to be heading toward one of those. Her speculation was confirmed as he reached the door and shoved it open. He gestured for her to walk inside, then slammed it behind her. Rex jumped. Her reaction was stopped as she found herself staring at a long row of bunk beds, with some girls lying down and others moving around next to them. The barracks.

Everyone turned to stare at her when the door banged. Seeing it was another recruit, they turned back to whatever they had been doing. Rex walked slowly down the aisle between the beds. She was just about to ask where hers was when she spotted her backpack on an upper bunk. Reaching up, she pulled it down to find that it was nearly empty. Whoever had taken it had left only a toothbrush and paste, along with feminine products. Her hand flew to her collarbone. Nothing. She scrabbled around, searching with growing concern. Where was her necklace? It was gone. The only link she had with her mother was gone.

She would never see her mother again.

"Hello, ya just came in? Welcome! I think we're bunkmates."

Rex turned to see a girl with red hair and pale green eyes smiling at her, holding out a hand. The open manner she had made Rex distrustful immediately. She shook the proffered hand warily.

"I'm Bridget," the girl said with an Irish accent. Her freckled face still bore a smile. Rex assessed her more thoroughly and decided the girl was probably innocent and genuine. Her distrust eased a bit.

"Rexala. Call me Rex." She allowed a smile to break through, just a little bit.

"This is my first day here. I arrived this mornin'. I can't wait for orientation to start! I'm itchin' to do somethin'." Bridget fidgeted and squirmed all the way down to her toes.

"Why are you so excited?" Rex asked, thinking even more that this girl must be very naïve.

"Because I want to train! It's been my dream, ever since I found out I was a cyborg."

"Nice that you knew ahead of time," Rex muttered, rifling through her backpack once more. Bridget seemed not to notice the sarcastic comment.

"Did ya get your uniform?" Bridget asked.

Rex glanced at her bunk again and realized there was a small bundle on her bed. She grabbed it and shook it out. A piece fell to the ground, and she hurriedly scooped it up.

"Ya can go to the shower room and change. It's right there, in that hallway to the back." Bridget gestured to an opening in the wall. "Then can I show ya around?" There was a note of childish excitement in her voice. "Ye'll love it here. I already love it, and it's not even my home yet. My mother said it takes three days to make a place your home, and I haven't even been here for a whole day."

"Hm." Rex nodded, not in the mood to be reminded about the home she had just left. Clutching her uniform, she snatched her backpack and strode to the hall, which took a turn to the right and opened into a room with a line of stalls and showers. She dove into one and shut the door. It had a real toilet—one like she had seen the one time she had gone into the city—rather than the holes in the ground that were standard in Ben-Valta.

She did her business quickly as the tea she'd had worked its way out of her body, and hopefully the drug along with it. She then changed into the lower half of the uniform, which consisted of sky camouflage—cargo pants covered in shifting blue-and-white patterns—and the boots Roth had given her. She was about to pull on the dark tank top when the door was pushed open, almost hitting her in the face.

"Oh, hey, didn't notice you there," the girl said. She looked Rex up and down with an expression of distaste on her face. "You really need to do something about those marks. You won't get any men like that. And we might be in the military, but you won't get points for looking like you've lost in combat already, either."

Rex's chest heaved with the effort of keeping herself from putting a right hook into the girl's perfect face. The bruises, slashes, and scars across her torso were something no one but her mother had ever seen. Still, she could have dealt with the intrusion if the girl had simply turned away. But for her to make a jab about Rex losing in combat, when she clearly had no knowledge of real pain, was enough to drive Rex to educate her on the subject in the future.

"I'm not here for the men." It was the only thing Rex could trust herself to say without spitting a stream of curses. She yanked her tank top down so hard she was surprised it didn't tear. Shouldering her pack, she stalked out of the stall past the girl, her fists shaking with barely controlled rage.

Several other girls had come in and were changing or washing up at the sinks. Obviously they didn't care as much about privacy. Some of them looked her way and mumbled a greeting. Others remained in conversation with each other. Moving past them, Rex splashed water on her face and stared at her reflection in the mirror. Her dark eyes looked haunted, staring out of pits in her skull. After having her entire life taken away, it wasn't surprising. She began slowly pulling her hair back into a high, tight braid, her gaze still fixed on her face in the mirror.

"Recruits, atten-hut!"

The yell almost made her jump. All the girls in the shower room hurried out to the bunks, some still pulling on pieces of their uniforms. Grabbing her half-finished braid in one hand and seizing her backpack with the other, Rex hurried to the doorway. She tossed her backpack up on her bunk and then stood beside it, hastily securing her hair before putting her fists atop each other over her chest like she had trained at the arts school her whole life.

A hulking American woman paced between the two rows of recruits. When she reached the end, she spun on her heel and walked back, stopping in front of a recruit down the line from Rex.

"Recruit, what's your number?"

"Zero-Thirty-Two," the girl replied in a subdued voice.

"Speak up!" the woman bellowed.

"Zero-Thirty-Two!"

"Good!" The woman continued pacing and stopped, looking toward the opposite row. "Keep those fists on your chest! Haven't they taught you the proper attention stance? Much better!" she said as the offending stance was corrected. "I'm Sergeant Kelly Bailey. You will address me as Sergeant Ma'am. Today is muster. I will be assessing whether or not you have what it takes to be an Airborne Elite. For any of you who didn't know, that's what you're training to be. Flying soldiers, the deadliest on this side of the world. If you pass muster, you'll go into the first phase of your elite training. Any questions?"

No one dared to speak after the sarge's bellowing had stopped.

"Good. We start immediately."

***

The first challenge was a one-and-a-half-mile run, to be completed in thirteen minutes and fifty seconds. The boys filed out of their barracks to join them. They ran the circumference of the compound four and a half times. A guard stood at the starting point to mark when they had completed one lap. Sergeant Bailey ran with them, yelling commands. Rex kept pace easily, as did most of the others. Two of the smaller girls fell behind. Rex felt sorry for them as she saw them both throw up. If they were already this spent, they would have a hard time passing muster. Then she turned forward and concentrated on breathing deeply.

After the run came the push-ups, crunches, and obstacle course—crawling under barbed wire, scaling a wall covered in loose ropes, and sliding between a rope framework. The framework was to test balance and flexibility rather than strength. After the grueling routine, Rex's muscles screamed as she tried to weave between the ropes. She eventually got caught in a backward bend, supporting herself on her toes and fingertips, and had to find a way to get enough momentum to slide through. Just as she was about to push off with her feet, she caught sight of a boy who had come up alongside her. He was ahead of most of the other recruits. In a moment, he would pass her.

He turned his head and their eyes met for a second. Then she felt herself tipping off-balance, and she collapsed onto the rope. It burned the skin on her back as she caught the fall on her elbows. Grunting in frustration, she wriggled up to a crouch and continued the course.

Finally, the routine was over. Rex was covered in dirt and grime and had a dozen small cuts all over her body. She had thrown up about halfway through, and the taste was still in her mouth and sinuses. When her turn finally came to shower, she reveled in the three minutes she had to bathe. The cool water over her back was glorious. She opened her mouth and let water flow in, flooding until it washed away the taste of dirt, blood, and vomit. She scrubbed the standard soap that was provided into her hair, then rinsed it out.

"Time's up!"

She stepped out of the shower reluctantly, conscious of the scars on her body and hating the lack of privacy for what seemed the hundredth time that day. But the girl who took her place in the shower barely gave her a glance. Rex looked toward the sergeant hopefully.

"No towel. Stand outside."

Rex went to take her place in the line of girls who were finished showering. She stood with every muscle in her body tensed, daring someone to make a jibe about her scars or the fact that she was naked. A couple girls glanced her way, but looked down quickly when they saw the sheer intensity on her face. Despite the vulnerability, she had to admit, this was an effective system. The relentless wind whipped around her, drying everything but her hair in less than a minute. Mercifully, the girls were quickly allowed to go back to the barracks and change. Rex found a clean change of underclothes on her bunk and gratefully donned them.

The command for dinner came soon after and the girls trudged wearily through the glass passageway, its walls now darkened, toward the mess hall. Rex noted that there was a separate passageway leading from the boy's barracks.

As they came to the mess hall, each girl had to stop and do three pull-ups on the bar set above the door. Rex did hers easily. She had more upper body strength than some of the girls in line, who struggled to complete their set. Once she was through the door, she caught sight of the girl who had walked in on her earlier standing with a group and throwing glances her way. The girl said something to the others, and they snickered. Rex set her eyes straight ahead so she wouldn't turn to confront them.

Her turn in line finally came, and she filled her metal plate as much as they would let her. By the time she dropped down at the nearest empty table, she was ravenous. Despite the fact that the pile of beef, potatoes, and greens looked old and less than appetizing, she dug in with gusto. Bridget sat down next to her and tried to get her excited about the tour of the compound that had been delayed, but she was too exhausted to make conversation with anyone. Just as the call for the end of dinner sounded, Roth came by and tapped her shoulder.

"You did good out there earlier, gorgeous," he said with a winning smile.

Rex seethed. It sounded like something her stepfather would say, but the only indication she gave of her anger was a tightening of her jaw as she stood up and brushed past the boy.

After she tossed her plate down in the dirty bin,

she turned to leave and collided with a girl who looked American.

"Sorry," they both said at the same time. The girl gave Rex a wry smile. "I've been here less than a day, but I already know Roth's an absolute pain who's way too important for anyone's good. Don't let him get to you. If he hits on you, hit him."

Rex raised an eyebrow at the girl's direct approach. It was exactly what she had wanted to do a moment ago. "Thanks." They strode side by side in the line out of the mess hall. Rex felt a strange sense of connection with the girl, as if she were an echo of Rex's thoughts. "What's your name?"

"Alelta. You?" The girl's grey eyes searched Rex's dark ones.

"Rex. Good to meet you." Rex realized she meant it. After everything that had happened in the past few waking hours alone, it was nice to have someone to share a problem with.

After brushing her teeth, Rex made a beeline for her bunk. She collapsed on the rough blankets, not even bothering to pull them over herself. The tears that had threatened to come all day had suddenly become clogged. She lay propped on her elbows, her face above the pillow, her cheeks dry. Her mind raced as she agonized about what had happened to her mother. The Ishmaks could have her stepfather as far as she was concerned—he deserved it. She imagined her mother's kind, black eyes filling with tears of fear as the Ishmaks did Lord knows what to her. Her mother would most likely be tortured in a way more horrible than Rex's stepfather had ever done. Her loving, soft-spoken, gentle mother . . .

It was a long time before she fell asleep.

0.3

"Recruits! Form up!"

Rex woke from her fitful sleep with a jump. She slid out of bed.

"Good mornin'!" Bridget chimed. "Ohhhh, it's a beautiful day outside!" she sighed, stretching.

Rex wished she could have such a positive outlook. She had to admit, though, the day was beautiful. The sun was out, bright and early, and the wind felt fresh as the recruits lined up for roll call outside. The male sergeant for the boy's barracks called out the names.

"Recruit Zero-Zero-One, Falhelm!"

"Present, Sarge!" Roth barked.

"Recruit Zero-Zero-Two, Planey!"

"Present, Sarge!"

When the sarge called for Recruit Twenty, there was no answer. "Recruit Zero-Two-Zero, Griffin! Are you present?"

A figure stumbled out from behind a companion and squeezed between two of his fellow recruits. Rex recognized the boy she saw at the rope course the day before. His dark hair was tousled, and it was obvious that he had only just managed to get his shirt on.

"Present, Sarge!" the boy said.

"Don't hide behind your fellow recruits like a pork chop! Stand up in the front! Show me that inner wolf!"

The boy's puffed-chest attempt to look like his "inner wolf" was met with subdued laughter. The sarge rounded on the other recruits. "No laughing!" The grins were quickly hidden, although several pairs of shoulders still shook.

"All recruits, a mile run! Go, go, go!"

As they ran, Rex kept pace near the head of the pack. Not the very front; she didn't want to tire herself out. But close enough to avoid being seen as weak or a slacker. She caught movement in her peripheral vision and turned her head to see the girl she had met at dinner the day before—Alelta—drawing up alongside her.

"Hey there, comrade," Alelta smiled. Rex smiled back. The connection she had felt the previous night returned. There was a respect that Alelta conveyed that Rex liked. It reminded her of Kani. It was easier to trust someone who respected you. Rex hadn't made many friends in her lifetime, but she knew good friendships always started with respect. She nodded.

"Comrade."

Alelta gestured toward the front. "We should move up after the third lap. No sense eating everyone else's dust the whole way."

"I like the idea." Her breathing was still light and

relatively easy. She hoped it would stay that way. "Speaking of which, how did they make this training ground? Did they just transport a load of dirt from down below and dump it over ... whatever this facility is constructed from? Blue steel? I'm assuming it's blue steel."

"Yeah, this whole thing is on a steel platform."

"How do they make it airborne?"

They were interrupted by the male sergeant. "Shut those bear traps back there! If you can talk, you're not running hard enough! Pick up the pace!"

The girls exchanged another smile, this time rueful, and stepped up their pace.

As they came into the last lap, they both nodded and ran even faster, passing one frontrunner, then another as the first recruits began to tire. They were both at the head when they completed the mile. They stood bent over with hands on their knees to catch their breath.

"Good job," Alelta said between breaths.

"You too." Rex nodded. Their push to the front had been spurred on by each other's competition. Rex loved friendly competition.

Bridget made her way toward them and smiled. "That felt good! I hope they don't make us do anything else before breakfast, though. I'm starving!"

Fortunately for Bridget, breakfast was served immediately after the run. It consisted of barely warmed beans and meat with dry biscuits and a metal cup full of milk. Rex let the milk run down her dry throat slowly so she wouldn't feel sick. She loved milk. Even though this was a powdered mix that couldn't compare to the fresh goat milk from her town, she appreciated something that reminded her of home.

"You had asked how they get this place airborne," Alelta said from beside her. "From what I heard, I think it's some kind of new tech. It's also top secret, so no one can know any real details about it or where it comes from. Or where it's at," she added, biting into a biscuit.

"Secret like everything else. Hence the nausea drug," Rex said through a mouthful of her own biscuit. Alelta laughed, almost choking. She had to cover her mouth to stop a spray of crumbs.

"That's a good name for it! Didn't think of it like that. Although I didn't feel too bad afterward, fortunately. Did you?"

"Yah, it wasn't so bad. I threw up, but then pretty much felt better."

Up to this point, Bridget had been silent. Now her eyes widened and she opened her mouth slightly. "Really? I threw up twice, and I still felt bad after." She giggled. Rex wasn't sure why that would be funny, but she figured it was in keeping with Bridget's optimistic attitude in general. She gazed around the table. She hadn't had any real friends growing up, except Kani and a few other sparring partners at her arts school. It was nice to have people who would sit with her and laugh at the things she said. With a jolt, she reminded herself that she still had to be careful. This was only the second day, and there was still a lot of character to be assessed before becoming too familiar with anyone.

"Where are we, anyway?" Alelta went to pick up her cup, tipped it, and caught it before it spilled its contents all over the table. Rex raised an eyebrow at the girl's reflexes.

"No idea. The last thing I remember was being handcuffed to Roth and dragged into the sky. I'm assuming that if he pulled me all the way here, we can't be far from Jerusalem."

Alelta and Bridget glanced at each other. Bridget held a hand to her mouth, obviously hiding a smile.

"What?"

Alelta gestured for Bridget to answer and leaned back in her chair.

"Well . . ." Bridget began. She ducked her head as if embarrassed. "Ya were in a carrier when Roth brought ya in."

Rex frowned at her. "What's a carrier and why does it matter?"

"A carrier is a sort of harness they use to carry people up here. Like, on their backs." Seeing Rex's scowl at the image of herself on Roth's back, Bridget hurried on. "But that's not the good part. When ya were brought in . . ." She choked and her words subsided into bubbling giggles. Rex waited for her to regain her composure, unsure of what was going on. Alelta interjected.

"Roth had trouble getting you in. You thrashed like a demon. Do you have something against harnesses?" She was joking, but Rex decided not to touch on that subject.

Bridget finally got control of her laughter. "He's this huge lad who goes around actin' mysterious and intimidatin' and weird, but he couldn't stop ya from beatin' him up when ya weren't even conscious! It took three guards to get ya to the medical wing."

"Wow." Rex was surprised that she had been so damaging. The worst part was that she didn't recall any of it. Not a single bit. She didn't like a drug that could make you go savage and not even remember it. Now it made sense why the doctor had strapped her down to the exam table. Despite herself, she felt a small flare of pleasure that she had been an annoyance to Roth. "Why did he bring me in, anyway? Didn't everyone just get here today or yesterday?"

"I think Roth's been here longer. Not sure why. But in any case, he's probably going to be sore for a while—physically as well as emotionally," Alelta mused. "The point is, he could have carried you pretty far in the harness. I've heard that most of the Israeli recruits are brought in that way. I was brought in by plane from America. So I'm assuming we're somewhere in the Middle East, but it could be anywhere."

"Doesn't narrow it down much," Rex agreed.

"Form up!" Sergeant Bailey's command brought them to their feet.

Rex tossed her dishes in the bin and headed outside. Bridget struggled to gulp the last drops of milk from her mug and then caught up with Rex. They fell in beside each other, joined by the others as they formed ranks. Rex guessed that this was the moment she would find out if she had passed muster.

"Recruits! Today you begin your training as Airborne Elite assets." Sergeant Bailey paced in front of the three rows of recruits. "You've passed muster. You've worked your whole lives for this moment in your arts schools. There are only two unfortunate souls here who didn't make the cut." Sergeant Bailey turned, her finger outstretched, and all the recruits held their breath. Her finger stopped in front of one girl. "You." Before the girl could react, she whipped about and pointed at another girl. "And you."

Crestfallen and ashamed, the girls slowly stepped out of line. Rex could see tears forming in the eyes of one of the girls.

"Instead of combat, you'll be trained in cybertech maintenance. The physical training is less demanding in that field. As for the rest of you lot, you're probably wondering what the hell you're doing here, why all the secrecy, what's with the technology, all that dump-crap. Since the State won the war, the Alliance has been forced to live in subjection to their laws while there's been a fight amongst the enemy over who will be the main ruling country, yada yada; you all know that. What isn't commonly known is that China's sole objective is to establish a one-world government where they're on top. Right now, the State members are all allied, but eventually, China's going to demand subjugation. The other countries will either cooperate or they'll go to war and ultimately lose to China because Drachu Kuan is a murdering dictator with no remorse and a giant army.

"The Alliance has seen this coming and we've been planning for it for over two decades. The Stratotech Project is what you're all part of. It's basically a military experiment. Your parents were chosen based on prior military service and physical health and asked to birth a kid that could be part of this project. You were trained your whole life to fight, to be tough, and to live hard. Now, you'll spend the next ten weeks honing those skills so you can ultimately strike China at its crucial points where no one else has succeeded. Basically, you're all the key part of the Alliance's plan to overthrow the enemy nation before they gain complete and absolute governance over the world. Any questions?"

Absolute silence fell over everyone assembled. Just over fifty years ago, Rex knew, the sergeant's speech would have made her sound like she was a madwoman living in an adventure screening. Today, after the millions dead in World War Three and with the communist Chinese objective being one-world governance, it was a terrifying reality. How powerful was China? The sergeant made it sound like the other State countries would be defeated in a week. If that was the case, how could a bunch of new adults thrown together for ten weeks make any difference?

The sergeant shrugged at the lack of response and continued, "Starting today, you'll enter the first of three stages of your training—the compatriot phase. In this phase, you'll be tested on your ability to cooperate in teams to prepare you for teamwork in the field. Your teammates will become your family. You will trust them with your life, because when you're on a mission, that will be the reality. Teams will be assigned shortly. The other two phases will be the competitor and alpha phases. They'll determine who leads the units in the field."

This caused glances to pass between recruits.

"The cooperation in this compatriot phase will count toward your overall score. Depending on your score at the end of training, you will fall into one of four categories—alpha, beta, delta, and omega. You will become part of a pack with one alpha male and one female."

Rex felt a surge of pride and anticipation. She had always admired the beauty, speed, and cunning of the desert wolves that roamed in the wastes beyond her fading edge town.

"The Alliance knows the backgrounds and histories of each of your personal lives. It's a tough world since the State took power, and each of you has suffered something or has had some secret hidden from you. And . . ." Sergeant Bailey paused once more, her heavy gaze roaming over the recruits. Rex could almost hear the others holding their breath. "If you become alpha, you will have access to our entire intelligence arm, which should contain any and all information regarding whatever you want to know."

That caused a stir. The recruits couldn't help murmuring to each other or giving small gasps of astonishment. The appeal of full knowledge about any personal tragedy or family secret was a long-coveted thing.

For the first time in over ten years, Rex felt real hope rising in her chest. All the years of secrecy, of cowering before her stepfather, of unanswered questions—all of it would be over. She could find resolution to mend her broken pieces if she only knew how her father had died. And if he wasn't dead...

Obviously sensing the motivating effect of her statement, Sergeant Bailey didn't reprimand the recruits. She waited a moment, then continued, "Your scoring starts today. Am I understood?"

"Yes, Sergeant Ma'am!" the recruits chanted.

"Any questions, Compatriots?"

Rex was about to salute to get the sergeant's attention, but a boy's hand had already shot up.

"How do we know what to do to score well?"

"Good question, Compatriot. For each phase, there are general rules to score well. In this phase, cooperation and respect toward all your fellow compatriots will earn you points in the day-to-day lessons. You'll be given instructions before each test. Following directions closely will determine your rank."

Someone else asked a trivial question. Rex wasn't listening. Her mind was racing. The first phase was based on teamwork. She wasn't sure how much she could trust her teammates, whoever they might be. But she guessed the sergeant wasn't mentioning that even in this first phase, being part of a team would take some leadership. Most likely, she was testing the recruits—compatriots—to see which of them would go the extra mile in training. Leading? That Rex could do. She wouldn't be some delta or omega, running missions at someone else's whim.

She *would* be an alpha, and she would find out what happened to her father.

0.4

Rex turned out, by a marvelous stroke of luck, to be teammates with both Alelta and Bridget—or perhaps Sergeant Bailey had been watching them and saw that they got along fairly well. There were three boys and two other girls on their team. One of the boys was the recruit she had seen at the obstacle course the day before and who, just earlier, had been called out by the male sergeant. When Bailey assigned him to Rex's group, he strode up to where she, Alelta, and Bridget stood together.

"Hey. The name's Rideout Terrault Griffin, or Rider, if you can't get your mouth around all that." He reached forward and clasped each girl's hand. Rex shook hands warily. This boy was confident—she could tell by his firm grip. That could be a good or a bad thing.

"And you're..."

Rex realized the other two girls had given Rider their names. "Rexala. Well, Rex."

"Rex." Rider nodded. "You know, I've never met a girl called Rex. Did your parents think you would be a boy, and when you came, they were just like, 'Oh well, close enough?'" His gaze and lopsided smile were easy and full of energy. Rex searched his eyes for signs of insult, but saw only warmth and mirth there. She raised an eyebrow.

"Not exactly."

Rider's grin widened. It straightened out the smile until the corners of his mouth were something close to even. "You probably have a bunch of interesting middle and last names. Don't all Israelites get something like thirty? Like, in the Bible, they sometimes refer to the same person by three or four different names."

"It depends on your tribe, your family, and your social status, as well as your personal achievements. If you're important, you usually get more titles."

"Cool stuff," Rider said, nodding thoughtfully. "So what's your tribe, family, social status, and personal achievements?"

Both of Rex's eyebrows came up. She was about to make a retort along the lines of "none of your business" when Rider's attention was diverted as he caught sight of someone he apparently knew.

"Tanner!" He jogged up to a tall, well-muscled boy and grabbed him in a fierce hug, slapping him on the back. "My man! Where's Cal?"

"He's on a different team," Tanner said woefully. "Although it's probably better since I won't have to look after him all the time."

Rider nodded vigorously. "That's it, make the best of it. Ladies!" He turned back to Rex, Alelta, and Bridget. "Meet Tanner, one of my best pals! He's got a twin who unfortunately won't be joining us. Tanner, meet Brigette, Aleleelelta, and Rex with thirty names."

Tanner spread his palms in a gesture of resignation. "I guess I'll have to try and learn your names on my own, since this hawk won't tell me." He shoved an elbow into Rider's ribs. Rider shoved back.

"Who's a hawk? I'm nice enough to tell you their real names, unencumbered by the fact that I am perfectly not dyslexic."

Alelta frowned thoughtfully, turning away from the jostling boys to Rex and Bridget. "What in precious burning cities is that all about?"

Bridget giggled. "Who cares? It's a lark!"

Eventually, the whole team was assembled, though they didn't have time to really meet each other before they were herded across the training ground toward the tall building with the glass side. Rex stared up at the darkened glass, wondering what lay inside the structure that was taller than the rest. She caught herself from bumping into the recruit in front of her just in time as the sergeant called a halt at the door.

"Some of you know this is the training facility. The first chamber is the weapons room, and the level above that is for the first phase of your training. No one can get to the higher levels until they pass the first. Anyone who tries to go higher is automatically recorded as a cheater, and believe me, you don't want to be known as a cheater. Any questions?"

"No, Sergeant Ma'am!" the recruits chorused.

"Good. Follow me at a walk inside."

The weapons room was large and open compared to the barracks. The walls were lined with row upon row of shelves, filled with training pads, gear, guns, knives, and anything else Rex could imagine as a weapon. There were benches in the center of the room for tired recruits to rest or gear up.

Sergeant Bailey gestured to a figure who stood in the back of the room. "This is Master Ekeli. He'll be your trainer in the arts. Today, he'll oversee your arts assessment and give me a report. Obey him. Just because I'm not here doesn't mean I won't hear."

Master Ekeli stepped forward and clapped both fists to his chest. "Attention!" His hazel eyes peered out hawklike from under his dark brows, searching through and scrutinizing the recruits. His skin was tanned, and he had a scar running from his right temple to his chin, and another above his brow. His eyes met Rex's and his jaw tightened slightly, showing a vein on the side of his muscular neck. "You will start your assessment immediately."

The recruits hurried up the stairs to the first training level. Rex took the stairs two at a time, eager to be on the mat. It was something she was familiar with.

She stopped dead in her tracks as she reached the top of the stairs.

The entire room was white, with walls that soared up to a ceiling some fifty feet above. Strung from the ceiling were striking bags and rings in uneven placements. Metal bars of varying thicknesses lined the back wall, reaching from floor to ceiling.

Light flooded in through the glass side of the room. It was totally unlike the black mat training rooms Rex had practiced in all her life. And why was the equipment in the air? The rings were the only thing traditionally strung from the ceiling, to develop flexibility and strength while using them as a support. Striking bags were never hung that high up. No ceiling she had ever seen was that high. She realized the other recruits around her had stopped as well and were staring. Quickly, before Master Ekeli could issue an order or punishment, Rex strode forward into the training room.

The master called for them to join him on the floor. Rex smiled in anticipation. She could do the arts the same way she could breathe or swallow or even sleep. It had been drilled into her from the time she was a little girl. The master's next words took her by surprise.

"Activate your shoes and meet me in the air." He shot up toward the ceiling and was lost in the jumble of punching bags.

Rex realized they would be doing the arts airborne. How? There was no support in the air, no floor to push off and gain force for a strike. Air didn't provide the solid platform needed to stay grounded and balanced or a place to hold down an enemy's body. But, if the master was asking them to do it, there had to be a way. With an effort, she stepped forward and pressed the central control on her belt buckle to activate the shoes.

"Whoa!" The sudden floating action brought

back the memory of being pulled up into the sky as her town burned beneath her.

Her mom...

She shut her eyes tightly, took in a deep breath, then opened them before tightening her jaw with resolve and twisting the buckle like she had seen Roth do. She rose slowly, jerkily, with her arms slightly out for balance, marveling at the floating sensation beneath her feet that simultaneously felt like a solid surface. Her boots emitted a steam-like vapor that disappeared as she rose. Shaking her feet slightly, she found that pointing her toes caused her to go up and sinking her heels caused her to go down. She could get used to this.

When all the compatriots were airborne, Master Ekeli began calling out the motions that Rex had just discovered. "Up—toes down. Down—toes up. Side—heel out..."

She saw Alelta struggling. She met her gaze, then proceeded to go through the motions smoothly so the other girl could see how it was done. With a few more tries, Alelta got it more or less right. She flashed Rex a grateful smile. Rex gave her a nod. It was basic good manners at an arts school to help another student. Once a week, when other people from her town came to train at what they thought was a simple self-defense school, she would help them —without giving away how experienced in the arts she really was. There wasn't anything particularly friendly about it. Alelta seemed to think it was some favor.

With a bit of practice, the airborne boots turned out to be easier to operate than Rex had first expected. They required the same type of balance as when they practiced the arts on the ground. Being in the air actually forced her to make her movements a bit more fluid and coordinated as she went through the motions. They only practiced the three most basic movements. Fight stance was the same, she thought, except you had to keep your toes up slightly. The key was to breathe and relax your weight into the balls of your feet, keeping centered above them through your core. If you did that, the pressurized air from the shoes pushed against the air below, creating the feeling of an almost solid surface underneath your feet. Basic strikes on the bag were a bit of a challenge, but the years Rex had spent under Master Juko's sharp reprimands to not overextend herself paid off.

She blinked hard as she thought of her old master's swarthy, bearded face, more conscious of it than of the girl who stood on the other side of the bag, waiting her turn to strike. Where was her master now? Had he survived the invasion? Her fists struck the practice bag as memories flooded over her.

Right-left. Right-left. Right-right-right, low left.

Her mom. Was she captured? Had she died, like Rex's father, and would now simply be added to the total number of casualties reported since the war?

Master Ekeli stalked through the ranks of compatriots, passing close by her. He stopped and scanned the people around her. She was conscious of his gaze lingering on her, and she struck the bag with renewed energy to show him she was no slacker.

And her toes went down.

An undignified howl was torn from her throat as she rocketed upward and thudded against a practice bag. Pain exploded in her back and she plunged forward. Arms flailing, she tried to gain her balance. She could hear the practice bag rocking back and forth on its chain, and she tried to avoid it. A ripple of laughter ran around the room as she groaned and slowly eased her weight onto her heels. As she floated down to her former position at her bag, Master Ekeli's gaze was still on her.

"Zero-Twenty-Seven. Stay on level."

Rex gritted her teeth. Despite her embarrassment, she stood tall. "Yes, sir."

"Good." His eyes remained locked on hers for another moment, then he turned away. Rex let out a sigh of frustration. She couldn't leave her master with this impression of her on the first day of training.

She readied the muscles all over her body. Then her head came up and she leapt, the airborne shoes carrying her level with the top of the bag. Her foot drove into the rough canvas so hard that she could feel the sand inside crunching together as it was compressed by the force. There was a cry of alarm from the girl behind the bag as she jumped out of the way, the bag's chain rattling as it swung up and rocked back into place. Silence flooded the room. Rex glanced at the faces around her from where she had fallen into a half-crouch, boots steaming slowly, hands raised in fight stance. She straightened, holding her head high, and turned to face Master Ekeli. His expression was unreadable. But he inclined his head, ever so slightly.

"Again."

Exhaling, testing her balance, she readied herself and leapt at the bag again.

***

By the time she was done demonstrating her skill, Rex was met with several envious glances from her fellow compatriots as they took a three-minute water break. To be singled out by an arts master was a rare commodity. But as they fell into line at the sound of Sergeant Ma'am's voice, in their eyes she also saw awe, fear, and even respect. To her, those who were in awe were inexperienced, those who were in fear were weak, and the few who respected her . . . well, given time, they might turn out to be allies.

The thoughts ran through her mind as she looked at the back of the row of heads in line. As her turn came, she stepped up to the fountain and took a long, deep draft.

"Keep it moving!" Sergeant Bailey barked.

Rex stepped away, wiping her mouth on the back of her hand. She brushed past a group and sank onto a cold steel bench.

"Recognized by the master? Pretty sharp for the

first day."

Alelta's voice carried a note of respect, and... was it envy? Rex couldn't be sure. The other girl dropped onto the bench beside her, polishing one of two steel wristbands she wore. The metal gleamed as the rough material of Alelta's tank top smoothed over it.

"What are those for?" Rex asked.

"A gift. From my mother," Alelta said. A pang went through Rex's chest.

"When?"

"Four weeks before I was recruited. She said they'd be my best weapon. Not sure how." Alelta turned the band toward the light, and Rex could see lines of darker metal running across the surface.

"Did you know when you were going to be recruited?"

"Of course." Alelta glanced at her sideways, her dark, choppily cut bangs falling across her face. It made her look somewhat severe. "Didn't you?"

Not for the first time, Rex smiled in frustration. "No. I knew it would be soon. But I didn't think it would happen the way it did. I guess no one could have predicted the attack."

"What attack?" Alelta paused for a moment.

"The Ishmaks. They moved in on our town. That was when I was brought up here."

"That's one damn way to be recruited," Alelta laughed.

Rex turned her lips up in a humorless smile as she bent down to stretch out. "I'll deal with it."

"Compatriots! Form up!"

Alelta smiled. "Guess it's back to the bags."

***

"You've all been cybernetically altered. Some of you may have been wondering exactly how we survive up here in the sky. Most of you don't know how your cybernetic bodies work."

The doctor—Leah was her name—had reappeared from wherever she had been hiding since recruitment and was now facing the compatriots on the ground in the training room. Her black hair was pulled back, and she wore a training uniform just like them—a tank top and cargo pants with airborne boots. "I'm here to show you the basics of how to operate cybernetically. I work with Master Ekeli."

Rex wondered why the master had deferred to the tall, lean woman standing there. It didn't take her long to figure out why.

"Activate your boots. Let's fly."

The sky was huge. It yawned open for miles under Rex's feet as she stood atop the fence of the compound after Leah had shut down the invisible barrier. She had never been afraid of heights—until now. Realizing that she would be reprimanded if she kept hesitating, she swallowed hard, twisted the buckle on her belt, and stepped off the edge. Her heart lurched at the brief drop, then the boots steadied her and she floated with the sky yawning open at her feet.

"Master Ekeli has already gone over the basic positions to move up, down, and so forth. I'll be teaching you how to fly smoothly and operate your cybernetic implants."

Alelta came level with Rex, and the others on the team made their way through the crowd of recruits to group around her as well. They barely had time to form up before Leah gave the next order.

"Lean forward! Toes back! Arms out!" She shot away, and the compatriots hurried to follow, some of them jolting awkwardly as they found their center of balance in the new flying position. Rex found hers easily. She sped forward with growing confidence, watching the heels of the compatriots ahead of her, and found that the drop didn't seem quite so threatening now.

"Your arms are for balance," Leah said. Rex realized the woman's voice was at regular volume, but she could hear her normally. As if reading her thoughts, Leah said, "You should be able to hear me and ask me questions despite the wind. You all have cybernetic implants in your ears and eyes to hear and see properly." She slowed a bit and turned so that she was flying backward, facing the front of the pack. "The drug you were given when you were recruited activated your basic airborne functions like enhanced hearing and your third eyelid."

Rex recalled the itching sensation she had felt when she had first arrived and realized it must have been the third eyelid activating.

"Now . . ." Leah fiddled with something on her wrist. "Your training and combat functions have been activated."

Rex started as a screen came up in front of her

eyes. Letters and numbers whirled, glowing blue.

Ready, Soldier 027? the screen asked.

More numbers whirled, and the screen adjusted focus rapidly. Dizzy, Rex blinked—and gave a small yelp of alarm as she saw a sand viper devouring its prey when she opened her eyes. She looked up and realized they hadn't shifted in altitude. Looking down again, she witnessed the sand viper gulp up the last remains of the small animal, miles below her. Judging by the mixed cries of alarm and excitement from the others, she guessed they were seeing the ground as well. Rex looked up again just in time to prevent a collision with the person flying in front of her. She snickered slightly as she heard several thuds, indicating that others hadn't been so lucky. Leah gave them another minute to get used to the vision change and to straighten their flight paths. Then she continued.

"Your cybernetic implants are extensions of your bodies. They respond to commands exactly as your nerves and muscles do. If you focus your eyes on something, the screens there will focus too. Strain your ears, and you'll hear three times as well as any normal human being. If you encounter a noise that's louder than a hundred decibels, your implants will deaden the sound."

"Question," Bridget said, from somewhere behind her. "Are these the only implants we have?"

"No," Leah replied. "Your lungs and airways have them as well. All of them emit a serum to help your blood and temperature levels adjust to the cold air up here. Near the end of your compatriot phase, you'll undergo an operation where I'll add cybernetic implants that enhance your best natural combat or defense ability. For instance, if you're the best arm wrestler, I'll reinforce your arm. Or if you can read three enemy languages, I'll give your retinal implants access to a selection of documents recovered by the Alliance from enemy forces. Our force is about combat, yes, but you can't win a fight if you don't have the strategic and tactical knowledge to back you up. On the missions that you'll fly, you'll have to be able to assess situations quickly and make appropriate decisions. Each member of the force can contribute something besides just gunpower. You'll receive your final implants accordingly."

"Amazin'," Bridget murmured. It sounded loud to Rex.

"Focus on something below you and get a feel for your implants," Leah instructed. "Keep your flying position."

Rex shifted her head to look at the ground once more. Nothing but sand dunes stretched away for miles. She focused on one dune, noting the shift in its crest as the hot wind blew over it. She suddenly realized that she missed the heat on the ground. But she had to admit, up here was gloriously free and cool. She raised her head, reveling in the feeling of the wind on her skin, lifting her up. She was soaring. Her hair, though it was braided according to regulation, whipped behind her as the wind caught it. The clench of her stomach, when she had first seen the height, was gone now. A smile broke out on her face, and her eyes half-closed as she breathed deeply. For the first time in a long time, she felt in control. Away from her stepfather. Away from the dirty little town where he'd hunted her. Free.

Too soon, Leah began a large circle back to the compound. As it came in sight, Rex took another deep breath, savoring the feeling of the open air and the jewel-blue view all around her. Then it was over. One by one, the compatriots stepped back onto the compound earth.

"You may have some difficulty sleeping tonight," Leah called as Sergeant Bailey prepared to resume command of the compatriots. "Come to the medical bay if you want earplugs."

As they filed back toward the training building, Rex's thoughts were far away from the training room or the practice to come. There was one thing she had to know. She would ask Sergeant Bailey as soon as she could get away from everyone.

***

It turned out to be nighttime before she had a moment to talk with the sergeant. As she came out of the shower to air-dry, her other compatriots went into the shower room. The other girls were some distance away to maximize the effects of the wind. Rex approached Sergeant Bailey, overwhelmingly conscious of the fact that she was not in uniform —or anything else—and clapped her fists together over her chest.

"Sergeant Ma'am. Permission to converse."

Sergeant Bailey looked her over skeptically. Rex wasn't sure if it was because of her scars or because the sergeant disliked being bothered. "Start talking."

"My town was attacked. I don't know what happened to my mother or my friend. Do you have a record?"

"What's your city and family name?" Sergeant Bailey uncrossed her arms and tapped her black wristlet. It lit up. Rex caught her breath. She had thought that all tech—including wrist-screens—had become obsolete since the Blackout.

"Bat'hai. I lived on the fading edge of Jerusalem. My town is called Ben-Valta."

"Fading edge . . ." Sergeant Bailey searched the names in her wrist-screen. Rex waited, heart pounding, for the woman to give the answer she had been wanting to know for what seemed like forever, though it had only been two days. Sergeant Bailey nodded once. "Your mother and stepfather are still in Ben-Valta. The Ishmaks were repelled by the Israeli standard military."

Rex closed her eyes in a rush of relief. "And my friend? Her name is Kani Sellom."

"We don't have records of anyone by that name." Bailey tapped the wrist-screen and its light died.

Rex nodded, understanding. Of course the Alliance wouldn't have a record of someone without a legal family name. But if Kani had stayed with Rex's mother, then Rex was sure she had made it. "Thank you, Sergeant Ma'am."

"Dismissed, Zero-Twenty-Seven."

As Rex went to her bunk, her mind whirled. Her mother was safe, at least for now. But another thought was foremost in her mind.

If the Israeli military kept a record of her mother, they definitely had a record of what happened to her father.

***

"Sir, I've sedated the asset. Do you want me to let you preview?"

Sekhmet, as she liked to be called, fidgeted from one foot to the other behind the figure on the dais, her luminescent green eyes lowered. She breathed quickly, her long, black steel fingers flexing and unflexing in excitement as she waited for a response from her leader.

His back was turned toward her, with one foot propped on the table before him and one hand playing idly with a wooden carving he had finished some days previously. Despite his casual position, she knew he had heard what she said. She smiled to herself, feeling her lips curl back over the long canine teeth that were still unfamiliar to her. He would be pleased with her work.

Without looking back, the figure gave a smooth gesture with his hand. "Yes, bring it."

Flanked by four guards, she hurried through the dark hallways to the vertical speed transit. Almost without pausing, she spread her palm over the scanner and raised herself up on the balls of her feet for the retinal scan, then stepped into the elevator. The guards did the same. As the black doors closed in front of her, she held her breath and waited for the stomach-lurching drop. The transit shot downward, lights flashing past as it descended one level after another in lightning succession. The sensation, which had only a few months before been nigh unbearable, was now merely uncomfortable. She guessed that the guards were unaffected.

The doors shot open. Sekhmet dashed out, leaving the guards to catch up with her. As she passed the rows of barred cells, nightmarish forms reached out at her—twisted faces; a gaping mouth filled with teeth snapping; scaly limbs clawing out at her; and glowing eyes like her own, some filled with anger, others with pain. The noises of barking, scratching, fluttering, and thumping filled the space, but she had dimmed her ears to it all long ago. She was intent only on the cell that was separated from the rest. After a palm and retinal scan and a voice command, the door buzzed open.

"Asset Three. Come with me." She gestured with her long foreclaw at the figure.

Amber eyes gazed up at her from under lids heavy with the effects of the sedative. The figure stood slowly. As before, every time he—it—moved, Sekhmet marveled at the perfection of its physique. It was a man in its prime, with full, sinewy muscles that rippled as it stood, naked but for the leather bound over its loins and the cords about its wrists. Long, dark hair flowed over the broad shoulders. He was beautiful—her own creation. *It,* she reminded herself.

The guards jumped forward to restrain the asset as it lunged toward her despite the multiple sedatives Sekhmet had given it. It gave a low growl, its face less than a foot from hers when the guards stopped it. A laugh of wild delight broke from her blood-purple lips. She could taste its power, its anger. It was pure, unbridled potential.

"Follow." She gestured to the guards and skipped down the hall, giggling. The master would love the progress she had made.

0.5

"Your call."

Rider and Nigel sat facing each other, with three other boys close by them. Nigel was hunched over, his face contorted into a frown of concentration while Rider was just barely containing a huge grin as he fanned his cards. From where Rex sat on the mess hall bench, she could see the ace of spades poking out from its hiding place under the two of diamonds. The band of light that ran around its margin glowed faintly blue.

They were allowed to take an hour to rest in the evening, after a long day of practice with the airborne shoes and a perfunctory practice at the shooting range. The real training in that area would commence tomorrow. The day was more tiring than Rex had anticipated it would be, given that they hadn't even sparred with each other. No doubt that would come in the next day or two. Sergeant Bailey had told them that tomorrow they would practice skills of teamwork and cooperation.

In the meantime, Rex had decided to get to know her fellow teammates—and scope them out. Besides Rider, Tanner, Alelta, and Bridget, there were three others—eight total, including Rex. Nigel was a short British boy who looked like he had lost the battle with puberty, but still managed to display amazing agility on the rope course. A tall girl, whom Rex had assumed was Israeli, turned out to be a Native American named Zyanya. She was perched on the back of a chair, straight-backed and graceful, as she watched the game from a distance. Her waist-length hair, taken down for the night, still had several braids running through it. The last person was an Israeli girl named Abihail, Abbi for short. She sat in a corner next to Bridget, who was trying to bring the shy girl out of herself. She was smaller than any of the others, but she had held her own in their exercises.

Her thoughts were distracted as a male sergeant strode past her, keeping an eye on things in the hall. Rex thought that "free time" wasn't very free with a commanding officer breathing down their necks, but maybe it would be different during daytime. She knew there was a platform outside the training room where people went to take breaks throughout the day. Some of the others called it the Ledge. It was a rather basic title—probably given by a boy.

She sighed and turned back to Nigel, who was still deciding what call to make.

"Spades . . . ?" Nigel asked.

Rider chortled and slapped the two of diamonds onto the table. "Not this time!"

Nigel gave a groan.

"Two wins for me! Hand it over."

Rex caught her breath as Nigel pulled something from around his neck.

Her necklace.

Scatting to himself, Rider slipped the medallion over his neck, unaware of Rex's gaze riveted on the precious item. Rex flexed her jaw, unsure of what to do. She wasn't sure she wanted to explain its value in front of a group whose members she hadn't fully evaluated yet. If untrustworthy people knew you cared about something, they had a weakness to exploit. She decided the best way to get it was to join the game.

"Mind if I have a go, boys?" she said, casually dropping into a chair.

Rider gestured to the deck. "No problem. Just pull yourself a hand. Six cards."

"What's the stakes?" she asked, though she already knew.

Rider tugged at the medallion around his neck. "This beauty right here."

Rex knew she could win her necklace back. She had played Full Sixes many times before, when an American soldier came every day for two months and showed children card tricks in the streets of Ben-Valta. Each player drew six cards. The players split into pairs, with one person showing only five of his cards to his assigned opponent. He would then rearrange his cards, trying to make his opponent lose track of where the sixth card was. The opponent had to guess where the sixth card ended up, as well as its suit, while not knowing if they had even guessed the right card. Then the positions would be reversed, and the opponent would become the cardholder. If one person won as both the cardholder and the opponent, they automatically won the whole round, or they played a tiebreaker if someone from another pairing had won both positions as well.

If you were skillful, you could keep track of the placement of the five known cards and when the cardholder moved them. If not, you lost. It was the ultimate game of sleight of hand.

Rex knew that her instincts and hypervigilance, developed over the years from hard experience, would catch the slight signals she needed to. She drew her cards.

"Ready."

Rider settled back in his chair with a deep sigh of contentment. He showed Rex a glimpse of five of his cards, then slid the sixth one in among them and began switching their positions rapidly. Rex kept her eyes leveled slightly above the moving cards, knowing that her peripheral vision would keep better track of the sixth card than if she glued her eyes to it. Staring at the card was a good way to fall prey to one of the cardholder's misdirection tricks.

Rider fanned his cards with a smile. "Take a guess."

"This one," Rex said without hesitation, tapping the card in the middle. Rider's mouth twitched ever so slightly, the smile breaking for a split second. She had chosen the right card. Now to figure out the suit. "Spades hearts clubs diamonds," she rattled without a pause. She didn't know how she knew it, but something in his body language changed when she said "hearts."

"Which is your answer?"

Rex smiled the most winning smile she could manage. "Hearts."

Rider's eyebrows rose in surprise. The queen of hearts, beautiful and neatly rendered, glowed red as he set it face up on the table. "Good guess. How did you know?"

"Not telling. Here." She revealed five of her cards, then pulled them back and rearranged them. Rider picked the wrong one, and Rex gave him a wolfish smile.

"Let's see if this hawk can do any better. Tanner! You're up." Rider relaxed back and put his boots up on the empty chair to his right. They fell into place with a loud clomp, and dust from the training ground spiraled up.

Tanner smiled at Rex. "Guess we're playing a tiebreaker. You want to be cardholder first?"

Rex shrugged. "Sure." She arranged her cards and held them up for the other boy to pick.

"You know how Tanner got his name?" Rider asked as Tanner's hand hovered over Rex's cards. "When he and Cal were born, his parents weren't expecting twins. So they literally just looked at the two babies and decided to call Tanner 'Tanner' because his skin was darker."

"Shut up, hawk," Tanner said, tapping one of Rex's cards. As it turned out, he chose the correct card, but couldn't guess the suit. Rex held out her hand for the medallion. Reluctantly, Rider passed it over.

"You're too good at this," he said, scowling in mock disapproval. "Let's see how you do on the next round."

Rex shook her head. "No more rounds. I keep the necklace."

"Oh, come on. Not going to let us redeem ourselves?" Rider sighed in frustration but reached out a hand. "Good game."

Rex paused, unsure. The soldier who taught her the game was the only one who had ever done that. All the people in her town were the kind who would damage something of yours after losing to you. But she shook his hand.

"Good game, Compatriot." In this context, the word felt strange on her tongue.

"Well tha' was the pits!" Nigel exclaimed unexpectedly. Rider burst out laughing. Rex couldn't help smirking a bit, too. Nigel looked so disappointed, like a child.

Rider clapped Nigel on the shoulder. "Better luck next time, Compatriot." He swept the deck of illuminated cards off the table and proceeded to shuffle them through the air without even looking.

"Luck?" Rex asked. "Luck has nothing to do with it."

Rider spread his hands wide, the deck dangerously close to collapsing and spilling all over the floor. "I believe there's a bit of luck in everything. But

I tend to agree that it's in the power of concentration and slippery hands." He set the cards on the table. "Another game? What about Kill the King? Stakes are . . ." He searched around for an object. "Nigel's extra blanket."

Nigel groaned inarticulately. Rex was about to reply that it was almost certainly against regulations for her to use a blanket from the male barracks when the male sergeant's voice blared across the hall.

"Into the barracks! Jump to it!"

As they filed out of the mess hall, Rex drew up alongside Rider. She whispered in his ear so the sergeant couldn't hear, "What's that sergeant's name? He acts like an overgrown rooster. He even struts like one."

Rider visibly struggled to keep a straight face as the sergeant's eyes fell on them. He waited until the man looked away, then whispered back. "His name is . . ." his shoulders shook, "Rangorazi."

"What?" The word burst out louder than Rex had meant it to. But she couldn't help it. It was such a ridiculous name. "Who in Gehenna named him that?"

"Gehenna?"

"Hell," she explained.

"Oh!" Rider's voice was so choked with laughter she could barely make out his words. "We call him Rango-tango, the Rango-nazi, and Rango-paparazzi, among other things. Never to his ugly mug, of course."

"I bet he wouldn't like that," Rex agreed. "Where

did you find the necklace?" she asked, changing the subject. She kept her eyes riveted on his face as he answered.

"It was just lying on the ground in the medical wing. It didn't look like it belonged to anybody, so I pocketed it." He paused. "Does it belong to you?"

Rex was momentarily taken aback by his perceptiveness. "Yes."

Rider nodded. "Good thing you won it back, then. I was starting to get attached to it."

Rex allowed a smile to turn up one corner of her mouth. Then she frowned. "Why were you in the medical bay, anyway? Did you get recruited after me? I thought your number was Zero-Twenty."

"Weeeell . . ." Rider shrugged expansively and spread his palms. "I have a tendency to go places I'm not expected."

"You mean where you're not wanted?" Rex couldn't help a smirk breaking out. Rider's face was so full of unapologetic mischief.

"Yes, basically."

The sergeant—Rangorazi—barked an order. "Come on, Compatriots! We don't have all night."

Rider shrugged again. "Well, looks like I've got to go to the place I'm wanted. See you, Rex." He tapped her shoulder and strode off toward the boys' barracks.

Rex froze, tension seizing her in the reflex she always had when someone touched her unexpectedly. She supposed the gesture was meant to be friendly, though she couldn't be sure. But, given how friendly

Rider was in general, she decided to relax and keep an eye on him—for better or worse.

0.6

"First rank, shoot! Fall back!" Sergeant Bailey's voice rang across the shooting range. Rex shuffled forward through the coarse dirt, wielding the large AR-15 in both hands. The target was a figure of a man rendered in some papery substance Rex had never seen before. She sighted on his chest at the mark near his heart and shot in a matter of milliseconds, then spun back on her knees through the dirt of the training ground.

Before the next person could shoot, Rex took in where her shot had landed—close to the mark, but closer to the center of the target's chest. Good, but not good enough. She clenched her teeth slightly in frustration. To be fair, gun practice at the arts school hadn't been the main focus. The program was far more centered around using your body as the weapon. Gun practice only happened once a month rather than five days every week. All the same, Rex knew that Sergeant Bailey was watching for exemplary displays of skills. She wished she had paid more attention to detail during gun classes at the arts school.

Someone brushed her shoulder as they passed,

and she smiled slightly as she recognized Rider. He and Alelta were side by side in the rank forming up to shoot. Rex watched as he sighted and shot in a heartbeat. She smiled wryly in admiration. Obviously, Rider had a natural ability for target practice in the same way that she had an understanding of the arts. As he fell back from the low wall and was replaced by the third rank, Rex caught his eye and nodded.

"Good shot, Compatriot."

He grinned. "Thanks! Let's see how you do. Bet you miss the mark."

With a raised eyebrow, Rex brushed past him at the sergeant's call. "The necklace says I hit it right in the heart." She touched the warm disc around her neck, but as she came up to a crouch in front of the trench wall, the memory of an explosion struck her: a man falling backward, then lying still on the ground, blood by his head. Her heartbeat roared in her ears. It was a childhood memory—or rather, one she had imagined when she had first learned of her father's disappearance. She heard the command to shoot, realized she was behind, aimed, and fired. The shot grazed the arm of the target, and she spun out of the way as a compatriot fell into place at the line.

Rider grinned at her. "I would tell you to hand over the medallion, but since I'm such a nice guy—and, you know, since it's really yours—I'll let you keep it."

"Are you guys going to let me in on whatever is going on?" Alelta cocked her gun as she passed Rex, was joined by Rider as she slid to the line, shot, and returned. "Well?"

Just having finished his shot, Rider stroked the handle of his gun lovingly. "She just lost her medallion. Hypothetically."

Alelta frowned. "Hypothetically?"

"If she was able to lose it, she'd lose it."

Rider's explanation obviously confused Alelta more than it answered her question. Her frown deepened.

Rex tilted her head and bared her teeth slightly. "I'll hit the next one, just for good measure. And the two after that." She tossed her head and brushed past them.

She made good on her assertion. All three of her next shots hit the sternum of the target. One was on the border of the left pectoral muscle—almost out of line—but in the inner bullseye nonetheless. As she fell back, Rider and Alelta seemed to be in a tense discussion. Rex soon caught on to what they were talking about.

". . . I'm going to be alpha," Alelta was saying.

Rider shrugged. "You and every woman in this place."

Alelta's silver eyes were locked onto Rider's dark ones.

"You don't get it. I *am* going to be alpha." She didn't look at Rex, but Rex heard the unspoken challenge in her voice. She would be friends, but only so long as Rex stayed out of her way.

It was something Rex would never do.

She set her features in a casual expression as Alelta looked her way at last. "We'll see. There's a lot of competition besides just you and me."

Rider cut in, "Relax, ladies. We're still in the first phase. Plenty of time to tear at each other's throats in the last two phases. In the meantime, let's just kick back . . ."—he cocked his gun—"relax . . ." —he swept up to the line, fired almost without looking, and returned—"and enjoy splattering people's paper target brains into the dirt," he finished. Rex raised both eyebrows as she saw that Rider's seemingly careless shot had nailed the space between the target's eyes. He smiled winningly at her. "Your go."

"I already hit the last three. But I'll hit this one, too, if you weren't watching before."

Just then Sergeant Bailey called a halt to the shooting. "Water break, three minutes!"

As Rex fell into the line trudging across the field toward the fountain by the nearest building, Bridget popped in just ahead of her. "Hi, Rexie!"

Rex was startled by the nickname. Her mother—and Kani, on rare occasions—were the only people who had ever called her that. After a moment, she realized that Bridget's greeting merited a response. "Morning."

"How have ya been? Are ya excited?"

"Excited about what? Training?" Rex hoped Bridget wouldn't notice that she'd avoided the first question; she didn't want to reveal that her emotions had been tumultuous with intermittent spots of escape during social time at night.

"Yes! It feels so good to me."

"Me too." Rex was still slightly unnerved by the younger girl's exuberance, but she still had the same sense that the girl was genuine. Just very innocent. "Where have you been the past few nights?" She had only seen glimpses of Bridget in that time.

Bridget's green eyes lit up. "I've been talkin' with my friend Alec. He went to the arts school with me. He's a good one!" The way she smiled from ear to ear told Rex the "friendship" was a little deeper, at least on Bridget's part.

"What've you been doing?"

"He tells stories. I've been listenin' to him. Nobody else does yet. He has a calm voice, so people in the mess hall just think he's havin' a regular conversation. But I'd give him three more days, and people'll start to listen. His stories are amazin'! Ya gotta hear one sometime."

Rex shrugged. "Sure, why not?"

As the compatriots filed back toward the shooting range, Sergeant Bailey called for them to march behind her. They stopped at the obstacle course, which stretched out before them.

"Your first assessment for teamwork begins shortly," the sergeant said. As confused mutterings ran throughout the compatriots, she raised both hands. "That's enough!" The mutterings faded. "I understand that we haven't trained you for this assessment. This is just to determine where everyone stands in their teamwork and cooperation skills, not to test skills learned. It'll only count for a small percentage of your final placement. Your scoring will be communicated to you before lunch. It'll give you a chance to understand where you need to improve. Now, let's get started."

The assessment was fairly straightforward. The obstacle course, as it turned out, was a maze created entirely of ropes. Each team was sent through a different pathway, which was marked by colored flags, and they had to undo the knots as fast as possible to clear their path. No one was allowed to climb over the tied ropes. In addition, there were various obstacles to navigate along the way. It was barely a minute before the order was given for Rex's team to begin. At the sergeant's command, Rex and her teammates ran down their assigned pathway through the maze. Rex raced to the front of her group as they followed the colored flags down the stretch of open ground.

"Come on! Here!" she yelled as they came to the first junction—three ropes intertwined and knotted together. Thinking back to the game she and the other boys had played the night before, she had noticed that Rider and Tanner had the fastest hands. She called to them, "Rider! Tanner! You two undo the knots on each end. Bridget and I will take the middle. The rest of you, stay back and let us work!" She plunged forward to the rope and began working at it.

The other recruits were taken aback momentarily, unsure if they should follow Rex's lead. She stared back at them, her hands still plying the rope.

"Do it!" she ordered.

They leapt to the ropes, fingers flying.

Rider groaned as he worked. "It's a cut-back swan," he said with a grunt. "These suck."

A cut-back swan was an intricate knot used primarily for binding prisoners of war. There was no easy way to undo them. They were hard to tie and even harder to untie. Rex's knot, thankfully, was a simpler one. In a short span of time she had worked it undone. That end of the rope fell away. Rider and Tanner were a bit behind, and Rex drummed her fingers on the taut part of the rope in a fever of impatience. They had to move. They had to make the best time.

"Hurry . . ." she muttered, low enough so the others couldn't hear.

"No need. I'm done." Rider tossed the rope down and grinned at her.

Rex raised her eyebrows slightly at his uncanny hearing and nodded, then glanced at Tanner. He was almost through. She looked ahead to the next junction but couldn't make out what was a crossing and what was the normal path. As soon as Tanner was done with his knot, she raced ahead, following the twists of the path.

She suddenly became aware of someone beside her—Alelta. The other girl smiled.

"The next intersection is a no-touch climbing zone. You'll need me to go first. I used to practice on these all the time at home."

"How do you—" Rex was cut off as the path gave a

sharp turn backward and to the right and her stomach slammed into the rope. The no-touch zone rose in front of her, a large wooden climbing structure that she had assumed was part of someone else's path. She reeled back, wheezing.

"That's how I know," Alelta chuckled. She leapt toward the structure. "Let me blaze the trail. Follow where I go. Unless I make a mistake, of course." With a bound, she cleared the first three feet of the obstacle and pulled herself upward, using handholds etched into the wood. Rex noted that a sticky substance coated certain areas of the wood. It was hard to see, adding to the no-touch challenge. Noting the most obvious places where the liquid was smeared, Rex was about to follow Alelta, but realized with an ache that she should go last. As the leader, she had to make sure the others cleared the obstacle. Sometimes leading meant following.

"Follow Alelta! Watch where she places her hands," she ordered as Tanner came level with her.

"Sure thing," Tanner said with a nod, and sprang up.

Rex watched as Alelta disappeared over the top of the structure, then glanced at the others as they arrived. They stood uncertainly for a moment. Rex drew breath to give another order, but Rider beat her to it.

"It's a no-touch zone. Avoid the sticky parts and use everything else to climb," Rider said. "Let's go!" He began climbing, and the others followed.

Rex was slightly miffed that Rider had taken over

command, but she decided it was no threat. There was a male alpha as well as a female. Rider wasn't her competition—but that didn't mean that she would lose command.

"I'll go last," she told Bridget, who was near the back of the group. "Just making sure all my teammates make it through alright."

Bridget simply nodded and began her ascent. When she had climbed a few feet, Rex started after her. The wood was smooth, almost slippery, and the spaces with goo were harder to see than she had expected. She began counting handholds as she made her ascent.

. . . Four, five, six . . .

She had to move faster. Her eyes darted up at the path she had to take. Above her, Bridget slipped.

"Keep going, Bridget!" she called. They had to move. *Faster, faster,* she silently urged the others on. That was when her hand sank into the sticky goo.

"*Chara*," she cursed in Hebrew as she yanked her hand free. The substance was surprisingly strong at keeping hold of her hand once she touched it.

Thinking that she might have seemed a bit inconsiderate to Bridget now that she realized how difficult the climb was, she called, "We're almost there!" It was as much encouragement to herself as it was to Bridget. After another near slip, when her heavy boots skidded on the slippery wood, she made it to the top. From there she could see the ground of the compound stretching away into the distance, where she knew it reached the edge and looked into empty sky beyond.

She took a moment to wipe her hands on her pants. It didn't do much except make her pants equally sticky. She muttered another curse in Hebrew. Fortunately, the way down would be easier. It was more or less a straight shot, with a rope to aid her purchase on the descent. She hurried down, her hands sliding roughly over the rope, then ran to catch up with her teammates.

The next obstacle was another set of ropes tied together, followed by a treacherous, deep sand pit. Rex decided immediately that she would lead this one. She knew sand traps like the calluses on her hands, having had to learn quickly as a child to avoid them in the desert just outside her town. Being American, Alelta wouldn't be so familiar with the trap.

"I'll go first," she called to the others. "I know sand." The others were happy to let her take the lead.

"Step lightly and stay on the balls of your feet. Take it slow!" she shouted back over her shoulder as Tanner leapt into the pit. She knew he was probably capable of moving quickly, but she didn't want to take any chances. As she had the thought, her boot slipped into a pocket in the sand, and she swayed slightly to keep her balance.

"If any of you get stuck, don't panic. Wait for your feet to settle, lift your foot high and wiggle it into the sand, then push yourself up slowly." She accompanied her words with actions and dragged herself out of the hole. "Watch what we Jews do. We know about sand better than you Americans." She flashed a grin back at her teammates to indicate she meant no offense.

"Yeah, the most sand I ever saw was a man-made beach," Rider grunted. "This is the pits."

The others laughed at his pun. Rex risked a backward glance at Rider. He was stuck rather deep, but was struggling valiantly to keep his movements slow and measured, his face contorted in concentration.

"Just keep moving," she said, then added, "but not too quickly."

"I can only move as fast as an amputated sloth," Rider said, drawing more laughs from some of the others.

Since she was the first one out of the pit, Rex helped the others who needed it, along with Tanner.

"I'll make it today, don't worry," Rider said. "If I wait till tomorrow, I don't think I'll have the motivation." No sooner had he finished talking than his legs shot out from under him, and with a loud *whoomph*, he hit the ground. Sand exploded in all directions. A small cloud tornadoed away and swept over Rex and the others who had already crossed the pit. They all coughed violently. Rex saw Rider lift his head and spit grit, a smile on his face.

"I'm unharmed, in case you were hoping I died," he said. Rex couldn't stop the smile tugging at the corners of her mouth, but that didn't stop the awareness that they still had a course to complete.

"We won't get points if you die halfway through

the course. It's a team effort. Come on!" she shouted as he slowly began moving again. "Just get to the edge and we'll heave you free."

With tremendous effort, Rider dragged himself to where Rex and the others were waiting.

After two more rope barriers, Rex could see what looked like the end of their course. Sergeant Bailey stood to one side of a dirt field, and a tire with a rope attached that had once belonged to some mammoth machine lay directly between them and the finish line. The meaning was obvious.

"It's a team effort. We'll have to drag it with us. Rider! Tanner!" She was about to order them to take the front when she realized that would be a waste of their strength. She amended the direction she had been about to give. "Take the base of the rope, closest to the tire. Bridget, Nigel, Alelta, and . . ." She hesitated as she struggled to recall the other girl's name. ". . . Zyanya, you all push from the back! Abbi will pull at the front."

An expression akin to fear clouded the small girl's sensitive face. Rex could see a question forming on her lips.

"You won't have to pull much, Abbi. We'll be taking most of the tire's weight since we're closer to it."

Relief lit up Abbi's features as she took her place at the front. Rex knew the girl had only barely passed muster and was terrified of failing her team. But there was no more time to think. Rex pushed her way just in front of Rider and seized the rope. "On three! One, two, three, pull!"

With a chorus of roars, the group heaved with all their strength at the tire. For a heart-lurching moment, it didn't budge. Then came a tiny shift in the dirt, followed by the whole thing shooting forward.

Rex had the rope slung over her shoulder to maximize her body's pulling force. As the tire gained momentum, the rope vibrated against her neck, scratching and chafing as if in protest at the group's efforts to move it. Gritting her teeth, Rex heaved harder. She almost stumbled as the tire began moving even faster than before.

"You're not so weak, for a girl," Rider said from behind her. "But that added boost of speed was"—he grunted with exertion—"largely due to my own merits." Just before Rex's temper rose, Rider added, "Of course, we could both be weak and the people from behind might be doing all the work."

Even though she wasn't totally familiar with Rider's mannerisms, Rex could hear the grin in his voice. She had to admit, he waltzed the line right between her amusement and her undying annoyance. Now wasn't exactly the time she wanted to decide which side he fell on.

"Cut the sallying and let's move this thing!" she shouted back. With another roar, the group refreshed their efforts.

The finish line was coming closer. Sergeant Bailey's hulking figure loomed at the edge of the field, her face in that sarcastic expression she perpetually wore. Rex's heart leapt into her mouth as she saw two other teams nearing the sergeant. One was moving particularly fast. Rex caught sight of Roth straining at the rope.

"Faster! Another team's about to beat us!" she yelled to her teammates. She felt a surge of pride when everyone redoubled their efforts yet again.

A high-pitched yelp of pain came from behind the tire, followed by a soft thud.

Bridget.

0.7

Rex heard cries of encouragement from Alelta and Zyanya as they evidently tried to help Bridget back to her feet. The others paused momentarily in confusion as they heard the noise as well.

"Come on!" Rex shouted.

The others threw themselves at the ropes again, and the tire began to move once more. But it was too late. With the momentary delay, and with Bridget most likely unable to help them make up the time they had lost, Roth's team pulled their tire up beside Sergeant Bailey first. Dismay hit Rex like a punch in the gut as she saw not only his team, but another and another reach the line before they did. With a final effort, the group dragged the tire off the dirt and onto the grass that marked the finish line.

"Your time is sixteen minutes and thirty-seven seconds," the sergeant said.

The group was too busy regaining their spent breath to groan. Rex let out a long exhale of frustration but elected not to say anything to make the moment more discouraging.

"Ooh, my arm hurts."

Bridget shuffled forward, nursing a cut on her

forearm, which was streaked with dirt. She must have gotten it when she fell. Rex knew she could help her—she had gotten good at treating cuts and bruises over the years with her stepfather. She moved forward, but Abbi had already gone to Bridget's side and was taking her arm in her hands gently.

"It's a bit deep, not too bad," she said. "But it's got dirt in it. I'll need to clean it." She gestured to Rex. "Ask Sergeant Ma'am if we can go to the medical bay."

Rex frowned. "I think she'll have to be treated by that weird doctor. She probably won't let you do it."

To their surprise, Sergeant Bailey agreed to Abbi's request. "You'll all be trained as basic medics, but if anyone wants to learn specifics, it doesn't hurt. What's your number, Compatriot?" she asked, gesturing to Abbi.

"Zero-Twenty-Three, Sergeant Ma'am."

"Zero-Twenty-Three . . ." Sergeant Bailey said softly into her wrist-screen. Rex smiled to herself as she saw several of the others give small starts of surprise at seeing the tech. The sergeant nodded decisively. "I'll let Leah know you want to shadow her. You're dismissed."

The group members began shuffling away, spirits low. Rex was about to go after them when Roth's voice stopped her.

"That was some good stuff you showed back there, gorgeous. Can we join up and celebrate later? I'd like to get to know my competition." Roth grinned at her. To anyone else, he probably would have seemed disarming. There was a light in his eyes behind the hazel coloring, like the glow of a fire ready to envelop her if she stepped too close.

Rex met his gaze, assessing him. Rage smoldered in her chest. Why did this *manyak* have to rub salt in the wound? Her team had already lost. "I think we know each other pretty well."

Roth brought his palms up in a conciliatory gesture. "Okay, I see the fire. I'll just wait till it burns out. Consider my offer a standing one. It'll be worth your while."

Rex held his gaze for another few seconds to hide her confusion. What could he possibly have that would make spending time with him worth her while? Was it a threat or an invitation? She wasn't sure which was worse. Finally, she turned away to where Abbi and Bridget were heading toward the medical bay.

***

"What should we call ourselves?"

Rider posed the question at lunch. He sat, finished with his meal, hands laced behind his head.

"A team?" Nigel ventured, not understanding.

There was an explosive snort of laughter. Rex was surprised to find that it was Abbi. Nigel turned a long-suffering look on her. Rider continued.

"No, I mean, if we're a team, we should have a name. You know, so we can have a war cry or something. It'll make us official."

Americans. They were always giving names to things that didn't need them. But, she had to admit, it would help the group feel more connected. That definitely couldn't hurt, especially after today's loss. She tried to ignore the board above the mess hall door that screamed *"Fourth Place!"* beside their group number.

"Ooh, I think that's a perfect idea!" Bridget said. It was easy for her to be so positive. Her back was to the door. She wasn't the one being perpetually reminded that she had failed as a leader in the first assessment. "Maybe we could be the Warriors."

"Hm, good idea, but it's a little too obvious I think." Rider flicked an unruly strand of hair into place. It immediately fell back down. "Any more?"

The others began throwing out names.

"The Raptors?"

"Swifts."

"Beta? It was what they called me on the arts mat back home," Alelta said.

Rex's interested was piqued at the last comment, drawing her mind away from the scoreboard. An idea formed. "Hold back, what's everyone's mat name?"

"I didn't have one. I guess I could call myself the Amputated Sloth," Rider grinned. Rex couldn't help giving a small snort of laughter.

"Mine was Hailstorm," Abbi said. "Since my name's Abihail."

"Gale," Bridget said.

Nigel raised a hand. "Mine's Fenris. Why?"

Rex nodded, acknowledging his question. "I'm trying to see if there's a common theme among some of the names. Maybe we could use that."

"We seem to have 'storms' and 'wolves' in common," Alelta said. "What do you think, Rex?"

Rex hesitated. Her name on the mat had been Stormstriker, but several of the others did have wolf names. And their placement would be determined according to the levels of a wolf pack.

"What about the Gaelwolves? It combines both."

Rider screwed up his face, considering. "Not bad. Gales and wolves. Wolves and gales. It makes me think of a gale of snapping teeth."

Bridget laughed. "That's fearsome!"

"It's a good name," Alelta said quietly.

Rex nodded as she saw they were all in agreement. "Gaelwolves, then. And that's g-a-e-l, not the normal spelling."

"Does it matter?" Rider asked with a raise of an eyebrow.

Rex regarded him seriously for a moment. "Gael" was the spelling her father had used in a love letter to her mother. *No fire, no wind, no gael, or rough seas could keep me from coming home to you,* had been his words. But she wasn't about to let Rider know that. Fortunately, Tanner cut in, elbowing Rider in the ribs.

"If the lady wants a cool spelling, let her have it, you hawk. It's the gentlemanly thing to do."

"It sounds just fine! I like it," Bridget said.

The others nodded agreement. And so they became the Gaelwolves.

***

Rider crept out of his bunk that night, tiptoeing gingerly to where his boots stood. He slid his feet into them. The soft click of the mechanisms locking onto his legs seemed deafening. He froze, listening. Quiet snores met his ears, along with the rustling of a blanket. Someone shifted in their bunk, and the metal frame squealed in protest. Rider waited, counting to thirty, knowing that anyone woken by the noise would go back to sleep in that time frame. He let out a low sigh. Now all he had to do was get past the bunks without arousing suspicion. And he knew how to do that.

Strolling casually—though quietly—down the aisle, he made his way toward the shower room, confident that anyone who saw him would assume he needed to take a leak. Inside the shower room, he stopped, his eyes focusing in and out as he scanned for any sign of another person. Nothing. With the same quiet steps, he crept through the door that led out to the hallway.

The glass around him was dark, as the new moon cast no light on the compound buildings. That was good; it meant no one could see him. Footsteps came toward him, and he leaned against the wall in the shadow of a support beam as the guard passed. After a few seconds, he slipped into the mess hall and stole into the darkness of the far wall.

"Hey, man, is that you?"

"Yeah, I'm here."

"It only took you twenty years. Are you good for it?" Roth scoffed.

Rider shrugged. "They took all my money when I got here."

Roth stepped closer. Rider felt him move rather than saw him. His eyes were still adjusting to their new focus. "No need to worry about that. I've got mine. It's . . . somewhere safe. I meant, are you good for the job?" Something in his tone told Rider it was more of a threat than a question.

Rider made a casual gesture. "Yeah, I've got it. Guts, if that's what you mean. But I'm getting my position, or it's all off."

Roth snorted. It sounded like a bull getting ready to attack a dog that had wandered into its pen. "What do you think, dumbass?"

Rider bristled. It was his turn to step closer to Roth. He spoke deliberately. "My position. Or it's all off. I'll need extra to convince him."

Roth made a dismissive gesture. "Sure, you'll get it. But you owe me every extra cent once we get sent out."

"Fair enough," Rider said. The breath was squeezed from his throat as Roth seized the front of his shirt and pressed him against the wall.

"You don't think I keep up my end of bargains? You think I'm not fair?" He hissed the words in Rider's face. Rider choked, trying desperately not to cough and alert the guard. Not for the first time, he scrabbled his mind for why Roth would set up a meeting in such a difficult place, at such a difficult time. Why not during the day, during training hours —anywhere but here? As Roth increased the pressure, he realized this was why. The other boy could control him easier this way. Anger boiled in his blood, but he couldn't fight back. If he did, the guard would come and they'd both be caught outside the barracks in the middle of the night. But he knew one way to fight back that had served him many times. He held up his hands in a placating gesture. Roth released him.

"Just an expression," he said, drawing air back into his lungs. "I'll get the job done. I've never let you down before. Have a little faith." He added the last with a winning smile. "I always make good on my end. You do, too," he said, before Roth could lunge at him again. He kept the disarming smile painted on his face, gritting his teeth against the dishonesty of his last statement.

"Oh, you'll make good on it. Because I'll make sure you never get any position if you don't."

0.8

Thwack!

Rex sighed with pleasure as her foot made solid contact with the striking bag. It only rocked slightly, but she knew that was how it should be. If her target had been human, the person's body would have absorbed the full, crushing force of the blow, rather than merely being pushed away.

She steadied herself with another long sigh, slightly crouching in fight stance, and leapt at the bag again. Another thwack echoed through the training room, joining with the storm of other sounds as forty compatriots took turns striking. Falling back to fight stance, she smiled fiercely in satisfaction as Rider grinned approvingly from across the room.

Despite her earlier reserves, she was beginning to find that opening up and receiving others' praise and respect felt good. It was much easier to be friendly than to constantly be on the alert. On the other hand, there was still that incessant internal battle going on—when to trust her teammates, when to take a joke, who to show interest in. Rider was someone she couldn't help but laugh with. He had a devil-may-care attitude that she secretly loved. It seemed to free him up from worry. Only yesterday, in a timed training exercise where they were supposed to climb bars over a stretch of water, he had abandoned the bars and chosen to run through the water. Though the penalty for touching the pool was an addition of ten seconds, he had reasoned it would take more time to climb over the pool than to run through it, even with the added seconds. As it turned out, he had been right, and their team received a better score. She respected his ability to think outside the arena. It was something she couldn't normally do.

"Zero-Twenty-Seven."

The voice was so close, she had to stop herself from jumping. She turned to see Master Ekeli standing—or rather floating—behind her.

"Yes, Master?"

"At ease, Zero-Twenty-Seven," he said as Rex saluted. She briefly wondered how he knew her number. "What is your name?" he asked, with a burr of an accent. She guessed he came from the south, closer to Egypt. It would explain how he had come to be a leader in an elite force. Only people with the hardest constitutions survived life near Egypt's border. It was the point of entry for all attacks made by the Egyptians.

"Rexala Bat'Hai," she replied, somewhat confused.

Master Ekeli nodded. "Rexala. 'The king's soldier,' in the modern Latin form. Strong name for a strong fighter."

Rex was taken aback for a moment. Then she inclined her head slightly. "Thank you, Master. I'm honored."

Master Ekeli tilted his head to one side, inspecting her. "Your eyes. They tell a story of their own." He said the words softly, and Rex wasn't sure if he was sympathetic or merely being observant. "It will serve you well. With all probability, I do not need to tell you this, but I will say it once: do not be afraid to fight back against an abuser—especially in this place. I breed fighters, and I expect them to fight back and prove their mettle."

Rex raised her chin. "Yes, sir." This was so different from her old life. Here, she could fight back.

Here, she was in control.

Ekeli nodded. "As it should be." He stepped forward and gestured to the bag. "Your form is good. Your power, even better. But being airborne has compromised both. Temporarily. I will show you how to improve." He stepped aside. "Stand ready to strike."

Rex took up fight stance.

"Your left fist. A little higher."

Rex had to suppress an annoyed sigh at the criticism. It was the same comment Master Juko had given her back home. She knew it was only a fractional distance, but the arts were about knifeblade precision.

"Better," Master Ekeli said. "What is your most powerful strike?"

Rex answered without hesitation. "High kick, left leg."

"Show me."

She turned to the bag. With a burst of tension, she pushed off her right foot, using her core, and shot her left leg out. Her foot smacked the bag and she pulled it back in a heartbeat, falling back into fight stance. She glanced at the master. His expression, as always, was unreadable.

"Do it with your whole body. Do not forget your basic technique. Yes, there is more freedom and mobility than on the ground. But you must feel as comfortable in the air as you felt on the ground—more comfortable, even. This air, this wind, this freedom is your life. Now, let me show you..."

***

The master's words echoed in the hallways of Rex's mind as she trained for the next few days. The technique he had shown her was something she had never been able to achieve on the ground. It combined all her best points of fighting—motion, speed, and accuracy.

She found herself drilling harder as her past haunted her. Visions of her stepfather pushed into her mind like a robber breaking in, and the world outside faded when she faced the punching bag. The arts had always given her comfort. It was how she had released the drive to fight back for years. Now, with the sky becoming her new earth and the arts at a level she had never experienced, she had a sudden burning desire to go back. An empty feeling weighed heavily in her chest as the unfinished scene played in her mind. She had the drive to finish it, to face him and obtain closure. But she was here, and he was there.

"An eye for an eye..." she murmured to herself. She leapt up to the left and, as Master Ekeli had taught her, let the momentum of her thrust and the weight of her boot carry her in a full spin through the air before she brought her left leg crashing into the practice bag. She fell to one knee as she finished the strike, floating, her eyes closed. "And a tooth for a tooth," she finished. "Closure..."

"Heyyy," Rider drawled, breaking through the fog of her mind. "That was a killer strike. Teach me?"

Rex blinked, wary of the praise, but everything she knew about Rider told her he was worthy of her trust. She shrugged, deciding there was no harm in helping a fellow compatriot with his technique. "Sure." She faced the bag. "Start in fight stance. Are you right-dominant or left?"

"You mean right- or left-handed? Right." Rider fell into fight stance beside her.

"And your most powerful strike?"

Rider hesitated. "Right uppercut, I guess."

"Alright. Push yourself off, slightly to the left, and let your momentum carry you. Like this." She leapt up, feeling the exhilarating rush of air as she showcased the 360-degree turn and the satisfying thunk of her foot on the bag. "And end like this," she said, glancing back over her shoulder from where she had landed.

Rider whistled. "Okay, I'll give it my best shot. Up and . . . to the left, you said?"

Rex nodded. Before she could say anything further, Rider had hurled himself into the air. He spun just over 180 degrees, then faltered and floated slowly down.

"Harder than it looks," he grunted.

Rex conceded the point. "It was for me, too, at first. The main thing is getting the momentum of your whole body when you leap, and letting it build up and carry you all the way through the spin. Once you get that, you have to figure out how to aim so that all that momentum hits the bag in the right spot. If you don't direct it properly, you'll just spin out of control. It takes practice."

"So does hitting a target dead in the heart," Rider said. It was all too obvious that he was keeping a smile off his face. Rex rankled a bit. Her stepfather used to demean her achievements—or what he saw as a lack thereof. In addition, she had suffered a blow to her pride when she lost the bet at the shooting range, even though she hadn't actually had to give him her medallion. But Rider's smile broke through just in time to stop her from flying away to another punching bag.

"Don't be too sore about it. I still can't get through a sandpit faster than an amputated sloth."

In spite of herself, Rex let out a burst of laughter. "I barely knew what a sloth was like before you started impersonating one," she said.

Rider looked at her questioningly. "Where did

you live before now?"

"In a fading edge town. I didn't go into the city much."

"Ah." Rider nodded. "That explains it."

Once again, Rex felt her temper rising. "Explains that I don't know anything about anything, you mean?" she asked.

To her surprise, Rider shook his head emphatically. "No, not at all. You don't know some unimportant things, but you know the important things. And that's what's important."

Rex considered the statement and realized Rider hadn't meant offense. She relaxed once again. "Thank you, I suppose."

Rider shrugged. "Sure thing. Now, let's see if I can do this move." He was about to leap into the air when Sergeant Bailey's voice cut through the room like a whip. Even though she was on the ground, it carried clearly up to the compatriots.

"Compatriots! Form up!"

That's odd. Master Ekeli should have been the one to call a halt to arts training. But then Rex saw him standing next to the sergeant and realized he had told her to give the order.

Rex swooped down from the ceiling in a rush of air. She was conscious of the other members of her team forming up around her. They seemed to do that automatically. Pride swelled in her chest at their recognition of her leadership.

"I have a briefing for you all." Sergeant Bailey's voice remained loud and commanding. She strode up and down the lines of compatriots, as she always did. And, as she always did, she wasted no time in getting to the point. "Multiple pieces of tech have malfunctioned. So far, it's been small things—the hologram siding on the training building, the force field on the upper platform, yada yada. But the instances are getting more frequent, and there seems to be a pattern. All the areas targeted are related to portions of your training. For instance, the hologram siding blacks out the upper levels of the training building, making sure that no one gets an advantage by looking at the upper levels before we move to that phase. The force field . . . well, you'll find out why it's important to a major obstacle in the second phase. Whoever's doing this seems to want to send the message that we don't have our training course under control, or that it isn't safe. Right now, it's merely an embarrassment. But at any time, something more serious could malfunction, and we don't want that to happen. Someone could get hurt."

Her eyes bored into the group. "Tampering with technology is a serious offense. Anyone with *any* information is to come forward with it. Meet me at headquarters after practice. Any questions?"

"Yeah, I have a question," Rider called. "Where's headquarters?"

"My office, just past the medical bay. There's a hallway to the right. Any other questions?"

Silence greeted her query. She nodded.

"Don't try to protect someone who's causing problems on purpose. It won't go well for you. Dismissed!"

Master Ekeli called for them to resume training. As Rex turned away, about to activate her boots, she caught sight of Roth leaving with the sergeant. He caught her eye and winked. With a snort of annoyance, Rex twisted the buckle on her belt and shot up into the air.

Glancing around, she saw Rider conversing with Alelta and felt a vague, unfamiliar longing in her chest as she thought of how her own conversation with him had been cut short.

0.9

In the next week, Rex got to know her teammates better. Bridget, she found out, loved to spend her free time flying everywhere she was allowed to go within the compound. At first, she went alone. The second time, Rex joined her to make sure she wasn't bothered by Roth or any boys with ill intentions. She knew that assault was heavily punished by the sergeants, but she wasn't about to leave Bridget alone until she had a better scope on who was trustworthy.

Zyanya, seeming to sense her thoughts, joined them as they flew out from the Ledge during a break. Bridget, in keeping with her bright attitude, made exclamations on how beautiful the sky was. Zyanya commented on how she missed seeing eagles—or any birds, for that matter.

They soon began talking about their lives at home while Rex listened, her senses still alert. Bridget had a fairly happy life on the fading edge of Dublin. The Irish had joined the Alliance to preserve their own freedom, which they knew would be crushed under communist rule. When the State had come to demand subjection, the Irish had fought like demons until the communists were forced to grant them one request: the ability to approve their own local rulers. Like the rest of the conquered world, the Irish were mostly grouped into major cities and fading edge towns. Bridget's town, it seemed, had a particularly independent population that smuggled weapons into Dublin.

"We've never been caught," Bridget giggled. "Every time the State comes to arrest someone, they can only hold 'em for a few days because the rest of us find a way to plant evidence or do somethin' else that takes the State off the scent. There was one time when we were able to pay off an officer with sheep's cheese and brandy."

"One of the State's men was bought off by cheese?" Zyanya was incredulous.

"*Sheep's* cheese," Bridget said, nodding meaningfully. "A small cartful. Aged just right, with rosemary in it. And some of the darkest red-gold brandy you ever saw. He reported that he had searched our cellars and found no weapons. Of course, he didn't say that he had found somethin' else he wanted much more."

"But State soldiers are ruthless. They are like wolves gone mad from hunger. They never stop hunting," Zyanya said. Rex knew that some Native Americans had moved back to the open plains after the Blackout. The State hated the fact that there were people outside of their cities, and they hunted the Natives to kill the spirit of independence that remained in their tribes. State soldiers who were assigned to the hunt were some of the worst—tough enough to survive the wild, strong enough to fight the fierce Natives, and driven enough to keep at it until their targets were dead. Evidently, the officers near Dublin weren't the same way.

"Where I live, the officers are more interested in going home to their cozy fires than in fightin' fire demons. That's what they call us! They're even scared of the children." Bridget broke down in a fit of laughter.

"The State killed the tribe I was born into," Zyanya said quietly. As Bridget stopped laughing, she continued. "Someone told them where our tribe was. My mother saved me by hiding me in a hollow tree we used for a guard post. I was adopted by another tribe. But I never discovered who betrayed us. I'm not certain if even the Alliance knows. If I become alpha, that is what I would like to know. And if the traitor is still alive, I will kill him." The intensity in her voice was a shock even to Rex. Zyanya was a serious girl, but she had never revealed anything so dark or personal as this.

"I'm terribly sorry," Bridget whispered.

"It's brave to tell that to other people," Rex said. She hoped it didn't sound unfeeling.

Zyanya gave her a searching gaze. "One warrior's trials are the trials of all her tribe. When we become braves, we tell the others the struggles we have and the things we fight for, so we can all fight for them together. It is strength."

"That's beautiful!" Bridget said. "We Gaelwolves

should do that."

"I don't think everyone will be as comfortable with that as Zyanya is," Rex said quickly.

Bridget's face fell. "Well, I'll tell both of ya, anyway."

A whistle sounded in the distance. Rex turned to head toward the training ground, where she could see compatriots gathering.

"It'll have to wait until later. We've got training."

When they reached the training field, they fell in with their group and stood facing Sergeant Bailey. Behind her lay the large, open space they would use for the assessment, which had a trench dug into it.

"Compatriots! Your assessment today will employ all the skills you've learned so far, and it'll prepare you for field combat. Each team will face one other in a mock battle. You'll have twenty minutes to break through the other team's front line and take their trench. Only training weapons will be used. If you're hit in any vital areas—that includes the chest, head, and stomach—your vest will shut off, at which point you have to stop, get on your knees, and put your hands behind your head to indicate you're out of the fight. Teams one and two!"

To Rex's surprise, the Gaelwolves were the first team. To her disgust, Roth's was the second. The tall, muscular boy was rolling his shoulders and cracking his neck, a grin on his face. The expression reminded Rex of a shark. He stood at the head of his group, as Rex had often noticed him do.

"That'll make shooting you easier," she muttered.

"Teams!" the sergeant called. "Gear up, full shooting equipment."

"Come on," Rex called to her team. They set out at a fast jog for the training building. The training gear was on one wall, and it only took a few minutes for them to suit up. As they filed out of the training room, Sergeant Bailey called to them and assigned them to the far side of the training ground. Taking in the layout, Rex addressed her team.

"Four of you will come with me to hold a line in front. We'll attack from there. Nigel, Bridget, Abbi, get down in the trench, just in case anyone breaks through. The rest of you, follow my lead." She paused as she felt a hand on her arm.

"We should use that war cry now, Captain," Rider said with a grin.

Rex nodded, seeing Roth's team forming up in her peripheral vision. "It'll boost morale. But be quick about it."

Rider took a deep breath and bellowed, "Hunters swift as winds that blow,"

"Bringing all our enemies low! Gaelwooolves!" the group howled as one. With that, they charged forward as Sergeant Bailey's piercing whistle began the fight.

Rex met an opposing compatriot head-on, wasting no time. She gunned him down and swung her AR-15 in a huge arc to bring down two other people. One of them went down, his hands raised. The other hadn't been hit in any vital areas, and he trained his gun on Rex. She ducked her head and brought it close to the body of her gun as she crouched to minimize herself as a target. Plastic bullets spattered off her training gauntlets. She squinted as one bounced off her goggles. With a yell fueled by adrenaline, she fired relentlessly until her opponent's vest died and he was forced to admit defeat. Rex moved forward, a smile on her face. There was something thrilling about gunning people down and watching them sink to their knees.

"Come on, this way! There's an opening!" She gestured to her team and led the way. Rider, Alelta, and Zyanya fell in behind her. A quick glance backward told Rex that Tanner was engaged with another opponent.

"Zyanya!" Rex called. "Help Tanner out!"

The tall girl nodded and fell back, hitting the defender from behind. Rex had no more time to watch as another defender plunged toward her, gun blazing. She had to drop to one knee to avoid the bullets, then fired up at the boy. He staggered as a shot hit him full in the forehead.

"I just won back that medallion," Rex said with a fierce smile of satisfaction. As she did, she noticed movement off to her left. One of the defenders was running in a crouch along the sidelines toward their trench. Rex swung her gun on him.

"No you don't . . ." She sighted and pulled the trigger.

The gun was struck from her hands, hitting her painfully in the face. She reeled back and heard the weapon thud to the ground some distance away.

Roth stood over her, his gun poised at her head. He shook his head.

"Too easy. I thought you'd have more fire."

"I'll show you fire," Rex growled. But Roth shook his head again.

"No, see, I have this gun here," he brandished his weapon, "And your head is there. If it had real bullets, they couldn't miss, and you'd be dead. Now, put your hands up."

Rex raised her hands and smiled wolfishly at him. "Except that you haven't fired it." Her already raised hands came up and shoved the gun upward. A shot exploded inches from her ear and she cringed despite her cybernetic implants blocking the noise. Roth darted in and tried to shove her away, but she recovered just in time. With a yell, she threw herself forward, countering his thrust, and brought her forearm crashing down on his wrist. Using the momentum of her body weight, she fell, yanking the gun from his hands at a forty-five-degree angle. She stood and shuffled backward quickly, aiming the gun at his forehead.

"I wouldn't move if I were you," she said, exhaling lightly. Roth stared at her, and she smiled back. He slowly fell to his knees.

"Keep those hands up," Rex said sweetly as she passed him, keeping the gun trained on him and giving him a wide berth to avoid any sudden lunges. She knew she would have to shoot him in order for him to be truly out of the fight. Just as Rex was about to squeeze the trigger, one of Roth's teammates slammed into her and knocked her to the ground. She fell over the gun as she broke her fall with her elbow. The gun fired. Pain exploded in her left leg and she screamed as a bullet—a real and very deadly bullet—tore through bone and muscle. At such short range, it went straight through. She dropped the weapon and seized her leg, giving a yell of pain through her clenched teeth.

"How . . . ?" The boy who had pushed her stood aghast, his legs spattered with Rex's blood. Roth shoved him.

"Go get the doctor!" Roth yelled. The boy turned and ran toward Sergeant Bailey.

Rex rocked back and forth, holding pressure over the hole in her calf. Tears stung her eyes as the excruciating pain racked her and blood gushed from the wound. She was no medic, but she knew by the bits of bone protruding from the hole that the bullet had shattered part of her shinbone.

"That looks pretty bad. Let me help you." Roth bent toward her, but she growled at him. Hands shaking, eyes streaming with unbidden tears, she slid off one of her gauntlets and placed it between her teeth. She bit down hard as she stripped the hem of her pants leg away, then wrapped it around the wound. It wasn't much of a bandage, but it would have to do. She pulled the binding tight, her cry of pain masked by the gauntlet in her mouth and the sounds of the others still shooting.

"Rex!"

Rider's hoarse cry carried to her across the field.

He came running and threw himself down beside her. "What happened?"

Rex clenched her teeth. She couldn't speak. *A lot of good I'd be in a battle.*

Roth answered Rider's question. "The gun had a real bullet in it." He paused, realization dawning on his face. "She almost killed me!"

At that, Rex found her voice. She spat the gauntlet from her mouth. "It was *your* gun!"

"No it wasn't," Roth insisted. "That's yours, and you tried to shoot me with it!"

Rex could see a red tunnel forming around her vision. She knew she was beginning to black out. But her anger clawed out of the tunnel and reached for Roth's lying eyes. "I. Disarmed. You," she spat deliberately. "And other people saw it."

Roth hesitated for a split second, and she could tell he was calculating the possibility of if, in the heat of the confrontation, anyone had really seen the sequence of events. "They—"

"I saw it." Rider rose to his feet. "She beat your butt and took your gun."

Roth's eyes narrowed and a calculating look came into them. He smiled. Even with her blurred vision, it was disturbing to Rex.

"Rider . . ." he said in a warning tone. But Rider pushed forward until his face was inches from Roth's.

"You liar," he hissed. "You leave her alone, or I'm out."

Roth laughed derisively. "You can't. It's already

started. I told you this would happen."

Rider raised his fist. It shook as he brought it up under Roth's chin. The other boy continued to smile. Rider's jaw clenched and unclenched as he breathed heavily, his eyes locked on Roth's. Abruptly, he turned away and fell to one knee beside Rex.

"The doctor's coming," he said. He placed a steadying hand on her shoulder. Perhaps it was the pain, or the half-delirious state she was in, but Rex reached out and gripped his arm. The pressure helped her hold on to the real world as the pain threatened to shut off her consciousness. Dimly, she was aware of Leah checking her leg. She gave a gasp as the doctor pulled off the makeshift bandage there and swabbed the wound with a clean cloth. A moment later, she was aware of Rider's voice echoing in her ears.

"Can you walk?"

Rex turned her head in his direction. The walls of the vision tunnel were closing in. It would be so easy to go to sleep . . .

"Rex? I know you can do it. Get up, Rex."

Get up, Rex. Her father's voice rang in her head. Suddenly she was a little girl again, sprawled in the sand. Her father bent close to her.

A true fighter always gets up.

There had been a training session. She had fallen. Had he been training her?

Get up, Rex.

Her eyes shot open and she gripped Rider's arm fiercely. With a roar of pain and effort, she heaved herself to her feet.

She was Rexala. She was her father's daughter. She was a fighter. And she would always get up.

With one arm around Rider's shoulder and one around Leah's, Rex stumbled forward past the enemy's trench she had so nearly taken, her head held high.

***

"I'm going to do it," Leah stated. "You know I have to." She selected an instrument from the tray, glancing at Rex's unconscious body. The girl breathed gently under the effects of the sedative, and she didn't stir when the robotic arm from the ceiling shifted the light above her face.

Master Ekeli sighed. "It will give her an unfair advantage."

"Which is why I'm going to do it to all of them. Fitting them early will increase their drive."

Ekeli fingered his chin. "I had hoped to practice more technique before adding cybernetics. But I suppose . . ."

"Whatever you had hoped for doesn't matter, as long as they're ready." Leah stripped the bandage from Rex's leg. She snapped her fingers, emitting a low whistle, and two assistant medical droids rolled into the room. Their cylindrical bodies shot up to head height and made a series of clicking noises as dexterous cybernetic limbs unlocked.

"Surgery, Pallios. Surgery, Manka," she said to the droids. "Brush." Pallios handed Leah an instrument, and Manka held out a cup. "And you said they're ready enough for fitting," Leah continued to Ekeli. "Besides, the girl's no good with one shattered leg."

"Such a shame." Master Ekeli shook his head. "But she will be even more powerful afterward. I assume you will use the chamber for the others?"

Leah didn't answer for a moment. She kept her teeth clenched in concentration as she used the glowing magnetic surgery paint to indicate where she would make incisions in Rex's leg. "Yes. But this one's special," she said with a smile.

Ekeli nodded. "Yes. Very special," he agreed.

010

Rex woke from the deepest sleep she'd had in years. She blinked slowly and turned her head. Rider's face leaned over her, and a smile broke out on it as she looked up into his dark eyes.

"Well, good morning, La Capitan," he said. Rex laughed. It sounded strange to her ears.

"Morning, Rider," she said with a yawn. Then she frowned. "Why are you in the girls' barracks?"

Rider chuckled. "No, we're definitely not in the barracks. Look." He gestured around the room. With another yawn, Rex sat up—and caught her breath. She was somewhere in the medical wing, judging by the reflective walls, but instead of darkness, the left-hand side of the room opened up to the outside. Sunlight fell through, and Rex imagined she could hear birds singing. Of course, that was fanciful. No birds lived forty thousand feet up in the stratosphere. Then she realized it was the wind. It sang through the open glass doorway with a beautiful, haunting voice.

She tried to rise and yelped as she felt cold metal on her leg. Horrified, she looked back and forth between her left leg and right arm—or rather, what had replaced them.

Her entire leg from mid-thigh down was comprised of interlocking panels of blue steel. Her right forearm was the same. No—her arm was only reinforced, not replaced like her leg. She turned her hand palm-up, then turned it back. The movement was smooth, and she could feel strands of something—she guessed it was metal cord—twisting inside her wrist.

"What . . . ?" She flexed her foot, feeling the cords there contract and elongate. Her leg—or whatever was left of it—ached. She looked to Rider. "What did they do? And why did they do it? And why are you here?"

Rider smiled reassuringly at her. "You remember your leg was shattered, right? You wouldn't have been able to train like that. The doctor lady 'fitted' you. That's what she called it, anyway. I'm here because Abbi needed to grab something. She's been watching what the doctor did so she can learn."

Rex shook her head, still shocked. "But why did Leah reinforce my arm?"

Rider nodded. "I asked her about it. She said that Master Ekeli said that that was your strongest asset. Other than your leg. We've all seen those high kicks you do."

Rex touched her fingers against her thigh, then opened and closed her fist, feeling metal meet metal as her fingertips pressed into her palm. Her ribs jarred painfully as she touched them. "What in the blasting fires of Gehenna . . . she replaced my ribs too?"

"No, definitely not," Rider hastened to placate her. "She reinforced your torso so other gunshots wouldn't decimate your organs."

"So I'm . . . what, bulletproof?"

"Well, more or less."

"Wow." Rex stood slowly, testing her weight on the new leg. Her thigh seized up in a cramp and she gasped, groping for the bed railing. Rider's arm seemed to materialize under her fingers. Rex froze, unable to turn and meet his gaze. There was incredible strength in his forearm alone—and yet he was supporting her in a moment of vulnerability rather than hurting her.

"Are you alright?" Rider asked. His arm remained steady under her fingers.

Wait.

Her fingers were reinforced with metal plating, and yet she could feel every hair on Rider's lean arm. She tried to ignore the sensation.

"I'm fine."

She gingerly set her foot on the floor. She flexed her toes, pressing each, one at a time, into the floor, absorbing the cold and the unyielding concrete under them. She did the same with her human foot. It couldn't be . . . but it was. The cybernetic replacement was more sensitive than her own skin. Standing to her full height, Rex surveyed her new body as best she could, from her toes to her elbows. Once again, she tested the range of motion for her right arm.

"Wouldn't Kani love to see this?" she mused, admiring the smooth motion of the armor she had been given. Armor wasn't something she'd ever anticipated having—especially not as a symbol of status. Typically, the only status indicated by armor was that of being disabled. Even the rich simply bought fancier armor to make their disabilities less shameful. Here, it meant she was strong. In fact, she was the strongest recruit at the compound.

She looked around suddenly. "Where's Roth?" she asked in a low voice. Rider stood, one hand raised as she moved toward him and the doorway.

"Don't mess with him," he warned. "He's not a good person to bug off."

Rex snorted. "He should have realized *I'm* not a good person to bug off before he got me shot and accused me of trying to kill him. Get out of my way." She pushed past him.

"Rex, I'm warning you! He doesn't forget. You won't be safe."

She locked her eyes on Rider's, and she saw fear there. It was not something she normally associated with him. "Whatever he's done to you, I'll make sure he never does it again." She vaguely remembered him saying something unusual to Roth the day before, but right now, she couldn't recall exactly what it was. "I'm not afraid." She stalked out the door.

Roth was propped on one knee on the training ground, breathing heavily. Several of the others were finishing their rounds of push-ups nearby. Rex strode past them, ignoring the darts of pain that shot into her thigh from her new leg. Before Roth had time to react, she grabbed him by the back of his shirt and heaved him bodily from the ground, using the new strength from her reinforced arm. She delivered two lightning punches to his face.

"That's for hitting me in the face with my own gun."

She kicked him in the shin with her left—metal—foot. Roth howled in agony and scrabbled to get out of her hold. Rex bit back the howl of pain she had almost released herself.

"That's for getting me shot."

She threw him back into the dirt and brought her knee down to crush his chest. She smiled savagely as he choked under her full body weight bearing down on him.

"And that's for lying to try and get me court-martialed," she finished.

Peep! Peep-peep-peep-peeeeep!

The male sergeant—Rangorazi—ran up, blowing his whistle. "Break it up! Compatriot!" He addressed Rex, "What is your name and number?"

Rex sighed, rising to her feet. She was getting tired of repeating her information. "Bat'Hai. Zero-Twenty-Seven," she said.

Rangorazi stood in front of her, quivering with rage. "Zero-Twenty-Seven, what is the meaning of this? Why in the black molding bowels of the universe would you attack one of your compatriots?"

Rex's mouthed twitched as she fought to keep a straight face after the ridiculous curse. She raised her chin in defiance. "This *compatriot* had a loaded gun in our training exercise. I disarmed him and ended up getting shot, but he tried to blame me by saying it was my gun that was loaded. He cost me my leg." She gestured to her cybernetic replacement.

"You do realize this will affect not only your score, but the score of your whole team? Fighting during the compatriot phase is strictly forbidden—forbidden!—d'you hear? You agreed to that on day one!"

"I believe Master Ekeli will agree that no points will be deducted for fighting an abuser. Ask him to come. He'll back me up."

Rangorazi smoldered for another moment, then turned as a voice called from directly behind him.

"Rexala is correct." Master Ekeli stepped up. "And as her trainer, I have the authority to pardon her."

"This incident is on my training field! I make the decisions! And she's broken protocol. I'll teach her to attack a compatriot! Her whole team will suffer for her disobedience. She'll be lucky if she has even a 0.0001 percent chance of becoming alpha . . ." he trailed off under Master Ekeli's steady gaze.

"Are you finished?" the master said smoothly. Rangorazi gestured furiously at the air and made an inarticulate noise. Ekeli continued, "I taught Rexala —and others—that fighting back when you are abused or cheated is noble and respected. She cannot be blamed for following my guidance—on your training field, as it may be."

"But the rules of the compatriot phase say that

fighting is forbidden," Rangorazi began. Ekeli cut him off.

"That is true, but let us examine the facts. This compatriot—" he gestured to where Roth lay groaning on the ground, "was the first to breach that rule by carrying a fully functional weapon during a training exercise."

Rex nodded slightly. It was exactly what she had been thinking. But Roth interjected, rising gingerly to a sitting position.

"I didn't know my gun was loaded."

"Oh, so now you admit it was your gun," Rex shot sarcastically. Master Ekeli raised one hand in a gesture to calm her.

"It was indeed his gun. The registration markings proved that." As he said it, Rex vaguely recalled being told that when a gun was claimed for training, the security system automatically cross-referenced the fingerprints of the user with the registration number on the gun.

"So why isn't he the one getting punished?" Rex asked.

"This seems to be another technological malfunction, although it is more concerning than the previous ones. Roth is not under suspicion for these malfunctions and, as he said, he did not know the gun was loaded. However, he did breach the rules of combat by not checking his weapon before the assessment. Your team automatically won the round, and you are not at fault for fighting a perceived abuse. In the future, though, I recommend that you ask me for my view on a situation before damaging another compatriot." He smiled slightly.

"But . . ." Roth and Rangorazi began at the same time. Master Ekeli held up one finger.

"Remember who is your senior," he said, with an unmistakable finality in his tone.

Roth scowled and Rangorazi muttered foul language under his breath. Rex inclined her head slightly, triumph swelling in her chest. Finally, finally, she had been able to fight back. The days of submission and secrecy, the days of hiding from her abusers were over. She smiled at Roth and turned away, ignoring his murderous glare on her back.

***

"Forty-five, forty-six, forty-seven . . ."

Rex grunted as Sergeant Bailey called the push-ups. After a meal and a short rest period following the incident with Roth, she had begun her training with her new cybernetics. The push-ups were the first part of the strength training. Rex pushed herself to fifty and sighed with relief as the sergeant called a halt. The exercise had set her muscles on fire where they met with metal.

"Water break!" the sergeant called.

Rex was about to rise when a hand appeared in front of her.

"Here you go, Captain." Rider smiled down at her. She clasped his hand and he hauled her to her feet.

"What're you doing here?" she asked. Out of the corner of her eye, she could see a small file of compatriots heading for the training room.

"Me and the rest of the team are getting fitted. Since you've been fitted, the rest of us will be at a disadvantage, so they're doing the operations early. The operation chambers are apparently on the second floor of the training building."

"Do you know what you're going to have altered?" Rex asked. Rider gave her a lopsided grin. She couldn't help smiling back.

"My arms. I'm going to get guns put in them."

Rex laughed out loud. "That'll be a cold day in the desert." She paused. "You're joking, right?"

Rider raised an eyebrow and shook his head, the smile still on his face. "Guns are my best asset, so I'm gonna get reinforcements where I can lock blasters into my hands. I'm pretty excited. They said there's some risk involved, so I just hope they don't chop off my arms and leave them that way."

Rex frowned. "I didn't know there was a risk. I mean, it makes sense. But then, I was unconscious and no one was worried about me." She said the last words with a small pang.

"I was."

Rider's warm, dark eyes had a soft look she hadn't seen there before. It was concern, she realized. Then she turned away. She was being fanciful. No one cared about her like that except her mother, and maybe Kani. She hadn't known Rider long enough for him to be concerned about her. She brought the focus back around to him.

"Well, we definitely don't want you to lose your arms," she deadpanned. "Then you'd actually be an amputated sloth."

Rider gave a short burst of laughter. "Definitely not," he agreed. "Well, I've got to go. The chambers of amputation call." He turned away.

"Rider?" Rex said. She suddenly had a surge of fear for the tall, lean boy. She noticed, as if for the first time, how perfect his physique was, and how devastating it would be if he lost limbs or, worse, risked his life. "I'll see you on the other side of the chambers?"

Rider gave her that easy, lopsided grin of his. "See you on the other side." Then he jogged off toward the training building.

**

As it turned out, the fitting took two hours. Once it was done, training started immediately for all the Gaelwolves. They raced back and forth between two markers on the field and touched each before running back. Next came push-ups, crunches, and pull-ups. Some of them struggled with their enhancements, stumbling or even falling as they became accustomed to new or reinforced limbs. Rex, having already done her training, sat watching them. She reveled a little in not having to work anymore, but her satisfaction was short-lived. Sergeant Bailey called a halt and ordered the group to report to Leah. Rex stood, brushing off her dusty cargo pants, and fell into step beside Rider and Alelta.

"So, you think Leah's going to let you practice with your new guns?" she asked Rider.

"Probably. I mean, since she's the head of cybertech, I would assume so."

A thought struck Rex. "If she's the head of cyber-tech, isn't she under suspicion as a possible cause for the tech malfunctions?"

Rider shrugged. "Yeah, I had thought about that, but I think Master Ekeli checked her out. Not that way," he chuckled as Rex frowned at him.

Rex recalled what Ekeli had said earlier about being Rangorazi's superior. "Why is he the head man here? I would have expected one of the sergeants to be in charge. I mean, Sergeant Bailey seems to take care of all the paperwork, and she has the office."

"Beats me," Rider said. "Maybe he's some legend from the war that the Alliance stuck here to keep fresh and relevant."

Rex ignored the good-natured sarcasm. "It just doesn't make a lot of sense. And who does he report to?"

Alelta cut in. "I know one of his superiors is someone high up in the Israeli government. Nobody is allowed to know who, but I think it's Aghbad Shalif." Shalif was one of the primary weapons managers in Israel. It would make sense.

"I'm just wondering who's checking in on us. Surely they don't just leave it all up to Master Ekeli. There should be checks and balances for each position of power. Otherwise you'll get a dictator, and then there's trouble. That's what's about to happen with China."

"There's probably more communication between Ekeli and whoever runs his life than we know about," Rider said unaffectedly. Rex had to be content with that, as they had reached the lower level of the training room where Leah was.

"Good afternoon, compatriots."

Rider raised a hand. "Gaelwolves," he interjected. Leah nodded.

"My apologies. Gaelwolves. Congratulations on being the first fitted team. While the others are still in the process, I'll show you how to operate each of your new features." She stepped toward Rex. "I'll start with you." Without further warning, the woman leapt toward Rex, launching a rapid series of strikes directly at her face.

It was only her lifetime of hypervigilance that saved Rex from a broken nose. She shot her forearms up just in time to avoid Leah's strikes. Despite her instinctive reaction, she couldn't avoid one punch that grazed across her cheek. Leah brought a fist toward Rex's neck; Rex batted it aside, but Leah kept Rex on the defensive, forcing her back. The woman's palm smacked Rex's shoulder. It was a move intended to mock and insult an opponent, but Rex refused to take the bait.

She knew she could keep deflecting blows. She also knew that she had trained her whole life for more than that.

She brought her reinforced right arm up, and Leah's fist slammed directly into it. Rex flicked her arm—and Leah's fist—aside and darted her own fist inside the woman's guard.

"Good!" Leah stepped back, still in fight stance.

"Block like that again, with the solid arm, and then strike with your other asset."

As the rapid-fire blows came at her, Rex pushed forward, maintaining her balance, and brought her forearm up. At the same time, she shot her left leg up in a high kick. Leah was expecting the move and brought her own arm up to block it, but the force of Rex's strike hurled her off-balance, and she swayed. Rex put her foot in Leah's stomach, pushing her back. The woman rolled to avoid injury and sprang to her feet just as Rex followed up with another foot strike aimed at Leah's throat.

It never reached its mark.

Rex felt a jarring impact as something stopped her leg in mid-swing. She realized it was Leah's leg. The woman's pants had rolled up to reveal blue steel above her ankle. Before Rex could react, Leah spun Rex's leg aside and drove in, stopping only when her fist was just under Rex's jaw.

"Never allow yourself to be surprised. Your killer will be a hidden monster. There's no room for hesitation." She stepped back. "Keep your advantage when you have it and don't let anything compromise your focus." While she was speaking, she brought a right hook up to catch Rex on the chin, but Rex was ready, and she swayed backward, knocking Leah's fist out of the way and striking a solid punch on the woman's face. Leah staggered back a pace. She raised her head, laughing as blood trickled from her nose.

"Very good! I'm not Ekeli, but he'd agree with me. Now, let me show you something." She wiped the blood from her nose with the back of her hand and crouched, one knee on the floor. Putting both hands to the ground, she took a stance as though she were about to do a push-up. With several deep breaths, she slowly raised her body off the floor. It was something Rex had practiced, though not primarily, at her arts school. She watched as Leah brought herself into a handstand, then shifted her weight to one arm, legs splayed for balance.

"You do it," Leah said. "With your right arm."

Rex frowned slightly as she bent to her knees and put her hands on the ground. "Why this stance? I thought the arts were supposed to be airborne. This is ground technique." Nevertheless, she raised herself on both hands. Her arms shook, and she had to touch her feet to the ground several times to push herself up into a handstand. Breathing heavily, she prepared herself to make the switch to one arm, conscious of everyone's eyes on her. She pulled her left hand off the floor. Her body swayed precariously for a moment, then pain shot up her arm and it collapsed under her. "I'm not entirely comfortable with this new arm," she said pointedly, glaring at the doctor.

Leah smiled slightly at her. "You never know when your boots may give out and you find yourself on the ground, so you need to know how to operate there as well. You'll get used to it, in time. This exercise is especially helpful. If your reinforced arm can do this, it can do anything. Try again."

Rex settled her body weight onto her hands,

hovering inches from the floor. She touched one foot to the floor and pushed herself into a handstand. Bracing herself for the pain, she slowly shifted her weight to her reinforced arm. It quaked violently under her. She remembered Master Juko's words: *When you shake, that is your body gaining strength. Keep your position.* With a supreme effort, she breathed deeply and centered herself over her hand. She felt the cold floor beneath her palm, the burning pain in her arm, and the weight of her body, then imagined a straight line from the ground to her shoulder. She raised her legs into a position that would allow her to deliver a kick. Then she opened her eyes and looked at Leah. The woman gave a small nod.

"Release."

Rex set her other hand on the ground and rolled forward into a crouching position. She stepped back, making an enormous effort not to groan.

"Very good. I'll train more with you later."

The other recruits took their turns exploring their new weapons and assets under Leah's direction. Alelta's wristlets from her mother turned out to be the key piece of a cybernetic implant that activated blades in her arms. As the American girl whirled her blades in a lightning sequence, driving Leah back toward the wall, Rex wondered how far ahead the Alliance had planned, and how they had known that Alelta would eventually receive these particular enhancements. Perhaps her mother had been a swordmaster, too.

More importantly, when the next phase came,

Alelta's skill would be a serious challenge for the alpha position.

Bridget had vocal cord implants that allowed her to mimic voices. The doctor had Bridget listen to several recordings of people of various nationalities saying everyday words. Rex had to hold back a smile as the red-haired girl rasped and croaked while Leah took her through voice exercises, trying to help her fit her mouth and throat around the unfamiliar tones. By the end of the session, however, Bridget could successfully imitate the pitch of a Chinese man saying, "Breakfast, friend?" Leah seemed immensely pleased, and Bridget joined the others with a smile on her freckled face.

Tanner had both his legs enhanced for faster running. After the first few minutes, in which he drew gasps from the others at the sheer speed he exhibited, the excitement wore off and there wasn't much to see that the quick-footed boy hadn't already shown in their training exercises. Abbi had a full armored breastplate that rendered her entire torso completely bulletproof, rather than merely being reinforced. Leah explained that it was protection for when Abbi became a medic.

"You'll have people shooting at you from every direction even when you're trying to save someone," she said. "Your best weapon in that case is to be impenetrable so you can keep doing what needs to be done." To demonstrate, Leah fired a shot directly into Abbi's stomach. The small girl yelped and doubled over as if expecting a shredded midsection, but when she stood back up, the bullet hovered less than an inch from the metal plating.

"It's magnetic. It stops the bullet before it hits you. Not only will you not be hurt, you won't even feel the shot hit. Because it doesn't."

This development was arguably the most revolutionary one of the day. When Nigel asked why everyone couldn't have magnetic bulletproof armor, Leah gave him the shadow of a smile.

"If you want to pay two thousand shekels to the Alliance, go ahead. That's how much it costs to get a four-foot sheet of this metal developed, not to mention getting it molded to the wearer."

Nigel subsided at that. However, his own enhancement was a wonder in its own right. He had a virtual computer system that could unfold from his hands. Microsensors in his fingers allowed him to project a floating image that could block enemy security cameras, and his system could both connect to the military communications database and allow him to try and hack into the computer system of an enemy. Glee lit up Nigel's face as he saw list upon list of coding techniques and hacker's loopholes he could explore in his free time.

"I'd recommend getting started on it at dinner," Leah told him. Judging by Nigel's expression, Rex guessed he would waste no time.

Leah called Zyanya forward and explained that she had a blow-dart mechanism in her jaw, similar to the blow pipes used by her native people. Zyanya had just fired her first two darts at a target when the alarm began.

As the high-pitched wailing echoed all across the compound, Leah wasted no time.

"Compatriots, follow me! We're under attack!"

011

The Gaelwolves followed Leah at a run toward the weapons room. Sergeant Bailey had just arrived with another team and was arming them.

"Where's the attack from?" Leah called, snatching a pair of handguns from the wall.

Sergeant Bailey strapped on a bulletproof vest. "The west end. They look like Egyptian assassins. There are twelve, maybe fifteen of them; probably scouts out to locate us again. We can't let any get back to the State with a report, especially not now that they've definitively spotted us. If we take these two teams along with a backup from Rangorazi, we should be able to beat them."

Leah sighed in frustration. "The compatriots aren't supposed to be put at risk like this. Blast these dogs!" She addressed the Gaelwolves. "Gear up! Combat suits are on the far wall, organized by sizing. Choose a weapon if you don't have one built in. You have sixty seconds!"

Rex raced to the far wall and grabbed one of the sleeveless combat tops, which had the same pattern as the pants she wore. She pulled it on over her tank top. The flexible Kevlar was reinforced with a harder material over the vital areas. A dull blue helmet rested on an upper rack, and she seized it and set it on her head. It locked into place, protecting her temples and forehead. Fingerless gloves, reinforced at the knuckles, completed the outfit. Rex strode to the weapons wall and selected a huge machine gun she had always wanted to use. Slinging the ammunition belt across her hips, she shouldered the gun and stood ready.

"Gaelwolves!" she called, not waiting for Leah. "Form up!"

The others fell into place beside her. Leah glanced them over and jerked her head toward the door. "Come on!"

The Egyptian force had just breached the outer wall by the time the Gaelwolves got there. The large guns that were mounted on the barracks roof had evidently held them at bay until now. They swarmed onto the compound, their black oxygen masks and dark goggles giving them a frightening look. Some flew, using their jetpacks, while others moved forward on the ground. Rex ran at the head of her team, and the others formed an arrowhead shape behind her, with Alelta and Rider to her right and left. She activated her shoes and rose into the air.

"Hunters swift as winds that blow," she yelled.

"Bringing all our enemies low! Gaelwooolves!"

Their line drove toward the first of the assassins. Rex hefted the huge gun off her shoulder, leaning her body slightly to one side to counterbalance its weight, and jammed her fingers against the trigger.

The first assassin was cut to smithereens under her onslaught. As she swung it in a horizontal arc, the next two men went airborne to avoid the shots. They fired back with precise blasters, and she felt one of the bullets rip through the thick fabric of her cargo pants. She spun as more bullets peppered the air around her. Rising higher, she leveled her gun at one of the men.

"Rider! Get the one on the right!" she said, keeping up a direct barrage at the left-hand assassin, whose body armor seemed particularly thick.

"Got it."

The man Rex was firing at twisted horribly as her shots hit him. But instead of falling back, he shook himself and began to make his way toward her, barely dodging the bullets from her machine gun. Slowly, inexorably, he closed the space between them. A jolt of concern caught in Rex's chest. The man wasn't going down, despite the crushing barrage he was under. He reached out, his long, clawlike fingers seeking her body.

Long, clawlike fingers.

Your killer will be a hidden monster. There's no room for hesitation.

Rex set her jaw and looked at her attacker's face. She brought her gun up to shoot him in the forehead.

Someone else's bullet found its mark. Rex started as the man's goggles were shattered and cracked by two shots in rapid succession. She whirled and saw Rider, whose twin blasters were locked into cybernetic cords protruding from his wrists.

"Don't fire at the body. Aim for the head," he said coolly, turning to where another assassin was going after Bridget. With two well-placed shots in the back of the man's neck, he felled him.

Rex had no time to reply as another black-clothed figure slammed into her, driving her to the ground. Just before she made impact, she twisted out from under him and shot to one side. He lunged at her, a karambit in each of his hands. She brought the gun up to block his strike, then shoved back at him, using the solid force of her right arm to propel him backward. He catapulted end over end through the air, then simply regained his balance and shot toward her again.

She was about to train her gun on him when a man rushed toward her from her right. She swung around and mowed him down with the machine gun. Blood spattered on her face. She spat it out and found herself facing the karambit man again. As he leapt at her, her ears caught the sound of a group of guns cocking in unison, and she sensed a group of assassins to her right.

"Get down!" she yelled to her team, twisting to one side to avoid the knife strike of the man before her. The assassins' guns rattled in unison. She heard cries of pain, but she couldn't look to verify who had been hit. She barely blocked her assailant's next strike by deflecting his forearm with her own and smashing the gun into his body. A grunt escaped the man, but she didn't pause. Instead, she let go of the gun and, throwing her weight backward, delivered a high kick to his face. His karambits came up, and steel shrieked on steel as they slid along her cybernetic leg. Rex's foot made contact with her opponent's forehead. She followed up her kick immediately, her fists seeking the man's face. She had to suck in her stomach as one of the knives whizzed by.

Slowly, she began to give ground. She realized that this was serious. The man was a deadly opponent, and if she didn't go on the offensive, she would very probably die. With a swift kick to the man's hands to distract him, she pressed her toes downward and launched herself higher. He tried to snatch at her leg, missed, and gave his jetpack a boost to follow her. It was his undoing. As he shot upward, Rex thrust her left foot out. It slid through his hands and connected solidly with his head, his own momentum lending force to the blow. He plummeted back to the ground. Rex swooped down, retrieved her gun and, flying backward out of his reach, gunned him down.

The line of her teammates had broken as they became airborne. She called an order and they resumed formation, all the while firing down at the assassins below.

"We've got to move, or they'll pick us off," Rider shouted. Rex nodded grimly.

"We'll rush them. At my signal, give it all you've got and fly forward. Ready ... Gaelwolves!"

They swept over the assassins. Rex smiled fiercely as she shot down two men. Another one dropped from Rider's gun. Rex heard something whistle past her ear, and realized it was one of the darts Zyanya had just learned to use. The Native American girl pursed her lips, and another dart struck a man in the neck. Alelta came behind with her blades to take care of any men the others had missed with their guns.

Then, suddenly, it was over. Leah's team, which had until now been engaged with a line to their right, pushed forward just behind the Gaelwolves. The line of firing assassins became a row of dead bodies in a matter of seconds. One of the last ones, Rex saw, was trying to slip back toward the wall unnoticed. If he was wearing the same type of body armor that some of the others had, her gunshots might not stop him before he escaped. Rex shot forward and homed in on the man. He turned, saw her coming, and increased his pace. But she dove, seized hold of him by the gun belt slung over his shoulder, and hauled him up with her right arm.

"Halt!" Leah called, her voice ringing across the field. "Disable him and keep him alive!"

Rex stopped herself just in time from flying up and dropping the man to his death. Instead, she smashed her left knee into the side of his head. The assassin's hand, which he had just raised to shoot Rex, fell limp and the gun dropped. Rex floated down to the ground, grunting at the dead weight of the man on her arm.

"Bring him to headquarters. We have a tidy little interrogation room there for him," Leah said.

Rex nodded. She gestured to the Gaelwolves, and Rider hurried up to help her drag the man toward detainment.

"That was some battle," Rider said as he took hold of the man's clothing. "How'd you like my new guns? Well, the second set."

Rex frowned. Rider was certainly in shape, but it was all lean muscle. He wasn't the bulky, powerful type. "You didn't have guns to begin with," she stated flatly.

Rider looked suitably offended. "Who tells a guy he doesn't have guns?"

"The girl who doesn't see them when she looks at the guy," she said. Then, realizing how that statement might sound, she added, "Not that I look at you."

Rider drew himself up with considerable dignity. "You're looking at me right now."

Rex scoffed, heaving the limp assassin's body up so she could get a better grip. "Because I'm talking to you. It's rude not to."

"But it's not rude to tell me I don't have guns?" For a moment, Rex thought Rider might actually be offended. But then his irrepressible smile broke through. "Well, now I do." He brandished his left arm, where the blaster still protruded from where it was attached to the cybernetic cords in his hand. Rex sighed and shook her head.

The interrogation room was a dark, low-ceilinged affair with a single chair flanking a table in the center. Greenish-blue light bounced off the walls in an eerie pattern. Rex and Rider heaved the man into the chair.

"Tie him up, then search him," Leah said, closing the door behind her. "Use cut-back swans. Here." She tossed Rex a length of coarse rope.

"They really seem to like making us tie and untie these," Rider commented. "They're torturing us more than the prisoners."

Nevertheless, Rex noted that he pulled the bonds securely around the man's wrists. She did the same. Once he was secured with both hands and feet tied to the chair, Rex began stripping off the man's body armor with her right hand. As she pulled the Kevlar away, she caught sight of a tattoo on the man's throat. It was some type of animal's head. It looked like a dog's, perhaps, though it was rendered in sharp, angular lines with no real detail.

"Rider, look at this."

"What?" Rider stood from where he was checking the man's boots.

"I don't recognize this symbol. It looks Egyptian, though."

Rider rubbed his chin. "Hmm, you're right. Maybe Anubis? God of the underworld?"

Rex shook her head. "No, his symbol is distinctive, everyone knows it."

"Could be a goddess," Rider suggested. He lifted the man's hand. There were long claws there, like the ones Rex had noticed on one of her attackers. "Judging by his manicure, this guy's probably not the assassin for a goddess of love and fertility. Unless she murders people after she seduces them."

"Shut up," Rex muttered, eyeing the claws. They looked cybernetic rather than genetic. "What is he?"

"Maybe he'll have something else on him that identifies him," Rider suggested. "Let's keep searching." He bent back down to pull off the man's boots. Rex tipped the chair forward slightly and searched with her fingers along the man's shoulders. Grunting with effort, she ripped the padding there away, then stepped back to figure out how to remove his vest, since he was already bound tightly. As her face passed his, his eyes shot open. She caught her breath in sudden fright. They were a luminescent green, deep and penetrating. He wheezed through his oxygen mask.

"He's awake," Rex called, somewhat shakily, to Leah.

"Just finish searching him, then I'll start interrogation."

Rex turned back to the man—or whatever he was—and set her jaw in determination. She took hold of his vest and half pulled, half ripped it off his body. The reinforced Kevlar came away with a tearing noise, and she had to take a step back to regain her balance as the cloth released. Patting down the vest, she found a thin, bumpy package made of orange plastic. As she held it up to the light, the assassin growled.

"I've got something," she called to Leah. The woman was taking off her gloves.

"Set it on the table."

As Rex moved to obey, the assassin spoke for the first time. "You just do what you're told, pretty. No mind of your own."

Rex whirled about. Her eyes bored into his. Anger pushed aside her fear of the glowing orbs in front of her. "You have no idea," she said.

The assassin coughed. Rex guessed that his oxygen mask might not be working correctly. "You've got to learn, practice it. Just make your move when the time comes."

"What in Gehenna's ugly maw are you talking about?"

Rex had to stifle an inconvenient smile at Rider's irreverent appropriation of her cursing. The assassin laughed out loud. It was a gurgling, guttural sound.

"So young, so pretty. So ignorant." He continued laughing.

Rex pulled the back of his chair forward so that he was leaning at an uncomfortable angle. She pushed her face close to his, baring her teeth and hissing at him, "Be grateful right now that you're ignorant of how hard I can hit you."

"That's enough!" Leah ordered, striding up. "Leave the intimidation to me, Rex." She took a casual seat on the edge of the table. "Finish up."

With another quick pat-down, Rex found only a pocketknife and some cord in the man's pockets. Rider had found an additional knife—though more deadly—in the man's boot. Both of them set their findings down on the table, and Leah dismissed them. As she turned past the assassin to go, he whispered, "When the time comes, make up your own mind, pretty. These people are not who you think."

Rex straightened and left the room along with Rider, hearing once again the gurgling sound of the man's laughter.

012

"Compatriots! This is the last week I'll address you that way. At the end of the week, we move on to the competitor phase. As of today, you'll be fine-tuning the skills you've already learned, and you'll have a final assessment to test all those skills before we go into phase two. Your scoring toward the alpha position will also be communicated to you. Any questions?" Sergeant Bailey scanned the lines of compatriots.

Bridget raised a hand. "Is everything safe? I just mean, after Rex's leg and then the assassins . . ." she said nervously.

Sergeant Bailey seemed to take no offense at the question. She nodded. "Security measures have been increased. The penalty for not checking a weapon before training is now a full day's confinement to the barracks—while handcuffed to your bed. Good luck doing your business if you're the unlucky soul who occupies the top bunk. As far as outside security, some of you have probably noticed that we're moving today. Since the assassins, scouts, or whatever you want to call them found us, we've changed the base's normal pattern of movement to make it harder for them to find us again. We're limiting radio communications with HQ and we'll only be getting food supplies once every three weeks instead of two." Seeing the looks of protest on some faces, she added, "Don't worry, you'll still get the same rations. Believe it or not, your food portions are carefully engineered to give you maximum energy, and security issues or not, we can't have you fainting during assessments. Are there any other questions?"

"No, Sergeant Ma'am!" the group barked as one.

"Good. Team drill starts now!"

The drill was easier than Rex expected. It consisted of practicing flying in formation above the shooting range and hitting targets below. She kept her place at the head of the group, the screens in her eyes zooming in as she focused them on a target.

"What d'you think our team score will be at the end of the week?" Rider asked. Rex aimed and shot before answering.

"We've won a lot of the other assessments, and we work well together as a team. When we win the last test, we should be the frontrunners."

"'When we win?' You've already got it planned?" There was an unusual steely edge to Alelta's voice. Rex glanced at her. The other girl's grey eyes were stormy.

Rex waited a moment, then replied, "Our team needs to do the best if we want to become alphas or betas."

Alelta fired an unnecessary amount of shots at the target below. "There's only room for one alpha."

"Well, one male and one female," Rex said. She didn't mention that she was determined to be the female, but she knew Alelta was going to make that difficult. As the time drew nearer for them to become competitors, Rex wasn't sure how she would maintain a friendship between them. She liked Alelta, but if the other girl got in her way, she wouldn't let that amity stop her from reaching her goal. From the look in Alelta's eyes, Rex guessed that she felt the same way.

"Shooters below!" Tanner called from the back of the line. Rex grunted in frustration as she pulled her mind away from the distraction with Alelta. Several guards, who were customarily stationed inside, were kneeling in a line and shooting at them.

"Do we shoot back?" Bridget called.

"Yes. But wait for my signal," Rex answered, feeling a plastic bullet whiz past her face. Since their guns were training weapons, there should be no danger to the figures below. She raised a hand.

"Ready ... aim ... fire!"

The Gaelwolves let forth a volley in unison. Two of the guards fell over, acknowledging Rider's and Alelta's accuracy, and let their guns drop. The others continued shooting. Rex held out one arm to signal a turn, and they made another pass. All of the guards except one fell, but Abbi was also hit. Tanner made up for her misfortune by shooting the guard directly in the face.

"Good shot," Rex murmured.

Tanner responded cheerfully, "Thanks!"

After a moment's confusion, Rex remembered that his ear sensors were just as good as her own. She gave a command in the same soft tone, and they followed her as she descended. She led the way to the training room, where they deposited their weapons. As she headed for the door, Rex was stopped by a low mutter from Alelta.

"Just because you got to be leader doesn't mean you'll be alpha."

Rex turned. She gave Alelta a long, dead-serious look. "I didn't *get* to be leader. I took the lead. If you want something, you have to take it and hold on to it. You should have challenged me on day one for the lead if you wanted it."

Alelta scoffed. "I didn't have much chance. They all worshipped you the moment you began ordering them around."

"They could have worshipped you more if you'd challenged me and won," Rex said. "Not that you would have."

Alelta's eyes blazed. She spoke in a fierce whisper. "You have no idea what I'm capable of. You think I'm just like everyone else, meek and weak. Well, I'm not. Did you see the people I gunned down just before your leg got shot? No. We would have taken the trench because of *me* that day, not because of you. Did you notice that I had shot out that assassin's jetpack thrusters, and that was why you were able to capture him? Of course you didn't. You're too busy taking all the glory. You don't care what the people around you do."

Rex stepped closer. "I've let you do all the frontline work along with me. You haven't been cheated. I've treated you fairly. If you want to lead, go ahead. Challenge me. See if you can do it better."

It was Alelta's turn to come closer, and she brought her face a few inches from Rex's. "You know what? I don't care about leading. But I deserve to be recognized! And if you won't give that to me, you'll find yourself short one loyal teammate." She shoved past Rex and stomped out the door.

Rex tightened her jaw. She knew that every other Gaelwolf had heard their conversation, despite Alelta's lowered tone.

"If anyone wants a different leader, now would be a good time to bring it up. I'll fight you for the position. Also, if you've got a problem with the way I'm doing things, by all means, let's get it sorted out now."

No one spoke. Slowly, heads began to shake. Rider was the first to break the silence.

"You haven't let us down yet," he said, "and you've got the guts to keep cool in battle. I'll stick with you. And I don't have any complaints, Captain."

Bridget stepped up. "Me too. I'm proud to be a Gaelwolf."

The others gave nods and interjections of agreement. Rex nodded once, decisively.

"Good. Because if we're going to win our last assessment, I need everyone to be on my team."

***

Alelta stormed across the compound toward the

mess hall. A guard at the door blocked her entrance, and she hastily did three pull-ups on the bar that hung above the door. The guard stepped aside, and she went in.

It was dark inside, as the room hadn't been lit up for lunch just yet. Alelta looked around, straining her eyes.

"Roth?" she whispered. She knew he was here. She had seen him slinking off while the Gaelwolves were still in the air. But despite her eye implants, she couldn't see much in the room.

She heard footsteps behind her and spun around. Roth stood uncomfortably close, a smile on his face.

"What did you want to talk to me about? Something with Rex?" He pushed in even closer. "Or did you just want to see me?"

Alelta was tempted to back away, but she realized it might be seen as weakness. She stood her ground. "Whatever you and Rider are planning, I want in."

Roth's eyes narrowed. "How did you know about that? Has he squealed?"

Alelta shook her head. "You're not the only one who knows things. Whatever he's helping you with, and whatever he's paid you, I'll make sure it's done twice as well and twice as profitable for you."

Roth chuckled. It was not a pleasant sound. "The money's not for me. I've got my eyes set on something much more important. But you'll still need the payment. Where will you get it from?"

"I know someone who'll be happy to back me up on my offer."

Roth nodded, considering. "Not bad. Though I might want a little convincing, just the same." His fingertips brushed along her face. She sighed and, in spite of herself, felt a tremor of pleasure. "But what's in it for you?"

Alelta locked gazes with him. "The alpha position," she whispered.

The lights flicked on, one by one. Roth stepped away from her as the noise of compatriots outside became louder.

"Deal," he hissed.

013

That night, Rex tossed her backpack onto her bunk and headed for the shower room. Bridget had already flopped down into bed and was asleep. Feeling lonely and exhausted, Rex began brushing her teeth.

The girl who had commented on Rex's scars on the first day—Rex recalled hearing someone call her Ilianayah—sidled up and turned on the water. She splashed some on her face and breathed an exaggerated sigh. Rex was instantly suspicious. She hadn't interacted with this *kelba* in weeks, aside from ignoring various comments directed at her from across a room.

"Feels good to relax after a day like that. Training to be alpha is tough." Ilianayah pulled a stray piece of hair out of her face. "Although, I guess you're a little less tired."

Rex glanced at Ilianayah's reflection in the mirror. She declined to answer, knowing that the self-important *kelba* would complete her own thoughts if given enough time.

"You've got some fancy gadgets to help you. The rest of us have to sweat for our achievements."

It wasn't even the competitor phase yet, and already this girl felt the need to try and scare Rex into backing down. It was pathetic. Despite what *kelba*-girl might say, Rex was tired, and bandying words with such a prig was not on her priority list. Aloud, she said, "You'll get fitted soon enough."

Still not making eye contact with Rex, Ilianayah checked her face from every angle. "It won't be soon enough. You've already had too much time getting pampered by the master."

"What?" The question burst out louder than Rex had intended. She had a special relationship with Master Ekeli, but he could hardly be said to pamper her. "Training someone isn't pampering them. He does the same for you."

"Really? He singles you out on the first day. Then, he gives you advice that conveniently saves you from getting punished for attacking another compatriot. And he spends more time ogling your techniques than he does with all the glances he gives us put together. I think that's a little unfair, don't you?" She made a clucking noise, as if speaking to a small child. Rex's anger flared, but she didn't want to bother with demanding respect from this overgrown peacock.

"Whatever the master does is his decision, not mine," Rex said, spitting out a mouthful of water and turning to leave. Finally, Ilianayah whipped around to face her.

"You could stop being such a show-off," she spat. "Your pretty circus tricks are the only thing getting his attention. You run at the head of your group, and you act like you're the best, but we both know you didn't get those scars from victories you won."

At that moment, four other girls entered the shower room. Three of them blocked the doorway to prevent Rex's leaving. The fourth girl managed to slip by just as they closed the gap. Rex realized it was Alelta. For a moment, Rex thought she was part of the group, but Alelta simply ignored the other people in the room and began brushing her teeth.

Some sixth sense warned Rex, and she ducked just as Ilianayah's fist came whistling by. Another girl went in for a punch. Rex caught the fist in midair with her right hand. She shoved the arm to the side and pivoted behind the girl's shoulder, using her as a shield as more blows came her way. The girl gasped as several of her gang's punches hit her. Rex leapt onto the girl's back and wrapped her arms around her throat. The girl stumbled backward into the wall, knocking the wind out of Rex's lungs, but she clung on grimly. Fortunately, the girl's attempt to shake her loose had only succeeded in getting Rex's back to the wall—where none of the others could slip behind her.

As Rex's victim blacked out and fell to the ground, Rex rolled forward and delivered a low roundhouse kick at the second gang member. The girl leapt up to avoid it, and the third girl grabbed Rex's left arm. Rex spun in the air, catching Ilianayah in the face with a kick as she came in for another punch. At the same moment, the third girl caught Rex in the face with two crushing punches. Rex gasped and staggered, blood spraying from her nose. But if the other girl thought she would slow Rex down, she was mistaken. As the girl lunged again, trying to bring her knee into Rex's chest, Rex blocked with her own metal leg and struck with a high kick into the girl's side. There was a cracking noise, and the girl collapsed, releasing Rex's arm and crawling away. Rex spun just in time to prevent Ilianayah's next blow, but her arms were jerked behind her as the second girl fought to secure them.

"Bad idea," Rex hissed, and wrenched her right arm free. She grabbed hold of the girl's hair and yanked as hard as she could. With a scream, the girl loosened her grip, and Rex spun in her arms and smashed her fist into the girl's jaw. She dropped like a stone. Ilianayah finally got in two punches to Rex's exposed back. With a grunt of pain, Rex spun and pushed her away. The two girls stood, Ilianayah breathing heavily with rage in her eyes, Rex smoldering with deadly confidence.

"One of these days your enhancements won't matter," Ilianayah spat. "Your team won't be with you, and we'll be equal; just you and me. Then I'll show you who's going to be alpha. You're not going to take that away just because everyone adores you."

The words were similar to what Alelta had said earlier that day. Too similar. Rex glanced at Alelta, who seemed to be avoiding eye contact all too obviously. Turning back to Ilianayah, Rex said, "Seems you're sabotaging your alpha position all on your own." She imitated the other girl's previous patronizing manner, although a little less dramatically. "Let's see. Attacking a compatriot without prior history of abuse . . . doing so with four times the number of people compared to the attacked person . . . and doing so in front of witnesses. I think that's a little unwise, don't you?" She clucked. Pleasure burned fiercely in her chest as she saw the other girl bristle with rage.

"What witnesses? It's your word against my whole group. And your teammate," she gestured to Alelta, saying the word with a sneer, "doesn't want to see you become alpha either."

Rex smiled like a wolf going in for the kill. "Not that teammate. What did you witness, Zyanya?"

From behind her, in the doorway, the Native American girl stepped up. Her expression was cold. When she spoke, her voice was quiet, but Rex could see fury in the lines of her body.

"I saw an attack on my leader with four girls to one. I also heard the leader of the attack confirm her own intentions. There was no previous abuse from my leader. The attack leader confirmed that herself through her own statements." She stepped forward until she was level with Rex, her dark eyes locked on Ilianayah's pale ones. "My people have a saying: 'The chief who brings his braves to a duel is no warrior, but a coward.' And in my tribe, all cowards are flogged with thornbrush. Don't tempt me to carry out our ancient punishment."

Ilianayah began speaking, but Rex cut her off.

"And that would be in response to previous abuse. We'll be reporting this to the sergeant now." With that, Rex turned and stalked off, past the unconscious and groaning bodies on the floor, past Alelta, whom she would deal with later, and out of the shower room toward headquarters.

***

Sergeant Bailey sentenced Ilianayah and her gang to toilet-cleaning duty for two weeks. In addition, their points dropped significantly. To Rex's frustration, she also lost five points—for what reason, she couldn't get a straight answer.

"This is the second time you've been involved in violent action in the past week," Sergeant Bailey said. "Try to avoid it in the future."

With that, Rex and Zyanya were dismissed. As they headed back to the barracks, Rex gave a nod to the other girl, keeping a cloth pressed firmly against her own nose to staunch a flow of blood.

"Thank you."

Zyanya nodded back. "I knew something was wrong when I smelled blood."

Rex frowned, adjusting the cloth against her nose. "You couldn't hear them, but you could smell blood?"

A smile touched Zyanya's pale lips. "It's something they implanted in me. It helps with tracking."

"Why didn't Leah help you use that when we were trying out our new fittings?"

"The alarm started before we got to that," Zyanya explained.

Rex reached the back door to the barracks, which led into the shower room, and pulled it open. "So, you can track?"

Zyanya smiled. "Yes, indeed. I've been trained to track since I was able to walk. It's something everyone in my tribe learns." Rex hadn't known that tracking was something that Native American women learned along with the men. She made a mental note to remember it in the future.

As they stepped into the shower room, they were met with the sight of a guard standing by while a little robot cleaned the floor. The bloodstains from the violent altercation slowly disappeared as the machine sprayed water over the floor and sucked it back up.

"Seems that thing does everything," she remarked, remembering the cup of tea the robot had brought her on her first day. She stepped carefully over the wet patches on the floor and strode ahead of Zyanya and to the bunk where Alelta lounged unaffectedly.

"Alelta," she said in a mock pleasant tone. "I have something to talk to you about." She pulled the cloth away from her nose so the other girl could see her face clearly.

Alelta's gaze came up slowly to meet hers. Rex narrowed her eyes, though she kept a smile pasted on her face.

"I know that *kelba* didn't decide to go after me on her own. If you want to fight me, get the guts to do it yourself."

Alelta's eyes narrowed, too. "Prove it. Why would I send someone else to do something I want to do?"

"Don't *khr shvr* me. You'd lose points. And you don't have people to back you up."

Alelta shrugged. "I don't even know what you just said. And you can't prove anything."

"Let me explain in common English." Rex leaned forward. "Don't give me that dump-crap. I know what you did, even if I can't prove it to the sergeant. But I can prove that you stood by and watched the whole thing. If you desert your leader like that again, I'll report you for betrayal and cowardice. Do you understand?"

"You aren't the boss of me. Training groups are flexible. You're not alpha yet."

"I'm your appointed leader."

Alelta scoffed. "Appointed by who? Not Sergeant Bailey. Not anyone else in authority. Just your pack of pups. So I don't have to do anything you say."

Rex's smile faltered as her patience became thinner. She twisted her fingers around the bloody scrap of cloth in her hand. "The entire group system hinges on teammates following their leader."

"No, the system hinges on teammates working together. You just want to order us around." Alelta took hold of the bedframe on the bunk above her and leaned out. "This phase is almost over, anyway. So until then, as long as I help my teammates and follow the sergeant's rules, you can't do anything to me." Alelta turned her back on Rex and shifted under her blankets.

Rex breathed heavily, but she was at a complete loss for anything else to say. She thumped to her bunk and swung up, ignoring the trickle of blood that made its way to her lips.

"I believe in ya, Rex." Bridget's timid voice drifted up from below where Rex lay. The tightness in Rex's chest softened a little at the girl's simple words, but she couldn't bring herself to answer.

014

"You leave her alone, or I'm out."

The thought flashed through Rex's mind as she lay atop her blankets, too hot and angry to sleep. It was what Rider had said after Roth accused Rex of trying to shoot him. She had only been on the verge of consciousness, but now, with her mind whirling in anger after Alelta's accusations, she remembered it.

"You can't," Roth had said.

Rider was in trouble. Judging by their interaction, Rider didn't want to be in whatever position Roth had him in—at least, not entirely.

"You won't be safe." Rider's face had been fearful when he said it.

Roth was blackmailing Rider or promising him something—either way, he was telling Rider to do something he didn't want to do. And something was holding Rider back from breaking away. Rage smoldered in Rex's chest. Whatever Roth was doing, she had to stop it. She had to protect Rider. Because she couldn't protect her mother, and because, for years, she couldn't protect herself. It was different now. Now, she could fight back. For herself. For the people she loved. A twinge of uncertainty rang inside her. Did she love Rider? Was he as important to her as her mother, or Kani, or even her old master, Juko? She felt a desire to protect him, just as he had protected her from Roth's accusation and the assassin in the attack. She owed him a debt. That was all.

"And I pay my debts," she whispered, nodding with finality.

***

She didn't have a chance to talk to Rider alone until the next afternoon, when they were allowed a breath of fresh air on the Ledge while several of the other teams were being fitted. Rex went some distance away from the crowd and gestured for Rider to come stand beside her. The other boys on their team were grouped together and in the midst of an impromptu arm-wrestling contest on the railing. Bridget was talking and laughing with her "friend" Alec. As Rider settled his arms on the rail overlooking the compound, Rex inclined her head slightly toward him.

"Tell me about Roth," she said in a low voice. She knew now was the time to ask questions, while Roth was detained in the fitting chamber.

Rider tensed. Rex felt it rather than saw it. "What about Roth?"

Rex gestured as if she were talking about any random thing, conscious of the proximity of Bridget and Alec. "How he's blackmailing you."

"He's not blackmailing me," Rider said, with just a little too much disinterest. "He's just a jerk."

"As your captain, I order you to tell me."

With a surreptitious glance around, Rider sighed. "He's promised me a high position in the pack."

"If . . . ?" Rex knew there was a condition. People like Roth didn't give out favors.

Rider's voice, when he spoke, was barely audible, even for Rex's ear implants. "If I pay."

"Pay him? How? There's no money up here."

"Evidently he's got some. In any case, we'll be sent on a mission after our training. That's what I've heard, anyway. I'd pick up the money then. I have a small sum stored up in a spot near Cairo. Was saving it for a motorbike." He sighed ruefully. "But he'll give me money he's got somewhere around here to pay off the master before then so I get a beta position."

"And he gets alpha, I assume." Rex snorted. Rider's silence confirmed her assumption. "I'm not sure the master will let anyone pay him off. Especially Roth."

"Oh, Roth's pretty close with the master."

"Hm." Rex nodded thoughtfully. "What money has he got? I seriously doubt that the master will take rainchecks on bribes. It's too risky."

"See, that's the thing. I don't think Roth's really paying the master with money. He's basically lending me his money, so I can go pay off Ekeli for my own position and make it look like there's some straightforward, honest bribery going on, when it's something different. From the way he talks about it, I don't even understand why I'm involved. It seems to be more between him and Ekeli than anything else."

"How did you even get mixed up with him? Did he just come up and ask if you wanted a higher rank?"

"Sort of," Rider said, frowning. "He said if I helped him with a job, he could make sure I got a position. Of course, all I saw was the opportunity: a better status, giving orders, maybe even eating better food. Whatever Roth was going to have me do was probably a one-time thing that would advance his interests. No one would get hurt. But the whole thing's become a hell pit of stuff I don't want a part of."

"Like what?"

Rider spread his hands helplessly. "That's just it! I can't figure anything out for certain. But it stinks of something much bigger than just paying off an official to get a position. I know that it involves Roth getting alpha, and Ekeli getting something else. I just happen to be the middleman."

"How so? And what is he threatening you with?"

"Threatening me? Who said anything about threats?" Rex continued to level her steady gaze on him until he spoke again. "I'm delivering the money."

Rex laughed out loud. "Just like him. So, he'll stay out of trouble in case the master isn't so receptive to his plan. What, did he threaten to blame it all on you if it slipped the cut? Somehow, I think Ekeli would see through that. If it was your idea, you'd make yourself alpha."

"It's the technicalities," Rider explained. "If I'm

caught trying to bribe the master, Roth can deny wanting the alpha position and say I'm making it up to throw suspicion on him. Since he's in such good standing with the officers—especially that rooster Rangorazi—they'll believe him over me. And of course, if Ekeli's getting something out of it from Roth, I'll take the fall and neither of them will be worse off for it."

"Why does he have so much influence?" Rex growled.

Rider smiled humorlessly. "He was the first recruit. He was the government's 'test run,' so to speak. They brought him here weeks before everyone else and ran final tests on him, making sure everything was perfect for the rest of us. He's a fighter—one of the best in the force when it comes to sheer willpower and drive. Even though he's a sick manipulator, they either can't or won't get rid of him. It's the psychology stuff that happens when you invest a bunch of time or resources into something. Even if it's not the way you want, you don't want to throw it out because you spent so much time on it. The point is, he's the Alliance's pet project. Anything he says goes."

"That makes sense. Unfortunately." Rex glanced around to make sure others were still out of earshot. "Why don't you just give it up? He can't accuse you without any proof. Right now, there's no evidence that you're trying to bribe the master. You could work your way up in the competitive phase and maybe even become alpha."

Rider's jaw clenched. Rex was conscious of the fact that his reaction to anger was the same as her own. "He'll hurt me if I don't do it."

Now Rex tightened her own jaw. "Not if I have anything to do with it." She cast about, looking for Roth's face among the crowd of compatriots, then remembered he was being fitted. She pushed back Sergeant Bailey's warning not to get into more violent altercations.

"Don't make him mad. I'll do what I have to do."

Anger swelled in Rex's chest. She had told herself the same thing for years when she had to hide her skills. "You don't have to put up with this. There are other ways. If you and I work together, we can beat him easily. Either we rough him up or we slip him up, and when he makes a mistake, we both testify against him."

Rider shook his head. "It's harder than that. You don't understand."

Rex snorted. "I understand beating the mess out of him and calculating his downfall."

"Rex—" Rider began, but Sergeant Bailey's voice cut in to call them back to training. Rex turned away.

"Let's go, we'll work this out later."

As the crowd of compatriots swarmed around her, Rex heard Rider call, "Don't do anything stupid."

Rex raised her eyebrows as she strode through the door to the training room. "Of course not," she murmured to herself.

015

The final assessment for the compatriot phase was not at all what Rex had expected. Rather than surmounting obstacles or fighting another team together, the team members were spaced out around the field. In the center was a black contraption with a keypad on it.

"You'll have one minute to complete the assessment," Sergeant Bailey called to them. "This thing here"—she kicked at the contraption with her foot—"is a replica of a Kharza time bomb. The real Kharzas were invented by ISIS during the war to target the best soldiers. The only way to stop this bomb is by holding it close to you and letting it kill you. Instead of a quick, violent explosion, Kharza time bombs emit a series of forceful micro-explosions that decimate the weaker parts of your body piece by piece and send sensors into your core at the same time. Once the sensors determine that you've lost three or more pints of blood because of the micro-explosions, the bomb shuts off. But until it senses that three pints of someone's blood have been lost, the bomb releases radiation waves that can cover a quarter of a mile.

"Typically, it takes about fifteen seconds for someone to die by holding a Kharza bomb, and it takes thirty seconds for a deadly amount of radiation to be released. So, unless someone sacrifices themselves by holding the bomb to shut it off, the rest of their team will die from the radiation. Of course, ISIS knew that the people who would be most likely to sacrifice themselves for their team would be the same people willing to do anything to make a mission succeed—usually the leaders. Eliminate the people with the guts to carry through with a mission, and you've crushed the mission."

She paused, letting that sink in. Rex breathed heavily, anger in her chest. Terrorists knew their business all too well.

"I've given you one minute for the assessment because you won't know exactly when the bomb is activated. You'll have some time to get to it and one of you will have to shield it. Once you're shielding it, it should vibrate three times to simulate three micro-explosions, then it'll shut off. If it only vibrates once or twice and then makes a noise like a gunshot, it means you took too long deciding to sacrifice yourself. If you want, you can talk about who's going to make the sacrifice, or one of you can just throw yourself on the bomb; I don't care. But don't let it make that gunshot noise, or you fail the assessment." Without further warning, Sergeant Bailey stepped away from the bomb. "Your assessment starts now." She strode quickly from the middle of the field.

For a heartbeat, nobody moved. Then, everything happened at once.

Rex activated her boots and shot toward the center of the field, zeroing in on the bomb. Across from her, Rider did the same. Zyanya reached the center ahead of both of them, but as she reached out for the bomb, Tanner came running at full-speed on his enhanced legs and seized it. Rex swerved quickly and snatched at the bomb in Tanner's arms. He turned away from her to prevent her grabbing it.

"I'll do it!" he shouted. "Get the rest of the team to safety!"

"No!" Rex yelled back. She knew that, if this were a real bomb, and Tanner sacrificed himself, she wouldn't be able to live with it. She grabbed Tanner's shoulder and jerked him around to face her, seizing the bomb and giving him a punch in the face—not hard enough to hurt him, but enough to startle him and make him release his hold. She clutched the bomb close, floating back away from the other team members as they tried to crowd in. She held up a hand to stop them from coming closer. "I'm responsible for you all. As your leader, I order you to stand down!"

The others paused for a split second, but before anyone could even blink, Bridget shot in from nowhere and snatched the bomb. Soaring into the air out of reach of the others, she curled up into a ball. Her body convulsed once, twice, three times as the bomb vibrated. Then, everything went still.

The Gaelwolves stared up in silence at Bridget as

she floated, completely unmoving, for several seconds. Then she let out a deep breath and straightened up.

"Well. I never had that much excitement in Dublin," she said.

***

It took Rex several hours to get over what had happened. Despite her excellent reflexes, despite the fact that she had been completely alert, she hadn't seen Bridget coming. It was unnerving. On top of that was the fact that it had been Bridget; sweet, nonviolent, obedient Bridget. She had gone against her orders for the first time—to do what, in a real situation, would have saved Rex's life and the lives of her teammates. Rex knew the Irish girl had a good heart, but she simply hadn't expected such an astounding display of sacrificial bravery.

Bridget was the center of attention around the Gaelwolves' table at lunch that day. The others clapped her on the back and acknowledged her bravery, asking her questions about her life on the fading edge of Dublin, and how she had helped smuggle weapons into the city. Bridget conversed with a huge smile on her face. Alelta, Rex noted, was quiet as Bridget received acknowledgement.

"People don't think that I know anythin' about weapons," Bridget said to the group. "But that's because I've learned to make 'em think I'm ignorant. When ya see our town, it looks like we're all just a group of farmers that make good cheese. That's the trick. If ya look like ya don't know one side of a pistol from the other, people will assume ya don't because there are so few weapons available to the common people."

"Brilliant," Tanner said.

"See, when I was a girl, my uncle would take me out to the barn when it was snowy. He'd have me huddle in with the sheep and look under the straw where he hid the guns a'fore his brother moved 'em into the city. He'd show me how to tell the difference between a shotgun and a rifle by looking at 'em closely. 'Don't pick 'em up until ye're older, lassie,' he'd say. 'T'aint safe. But if ye can tell the difference by lookin', ye'll be safe when ye do pick it up a' last.' So I grew up knowin' my weapons."

Rex marveled at how Bridget had turned out, considering the fact that one of her childhood games had been to spot the differences between separate types of guns. She felt a new respect for the red-haired girl. Bridget, though she had grown up with suspicion and instruments of destruction all around her, had chosen not to become part of it all. Instead, she was willing to sacrifice herself rather than hurt others.

As the meal finished and Bridget got up to leave, Rex leaned toward her.

"You were very brave today," she said.

Bridget's face lit up. "Thank ya! I knew I couldn't let ya die."

Rex frowned. "Why not me? I'm the leader. The captain who goes down with the ship."

Bridget looked at her with deep respect in her

green eyes. "Sometimes we need the leader to keep goin' because, if ya didn't, there wouldn't be a better one to replace ya." She gave Rex another smile and headed out of the mess hall.

Rex hoped Bridget's faith wasn't misplaced.

016

The next week hit hard. After twice the usual morning routine and miles of running around the compound, obstacle course training, and weightlifting, they had a brief respite. Just when Rex was beginning to regain her spent breath, they were ushered into the training room. She stood, head bent, as Sergeant Bailey addressed them.

"What you just did was the start of the competitor phase. These next five days—today included—require discipline, stamina, and drive. The Navy SEALs call it Hell Week for a reason. Boys will only be allowed six hours of sleep over this whole period; girls, eight."

Rex shrugged fatalistically. Some of the others gasped or groaned.

"Say goodbye to your teammates. The bonds you formed will and should sustain outside of training. But when you're with me, or Rangorazi, or Ekeli, everyone's your enemy. This phase trains you for the pits of disaster. In the air, on an attack, you may well find yourself alone. All your comrades may be shot down. Your survival instincts have to be like a knifeblade. It's what your home schools have been training you for your entire lives. For this reason, every exercise other than morning maintenance will be an assessment. The objective of this phase is alpha testing—to see who the best fighter is. The last day at the end of this week will be the final assessment, which will determine the alpha male and female. Here are your scores so far." She tapped her wrist-screen. It lit up and projected a list large enough for all the group to see without straining their eyes.

Team 1: Roth Command (Bayonets)
Team 2: Jonas Command
Team 3: Rexala Command (Gaelwolves)
Team 4: Elijah Command
Team 5: Ilianayah Command (Ascendants)

Rex heard cheers from some of her teammates. She exhaled slowly. Third place wasn't good enough. She would have to make up for that in this coming phase. She noticed with satisfaction, however, that Ilianayah's team was last.

Sergeant Bailey waited until the murmurs, groans, and cheers had died down before shutting off the screen. "Get ready, buck up, and fight!" With that, she let Master Ekeli take over.

Rex felt Alelta's gaze on her. She slid her eyes sideways to meet the other girl's and raised her head a little higher.

Alelta might be determined to become alpha, but Rex was hell-bent.

Ekeli stepped up. "Now that you have completed the compatriot phase, you all have earned the right to climb to the next training level. Follow!" He pressed his palm to the scanner at the edge of a doorway, waited for it to open, and led the competitors up the stairs to the second level of the training building.

The entire floor was a lake. Bubbles rose from the surface as the blue-green water—or whatever it was—churned and boiled around rock outcrops. The smell of salt and unfamiliar chemicals hit Rex like a wall. She caught her breath and her eyes watered. Zyanya, she noticed, had a hand clasped over her nose to negate her heightened sense of smell.

"When I whistle, your first assessment starts. Be the first to cross the lake. If you fall in it, you lose points. No flying. Take your weapons." He gestured to his left, where racks of training rods hung on the wall just in front of the lake. Rex surged forward with the others to select a rod. She tested their weight and balance, swishing two of them experimentally. They were identical in every respect.

"Good luck!" Bridget giggled as she grabbed two rods, almost smacking Rex in the face. With anyone else, Rex would have become ill-tempered at such an action, but she knew Bridget was just enthusiastic. Rex decided she would avoid fighting the other girl. Some people were too nice to hurt.

"I'll miss being a Gaelwolf," Bridget said, looking at the rods in her hands. "But we can meet up at dinner. Ya still haven't heard Alec's stories."

Rex frowned thoughtfully. "True. I'll give it a go." She stepped up to the edge of the lake. Zyanya, Nigel, and Rider drew alongside her. Zyanya gave her a nod.

Nigel groaned. "This is the pits. The abyss. A giant lake of bleedin', boilin' chemicals. Wot I wouldn't give for a noice, hot bath instead."

Rex's mouth twitched in a smile at Nigel's despair. The fact that the words were said in a strong British accent only served to make them funnier.

"This looks hot to me," Rider said. "If you ignore the fact that you're losing points, you could just swim across."

Nigel groaned again. Rider's dark gaze fell on Rex. He threw her a salute.

"See you on the alpha side, Captain."

Peep!

With Master Ekeli's piercing whistle, the assessment began.

Rex leapt directly from her position to the nearest rock and scrambled toward the top. A huge weight crashed down on her back, and her grip was torn from the rock. She tumbled down, ramming her ribs painfully against the stone. Bodies swarmed over her as other competitors leapt to the rock. Alelta—she was the one who had landed on top of Rex—was fighting her way to the top. With a grunt of anger, Rex leapt to her feet and bounded up the rock face, using other competitors as hand- and footholds.

Someone grabbed at her ankle. She spun it out of their grasp and kicked at them without bothering to look down. Her eyes were set on the summit, where Alelta had just disappeared from. Rex reached the top and scanned the lake quickly. One rock directly in front of her—that was where Alelta had gone. Two to the left, each with several people on them. One to the right, unoccupied. She brought her fist up to deflect a rod thrust aimed at her head from behind, struck with her own rod at the competitor, and jumped. She wavered as she hit the rock. Thrusting one rod into her belt and putting the other between her teeth to free her hands, she ascended and reassessed her position. The next leap, no matter which direction she took, would land her with other competitors. She spotted Alelta, ahead of the others, at the base of an outcrop. If Rex tried to follow, she would be slowed down by the other competitors. But there was one other way...

Two rods whipped down at her, and she swept out her own from between her teeth to block them. One jarred against her shoulder, but she ignored the stinging pain. That decided her. With a feint at her attacker's face, Rex plunged into the lake.

It felt like she was being clawed at by hungry desert lions. Fire raged against her skin as the chemicals bubbled around her and the breath was struck from her. She roared with pain, her eyes streaming. Squinting them, she could dimly make out what she thought was Alelta's form scrambling up the far rock summit. She tried to move, but her body shook and her legs seized up underneath her.

She would not lose like this.

With another roar, she struck out for the rock where Alelta was now battling with two competitors. She gritted her teeth against the hard rod to tolerate the pain. Her arms and legs moved faster, and the rock loomed closer. Just as Alelta hurled one of the competitors into the lake, Rex clasped the rock and hauled herself up. Clawing her way, inch by inch, she reached the point just below where the battle was going on. A rod whipped down on her outstretched hand and she yelped. With a growl, she dropped into a crouch as the other competitor struck out with two more blows. One whistled over her head. The other was deflected by her left leg as she brought it up in a roundhouse kick. It knocked the rod from the boy's hand, and Rex followed it up with a sweep at his legs. A quick glance told her that Alelta had fallen into the lake but was swimming for the last rock. Rex grunted in a mixture of pain and frustration as the boy's rod cracked down on her back. She didn't have time for this.

"Competitor, let me pass. You can still be the first male across."

The boy pushed out his bottom lip stubbornly. Rex sighed. Then, whipping out the rod from her belt, she disarmed him with two blinding strikes and kicked him into the lake. She didn't wait to watch his predicament, and instead took a flying leap and landed on the last rock—just ahead of Alelta.

Alelta rose to her feet and they stood, face to face, for a few seconds. Alelta broke the momentary impasse.

"Get out of my victory path," she hissed.

"Throw me out yourself," Rex shot back. With

that, Rex whirled her rods up, around, and sideways in a lightning sequence to disarm Alelta. But the other girl countered each stroke with one or even two of her own. Rex was vaguely aware of blows hitting her, but she didn't care. She just needed to distract Alelta long enough to buy the time to leap to the far side of the lake.

In her peripheral vision, Rex caught a flurry of movement. With sudden alarm, she realized it was Zyanya, moving past them along the side of the rock face. The momentary distraction resulted in a punishing blow across the head from Alelta. Rex cried out with the pain, then, in a burst of anger, shot two high kicks at Alelta. As the other girl reeled back, Rex ran to the top of the rock, leapt, and landed on the far side of the lake.

But Zyanya was already there.

Bitter disappointment filled Rex's mouth. *Damn Alelta!* If she had just had a few more seconds to get across, she would have won the assessment. On the other edge of the blade, Alelta hadn't won either. She flexed her jaw in a mixture of satisfaction and disappointment as she joined Zyanya, her boots squelching blue-green liquid.

"Good fight," she sighed.

"Good fight." Zyanya nodded. Her quiet respect was a slight comfort. At least she didn't crow about her victory, as Alelta might have. As Rex had the thought, Alelta's hand appeared over the edge of the lake. She hauled herself, dripping, out of it, and crouched on the ground some distance away. Past her, Rex wasn't surprised to see Roth already across. Other competitors made their way across the lake, one by one. When they were all assembled, there was a clicking noise, and a door behind them shot open to reveal the master.

"Competitors Zero-Zero-One and Zero-Thirty-Eight, congratulations." Master Ekeli addressed Roth and Zyanya respectively. "You receive full points for being the first ones to cross the lake without falling in it. All other competitors' scores will be determined based on the order in which they completed the course and how many times they were in the lake."

Sergeant Bailey stepped up from the stairway. "Alright, competitors. Water and rest, ten minutes! Then it's back to another assessment for Hell Week."

017

Hell Week was aptly named. After two and a half days of back-breaking assessments, with only two hours of sleep per night, nausea and dizziness overwhelmed Rex. Unlike Hell Week in the Navy, which was about endurance and survival as a team, the competitive phase was just that—competitive. Life seemed like an endless trudge of pain, sweat, and more pain. She had given up trying to expel the taste of vomit from her mouth. Currently, she was submerged in the chemical lake, trying to hold her breath as her head swam and her lungs felt ready to burst with the pressure.

Air, her mind called.

No, her will answered.

She knew that somewhere, to her right, Alelta was still submerged. She hadn't felt the water—chemicals—ripple to indicate that her rival had surfaced. In the sleep- and air-deprived state she was in, Alelta could have done a cannonball for all she knew, and she still might have missed it, but Rex couldn't take that chance.

Air. I just need air. Her mind and body called together this time. Pain shot through her head. She gulped chemicals, and her throat caught on fire as she swallowed.

Just a few more moments . . . for father. Her will latched onto her goal once more. She clamped her jaw as she shook from the effort of holding her breath. Blackness crept over her already closed eyes, and she clenched and unclenched her fists to stay conscious.

And then it came. That slight movement against her arms as the chemicals rippled. She whipped her head up, struggled in panic when it didn't immediately clear the surface, then pumped herself upward. With a giant gasp and a splash, she broke above the surface of the lake.

"Time! A hundred and eighty-nine seconds," Sergeant Bailey called. Rex barely heard her above her own wheezing and coughing. "Victory goes to . . . Zero-Twenty-Seven."

Alelta turned and glared at her, but Rex had never been so happy to have someone be angry with her. She had won, and that was what mattered. *Now to get out of this infernal pool.*

The next assessment came before Rex had even recovered her breath. The competitors were instructed to gear up with vests and training guns while the ceiling rearranged itself, bringing down a hanging maze of striking equipment and steel panels. With rumbling, whirring, and clicking noises, the new ceiling fell into place. Rex took a deep breath. She didn't know what was coming, but she felt sick just looking at it.

"Another torture device," she heard someone say. Dimly, she realized it was Nigel. Despite herself, she smiled. Nigel always had been a ray of sunshine.

"Competitors." It was Sergeant Bailey. "The rules of this assessment are simple: hide in the maze and shoot as many people as you can. If you're shot in either shoulder, you lose points but can keep shooting. If you're shot in the chest, your vest sensor will buzz, and you're considered dead."

"It's a giant game of laser tag," Rangorazi cut in. Sergeant Bailey threw him an annoyed glance.

"Call it whatever you want, but you're still expected to employ your best survival skills. The person who kills the most competitors—and doesn't die—wins. Get up to the entrance and I'll start the assessment."

Rex twisted her belt buckle and glided up to the ceiling, her gun resting on her exhausted shoulder. At least this was easier than being in that precious burning chemical lake.

"Zero-Twenty-Seven."

Rex couldn't stop herself from jumping. Her peripheral vision was compromised by her exhaustion, and she hadn't seen Master Ekeli approaching. But she nodded in respect. "Yes, Master?"

He inclined his head slightly, and his words were barely above a breath as he said, "Hide behind panel H-Six. It is the best position."

Rex struggled to keep a neutral face, cognizant of the fact that others might be watching. What Ekeli had just done . . . well, she wasn't sure it was entirely fair. But whatever the case, he thought she was worth breaking the rules. Ilianayah's accusations of being the master's pet irked at the back of her mind. She pushed the thoughts away.

She had an opportunity, and she wouldn't spoil it.

As the cover to the window fell down, blacking everything out, and the lights in the maze flared to life, Rex felt a thrill of anticipation. As her breath returned, so did her confidence. She would make her father proud. She would find out what happened to him. And if there was a chance, even the tiniest one, that he was still alive, she would save him. This game was the next step.

"Hey, Captain."

Rider floated up to her and jostled her with his shoulder. She flinched slightly, about to make an angry retort at the invasion of her space, then thought better of it. She knew Rider wasn't trying to hurt her.

"Want to team up?" he murmured. She looked at him. He raised his eyebrows in an inviting gesture.

"We're competing."

Rider screwed up his face. "Well, not really. You still get to be alpha. I'll win for the boys and you win for the girls."

"I'll lose points for not killing you."

Rider gave a shrug. "Kill me, then. Just do it after you've killed everyone else."

Rex laughed. "Like you'd let me live that long."

"Well, we both know it doesn't matter if I win. Roth still gets—" He gestured vaguely. "You know.

I'll get beta either way."

Rex twisted her lips in a savage smile. "Not if he loses every assessment."

"The money..." Rider began. Rex shook her head.

"It'll be too obvious as a bribe." She didn't explain further, but she saw realization dawn on Rider's face. She leaned in a bit closer. "I'll be behind panel H-Six. Keep it to your back, and I'll cover you. We can't let Roth know what we're up to." Abruptly, she shoved Rider away and hissed at him. After a brief moment of confusion, Rider adopted an angry look and headed away as if storming off. Then, there was no more time and the game began.

Rex plunged into the maze head-on, scanning right and left for the panel numbers. Her eye implants adjusted to the light, and she zoomed in on the upper right corners of each panel. A-2, B-4, C-3.

A shot whistled by her, and she swerved to avoid it. Twisting, she fired back, and was rewarded by a blink of light from the girl's vest, but the time cost her. Two other competitors overtook her. She managed to tag one of them. This was significantly harder than laser tag. At least in the crummy dump of an arena behind her town, she could see a laser beam searching for her and sight her own marks. She ducked again as a hail of training bullets peppered the air around her. She knew she couldn't make it to H-6 like this. First, she had to pick off a few more competitors. With a roar, she soared up to the top of a panel, pushed off with her feet, and shot straight toward the pack behind her.

She didn't go for accuracy. She simply clenched the trigger and mowed down competitors as she swept over them. An insane laugh broke from her mouth without her initially being aware of it. This felt good. After the past days of Hell Week, it felt really good. Shots fired up at her, and she spun in the air to avoid them. Sheltering momentarily behind a striking bag, she picked off another group, taking some out and causing the others to go to ground behind various obstacles.

"Hey, Captain!"

Rider was behind a panel some distance below Rex. He was fighting off a group of boys that were closing in on him, his locked-in guns recoiling in a rapid rhythm as one shot after the other found its mark. He glanced up at her again and jerked his head toward farther back in the maze, then gestured to himself and to the group as if to say, "I've got this."

"Meet you there," Rex murmured, and shot away.

She stayed as high up in the tangle of striking bags and panels as she could, her eyes still searching for H-6. A notification popped up in her right eye, and she blinked. Her vision screens didn't usually send messages.

Locating H-6 . . . located.

Her vision zoomed in on a panel forward and to her right. She headed for it, weaving her way around the obstacles in her flight path, and slipped behind its protective walls. Not that she needed the protection, but Master Ekeli had been right; it was an ideal spot for sniping lone competitors or destroying groups, as it was above where many of the other panels hung. To go farther into the maze, any competitor would have to pass along the same track she had—or risk following the main path and being annihilated by the dozens of other compatriots still stuck there. This was the smart choice. And in Hell Week, only the smart survived.

Rex breathed deeply to minimize her noise. The first sign of another competitor came in the form of a punching bag swinging slightly on its chain, followed by a thump against a panel. Rex raised her gun.

Two competitors whizzed into her field of vision. She pulled the trigger and shot them both down in a matter of milliseconds. With confused glances, trying to locate their shooter, they subsided toward ground level.

"Captain!" Rex heard the hoarse whisper before she saw Rider. "I've got a whole bunch of them on my six." He darted toward cover just as a group came into view, guns blazing. Rex smiled and pulled the trigger. Vest lights flashed, and the competitors went down in disappointment. When they were all out of earshot, Rex murmured to Rider.

"Roth?"

"Should be coming soon."

They waited in silence for what seemed like hours, though it could only have been a few seconds. Well, in the fog that was Rex's brain, she couldn't really be sure. Finally, another group came—the last, judging by the decreased noise at the front of the maze. Together, Rex and Rider demolished them before they made it halfway across the open space. But still, Roth wasn't there. Rex signaled to Rider to stay quiet, then floated just out of the cover of the H-6 panel to peer down the dark line of the maze airway. The neon lights made the backs of her eyes ache, and she squinted, straining harder.

Without warning, the shot hit her in the chest.

018

Rex recoiled in shock at the sudden impact. Her vest flashed wildly, then its light died.

Roth floated up from behind a low-placed striking bag, a cruel smile on his face. "Puts your fire out, doesn't it?"

Rex seethed. If she didn't know better, she would think Roth was out to get her just because he enjoyed thwarting other people's goals. But, even in her sleep-deprived, pain-filled mind, she knew it was because of Rider. Her entire life goal could be sabotaged by one friendship if she wasn't careful. On the other edge of the blade, perhaps she could protect Rider and beat Roth's face into the dirt at the same time. Roth's next words shocked her to her bones.

"Good job, Rider. Right where she was supposed to be."

Rex darted her gaze between the two boys. Roth's face was still set in that superior smile, but Rider's was blank.

"You did this? On purpose?"

"No . . ." Rider began, but Roth shot him a look. Rex instantly knew what was happening. And she wasn't going to let Roth get away with it.

"You're throwing shade on him. Just like you plan to do if the bribe slips the cut. And it's not going to work. You know why?"

Rider reached out a hand in warning to stop her. She didn't care. She thrust her body into Roth's space, confronting him.

"You can't make me hate Rider, because I hate you."

Roth laughed, a deep, nonchalant sound. "Oh, I'm so hurt. I was dying for your good opinion. And you don't have to hate Rider. In fact, loving him is so much better. There's a lot more to work with."

Rex took her turn to laugh, trying to force a carelessness she didn't feel. "I don't have to love him to hate you, either. Your bribe won't work. I'll tell the master everything. And Rider will back me up."

"I doubt it. He likes the way things are. Don't you, Rider? He wouldn't want anything else to happen."

"He's no coward," Rex growled. "He's not scared of you. And neither am I."

"How much do you know about him? And how much do you know about me? You're going to find out real soon what a coward he can be. Because I own him. He's mine. And there's nothing you can do about it."

"I can fight you. If I win, you leave him alone and never bother him—or me—again."

Roth's face contorted into something between a sneer and a smile. Once again, she was reminded of a shark. "And why would I pick a fight with someone as pitiful as you? I'd get in trouble for breaking you.

You're not worth the inconvenience."

"Scared. You're scared and trying to hide it."

"This is the part where you expect me to react to your accusation and agree to fight you to prove my courage. Well, I don't have to prove anything. So you can either go stomp off to the master and try your best to prove me guilty of whatever it is you're accusing me of, or you can accept the fact that I've won."

Rex ground her teeth in fury. She hated being helpless more than anything in the world. But how could she protect Rider? She knew Roth was right; nothing she could do would make him fight her. She looked at Rider, her gaze searching his face for some sign of rebellion, or explanation, or anything. There was only pain. He gestured helplessly.

"I have to, Rex. There's no choice."

And with that, Roth shot Rider's vest and they both turned away, leaving Rex smoldering and confused in the maze.

***

Dinner was a welcome respite. Now that groups were a bit looser, Rex had decided to finally take Bridget up on listening to Alec's stories. The Irish boy gestured broadly as he spoke to punctuate his words.

"So, it began when I was two. There was a time where I would throw up everything mah lovely mother gave me. Squash, bananas, avocadoes, ice cream . . . ya name it, I threw it up."

"Ice cream . . ." Bridget sighed dreamily. Rex

couldn't tell if the dreaminess was from the thought of the food or the sight of Alec.

"I got thinner and thinner until I was stumbling around, barely able to walk. I'd puke on chairs, rugs, furniture, but never in a dump or the toilet."

"Imagine having rugs," Rex muttered. Bridget shot her an annoyed glance, then immediately returned to adoring Alec.

"And then, one day, I could eat again. So I got nice and fat and grew up, but every once in a while I'd go through one of those vomitin' spells again. Every single time, I'd throw up somewhere I wasn't meant to. It would just come upon me and I'd hurl. So, years later, I'm at school, and I'm feeling nauseous. I run to the toilet room, thinking that for once, just once, this might be the day I puke somewhere appropriate. Get this: I'm *ten centimeters* from the toilet when I throw up everywhere."

The competitors around Rex roared with laughter. Exhausted as she was, she joined in. Anything to get her mind off the torturous day.

"It was bad, too!" Alec continued. "It was like, kinda green and spattered everywhere. The cleaner was mad. He comes in and he's like, 'Why you mess up mah floor, boy? Huh? That what that thar toilet for!'"

A chair clattered to the floor amid the raucous laughter as a competitor fell over, delirious and overcome with mirth. Rex threw back her head and gave vent to the pent-up tension in her body that she couldn't express through tears. Part of her wished she could vomit just to ease the knots in her stomach.

If I could just vomit and then fall asleep... sleep... sleep...

She looked at her plate with its pile of cold pasta and old chicken. The thunder in her stomach increased and she bent over, hoping for the first time in her life that she would throw up. She had been doing it every day for the past few days. Why couldn't it come now? Bile seeped into her mouth. She barely noticed the trickle of spittle that fell from her lips. Her limbs began to shake and she tensed, attempting to still them.

"You feeling okay, Captain?"

Rider's voice weaved through the fog in her mind. She turned to see him standing somewhat hesitantly behind her. She gritted her teeth.

"Don't call me that."

For the first time since Rex had known him, Rider looked genuinely hurt. He nodded slightly and turned away, threading his way back to the table where Roth lounged with a barely concealed smirk. Tanner was some distance away from them, looking like he wanted to pull Rider away from Roth but couldn't find a way to do so.

You and me both, Tanner.

Bridget looked between Rex's set face and Rider's retreating back.

"Ya know he's stumbling on his face for ya, right?"

Rex scoffed. "Him? Hardly."

Abbi chimed in. "I can tell by the way he tries too hard to be funny. That's what someone used to do for me."

"He acts that way around everyone."

"But he always stares at you when he does it," Abbi insisted.

Zyanya leaned in, resting her arm on the back of a chair. She wore an uncharacteristic smile on her face. "You can accept the fact that you've got yourself a boyfriend. It's not going to kill you."

Rex went to wipe her mouth on her sleeve, remembered she was wearing a tank top, and spat on the floor instead. "Well, my 'boyfriend' is scared of a *goel-nefesh ben-zonna.*"

"What?" Bridget frowned.

"Nasty son of a—"

"Alright, I get it!" Bridget said, covering her ears.

Rex continued, "He's scared, so, no, he's not my boyfriend. Boyfriends protect and stand up for themselves. And others. Especially people they supposedly care about. He doesn't." As she said the words, disappointment knifed through her chest. After all the trust she had built with Rider—after all the times he had watched her back, respected her, even made her laugh—in the end, he was weak. Victory over Roth had been so close, but he had given up. Roth had found Rider's Achilles heel and had plunged in a knife. His weakness was not trusting himself, not trusting his leader—Rex—to overcome their opponent. And a fearful person was not someone she wanted to be close to.

019

Rex's precious one hundred and twenty minutes of rest were over all too soon. She took a huge breath and heaved herself up from her bed, fighting the dizziness that swam in her head. It was the last day of the competitive phase—no, the last day before final alpha testing. If she could just make it one more day, she'd be one of the top two contenders for the female alpha.

"Almost there," she mumbled groggily, blinking hard and stretching to ease the agony in her cramped muscles.

"On your feet, Competitors! Step it up!" Sergeant Bailey ushered all the girls out of bed, through the glass hallway, up the dark stairway, and into the level two training room. When they and the boys were assembled, the female sergeant addressed them all. Her voice was overly loud for Rex's tired ears.

"Competitors! Today is your last day before two males and two females will move on to the alpha phase. Master Ekeli has given me permission to give you all an overview of where you stand in the pack as of today. We'll have three assessments today.

These are your chances to score higher and improve your position." She tapped her wrist-screen. "In the omega level: Melhi, Terae, Fthasad . . ." She belted out the competitors' last names, then moved on to delta level. As she came to beta, Rex's spirit fell as she heard Rider's last name called.

Well, that's all he'll get if he's too scared to stand up for himself. I gave him an option out. If he'd worked with me, he could be alpha. But a doubt pushed back. There was something wrong. There had to be. She wondered why she hadn't noticed it before; probably exhaustion. Rider was fearless. He laughed at the idea of being held back by anyone. He could run across a forbidden stretch of water and still get a better score than climbing over the puddle. Rider could give you a smile that melted your emotions into a puddle and hit a target between the eyes at the same time. He was carefree—because he was dangerous. Roth had to be threatening him in some way that didn't allow him to take the loophole Rex had offered him. And for Tanner to be unable to help Rider—Tanner, who was always ready with a comeback for any excuse or joke that Rider did to hide a mistake . . . there had to be a secret, some sort of blackmail.

With a start, Rex came back to the present as she heard her own name in the alpha contester group along with Alelta, another girl from a different team, and Zyanya. Rex felt a thrill of elation.

"These positions are subject to change depending on your performance today. Give it all you've got! Hold nothing back! Now, let's get to assessment one!"

**

Two assessments came and went, along with two meals. Rex couldn't remember if they were breakfast and lunch or lunch and dinner. The day blended into one amorphous fog of trudging through each challenge. Finally, the last assessment came. Master Ekeli let them ascend to the third level, and they grouped in the training room there. The room consisted of rows and rows of doors set along weaving mazes of shadowed hallways. The rules for the assessment were explained, but most of them went past Rex like sand in the wind. One rule she did hear clearly: they would be locked in separate rooms and have to find their way out. The person who did so the fastest scored the highest.

She swallowed hard. Memories of being locked in the service room at the back of her house, the low ceiling pressing down on her, the narrow walls giving her no space to lie down and sleep . . . the stench of old waste fermenting in the desert sun . . . no food for days . . . her stepfather's fist beating on the door. She would throw all her weight against it to stop him from giving her what he called "freedom"—a few minutes where he would drag her out, beat her, and use her. All the while, she couldn't fight back using anything more than a weak display of a twelve-year-old's normal struggling. And her fighting only resulted in more beating.

She pushed away the fear and replaced it with anger. This time, she could escape the room. This time, there was nobody to lock her in or pull her out for a "freedom" treatment. And this time, her temporary captivity would count for something.

Alpha.

Almost without conscious thought, she strode to a room and closed the door behind her.

The room was pitch black except for a red light that flashed in the far corner. Rex's eye implants adjusted to the darkness with a quick series of zoom-ins and outs and a brief vision of the walls bathed in glowing light. She heard a loud click as the door locked behind her and the assessment began.

She surveyed the room, analyzing what she had to work with. Steel walls with interlocking panels. On one wall, the word *"ALPHA"* spray-painted in different colors. A single black wall inset on the same wall. The red light on the back wall, still flashing. On the floor, a screwdriver with protective plastic over the end. Her exhausted brain struggled to piece together an escape plan.

"Nothing will get done by standing here," Rex muttered to herself. She picked up the screwdriver. Starting with the wall, she inserted the flat head of the tool into the grooves between the panels, then twisted. Nothing. Solid, unyielding metal met her efforts. She wiggled the screwdriver harder, jammed it, then yanked. Still nothing.

She crossed to the wall inset mounted on the right of the room and inspected it. There were four wires intertwined, all of them dark except a yellow one. It was probably a control panel of some kind.

Maybe try cutting the wires? She looked at the screwdriver, which had a protective covering over the metal end. It seemed to confirm the idea that it could be safely used to cut the wires. Without further deliberation, she set the screwdriver against the yellow wire and hammered at it until it broke with a snap.

Two panels from either side of the room shot out and began to close off the path to the door. With a muted yelp, Rex sprinted to the gap and thrust her cybernetic hand between the panels as they came together. She heard a crunching noise as her hand's metal plating and wires buckled under the intense pressure. Desperate, she tugged. With a ringing screech, her hand came free and she fell back on the ground as the panels interlocked.

"Stupid, stupid, stupid," she muttered, shaking her hand and hearing small gears clatter to the floor. She stalked back to the control panel, trying not to look at the smaller space she now found herself in. Her fingers shook as she probed the wires. Behind her, it was almost as if she could feel the wall creeping closer. It had blocked off the door that, though she couldn't open it, had afforded at least the suggestion of freedom. She searched the control panel frantically. If she could find out how to work it, she could get out. But if she made another mistake, the room would probably get smaller.

She looked more closely at the wires. At first glance, she had thought they were all black. Their coloring was so faint, even her optical implants had missed it in the darkness. The one to the left of the yellow wire was red, and the two to the right were blue and purple. Rex cast about the room again to search for some clue that would allow her to work the panel.

The red flashing light.

The red wire was the one to cut.

"That's too easy." Rex frowned. Even in her back-alley fading edge town, she had heard of old adventure screenings from before the Blackout where the hero had to cut a red wire to stop a bomb or some such disaster. It couldn't be that simple. It just couldn't. But the light . . .

"Oh, blast it." Rex took the screwdriver and severed the red wire.

Another click, and another part of the room closed off. Sweat broke out on Rex's face. Unwanted memories forced themselves past her angry defensive wall. In desperation, she cut the other two wires, hoping blindly for a reversal of events. Two more cut-offs. Now the room was not even big enough for her to lie down at her full length. Rex fell to the floor, a sob breaking from her chest. It was too much. The exhaustion, the brain work, the trauma like an army of tanks exploding in her head . . .

More intrusive memories flooded over her. She sat, arms clasped around her knees, rocking back and forth. Tears that she hadn't shed for months, years even, came flooding out. She was twelve again, crying alone. No one was there for her. She had to rely on herself. That was always how it had been, aside from those rare moments when her mother was able to get her out while her stepfather was gone drinking. Then she'd hold Rex in her arms, wash the refuse out of her hair, and give her day-old challah bread and beef. There was that brief moment of love and relief, but then her stepfather would return, and Rex would have to lock herself in the outhouse again so he wouldn't hurt her mother for letting her out.

The darkness and the cold closed in on her as she sat there. It was as if living demons prowled in the space that once again she couldn't escape. Sobs gave way to whimpers and shaking breaths. She had to get up. She had to keep going. For her mother. For her father.

Like a flash, the whole memory came back to her—the one she had briefly glimpsed when she had been shot. Her, falling into the sand face-first, arms bracing against the impact. Sand cascading like waves on a sea. Heat burning her skin. Blood dripping from her nose. Her father's firm voice.

Get up, Rexala.

He had been training her. She had gone for a high kick, which he had blocked. She had spun about in the air and taken a fall. Yet her father had not hurt her intentionally, as her stepfather later would. He was perfecting her technique. He was loving her. Even as she turned her head to gaze up at him, she saw approval in his dark eyes as he called her by her full name.

Rexala.

More tears came to her eyes, but this time, they

were love.

"I'm coming, Father." Shaking, she raised herself to her feet.

As she came to her feet, she stood directly in front of the wall marked ALPHA. She stared at it. Why hadn't she noticed it before? The *A*s were red, and the middle letters were yellow, blue, and purple, respectively. They were the same colors as the wires.

"*Zobie*," she cursed in Hebrew. She was supposed to have cut them in that order. Now that the wires were already severed, what more could she do? She glanced back and forth between the wall and the control panel and realized there was one difference. There were two red *A*s, and only one red wire. Maybe it wasn't about cutting the wires in order. Maybe it was about reconnecting them.

Hope burned in her chest, and she scrubbed a hand across her cheeks to dry them. She gingerly took hold of the two sides of the red wire and brought them together. She did the same for the yellow, blue, and purple wires. Then, for the final *A*, she joined the red wires once more.

The back wall shot open, and Rex stumbled out into the hallway. The dim lighting of the training room felt like a beautiful sunrise to her. As she took her place with the other competitors who had beaten her, her disappointment was overshadowed by a warm feeling of relief. She had escaped. She had beaten one nightmare from her past. And she had made her father proud.

020

Rex was astounded the next morning to hear that she would in fact be in the running for alpha despite her less-than-stellar performance in the last challenge.

"You have scored so well in every other assessment that you still have enough points to compete in the final challenge. You surpassed your friend, the Native American girl, by three points," Master Ekeli explained.

Zyanya took the news ruefully but with good sport. "*Tohki wanaphika ni*," she said, using an old Native American blessing. Rex nodded and gave her a smile.

"*B'hatzlacha*," she said in Hebrew. Zyanya frowned slightly, but from her nod Rex gathered that she understood it as a similar expression of goodwill.

Alelta was not so friendly. All traces of good humor were gone from her face, and her grey eyes were steel on Rex's dark ones as the news was announced. She was tense in every line of her body. Rex gazed back, alert but unafraid, and it was Alelta who looked away first.

The morning sun flashed off the steel roofs and glass tunnels of the compound buildings as Master Ekeli led both girls—followed by the other competitors—up to the roof of the training tower. The spire atop the roof had an elevator that led up to the glass platform at the very highest point. Only Master Ekeli and Sergeant Bailey accompanied Rex and Alelta to that platform. The sergeant gave each of them a training gun while Master Ekeli outlined the rules.

"In a moment, Doctor Haradth will activate a shield that will outline the boundaries above and to either side of this platform. Do not cross these boundaries. You will fight until one of you shoots the other in a vital area that would cause mortal wounding or gains a conclusively dominant position in hand-to-hand combat. These positions include holding down your opponent for more than four seconds or knocking them unconscious. You may use strikes, so long as no bones are broken. Competitor Zero-Eighteen will be allowed to use her assets with protective sheaths over the blades. When I give the word, you will begin."

Sergeant Bailey stepped up and clapped a hand over Rex's eyes. Rex recoiled in alarm at the invasion of her space. As the sergeant stepped back, a metal contraption closed over Rex's eyes.

"And you will be fighting blindfolded," Master Ekeli finished. Rex heard his and Sergeant Bailey's footsteps recede and she guessed they had gone to stand in front of the elevator, out of the way. The shield boundary grid hummed to life, and with a barked command from the master, the final alpha test began.

Rex reached out with her ears to gauge Alelta's position. She heard the other girl step to the left, and she took a corresponding step to the right. They continued circling. Rex strained her ears, flicking her eyes back and forth under the blindfold. Gone was the exhaustion of Hell Week—replaced by a lucid clarity she had never felt before. But if she felt it, Alelta did too. Her only advantage was to strike first.

She twisted her belt and leapt into the air, setting her finger to the trigger. She whipped the gun back and forth, hoping that one of the many bullets would find its mark. Alelta fired back. Rex ducked as a shot whistled above her head and another bounced off her bionic arm. Following the sounds Alelta was making, Rex stowed her gun and twisted toward her opponent, zeroing in on the other girl's position to bring her to close quarters. She kept her arms close to her body to shield against any stray bullets. Sure enough, several rattled on her skin before she rammed into Alelta full force, bowling her over. They grappled in midair. Rex struck with hands and elbows, searching for an opening in her opponent's guard.

Alelta pushed away. Rex heard the noise of Alelta's twin blades being unlocked. She hoped the training sheaths would activate properly, or she could lose more than a leg to a malfunction this time.

Alelta's blades whirled toward her body. Rex

avoided the first and the second strike, but the third caught her in the midriff, knocking the breath from her with the sheer power and ferocity behind it. Alelta seized her advantage and sent a blow crashing down on Rex's head. Rex let loose an involuntary yell, then her reinforced hand shot up to catch the blade before Alelta could pull it away.

They struggled there for a split second, Alelta striking with her other blade at Rex's side, and Rex refusing to let go of the blade above her head. She increased the pressure of her grip until she could feel the sharp blade penetrating its covering and biting into the steel of her reinforced palm. But Alelta drove a straight thrust into Rex's ribs with her free blade, and Rex was forced to let go with another yell.

Rex needed to get inside the reach of Alelta's blades. Doing that blindfolded, even with her reinforcements and a combat suit, would mean taking more punishing blows before getting inside the other girl's guard. Or it could mean taking a sword stroke to the head and being eliminated from the fight. Her only chance was to do it as fast as possible.

Covering her head with her arms to create a shield, she pressed her toes back and shot directly toward the sound of Alelta's breathing. Her elbows slammed into the other girl's chest, and immediately Rex circled her arms around Alelta's waist in a clench hold to keep her from getting away. Alelta bucked and struggled with a scream of rage. Rex pulled the hold tighter, pushing one hand against her opponent's chin and increasing the pressure on

Alelta's lower back so that she was bent backwards with her head and hips being pushed in two opposite directions.

She felt Alelta's gun being aimed at her head—a combination of muscle movements and slight noises—and her hand shot up, catching the gun just before it eliminated her from the fight. The shot exploded above her head, and she instantly yanked down, breaking Alelta's hold on the weapon and throwing it to the platform below. Alelta screeched in fury and hammered Rex with her fists. Rex grunted as the blows fell on her shoulders and face, then sent two carefully positioned blows to Alelta's ribs. The other girl gasped, and Rex took advantage of her competitor's lack of breath to yank the other girl's right arm forward and get behind her back. She wrapped her arm around Alelta's throat in a choke hold and began counting down the seconds.

1...2...

Alelta snarled. She brought her legs up and over, taking Rex with her in a complete flip. Rex's grip only loosened fractionally, but Alelta took advantage of it. With a violent twist, she wrenched herself free from Rex's grasp.

"Stop trying to take my position!" Alelta spat.

Rex scoffed. "Why do you always assume something's yours just because you want it? I've got as much right to have it, and probably more reason to than you do."

Alelta laughed sardonically. "The same right? More reason? Did the people at your school all treat you like crap when you were the best one in the class? Was your teacher always disappointed in you, no matter how hard you worked? Did your best friend *kill herself* because of—" Alelta abruptly fell silent, breathing heavily and growling like an animal. Rex kept level with her, hands raised, ready for an attack. Finally, Alelta spoke again.

"You may have a good reason, but you have no right to take away the answer to the question that destroyed my life."

Rex knew it was her turn to speak. "I have every right. Because you're trying to do the exact same thing to me."

With a roar, Alelta leapt at Rex, smashing her against the shield grid. Electricity crackled against Rex's skin and she grunted, bringing her knee up to push Alelta away. The other girl clung on. They spun end over end, striking the wall repeatedly as they hammered at each other. Rex felt a dozen bruises forming on her body. She blocked, struck, blocked, and struck again. There was something that could turn the fight in her favor. Not her gun—she hadn't had any success with that so far—but she needed space. She pushed away from Alelta. Steadying herself, she focused on Alelta's position and leapt up, feeling as if the air was a solid surface beneath her feet, propelling her upward. She spun a full 360 degrees and extended her leg to send a high kick at Alelta's head.

Her foot struck air. Rex spun almost out of control and had just managed to steady herself when

Alelta flew in. Now the other girl was giving it everything she had. She jabbed, hooked, kicked, used her knees and elbows—anything and everything to knock Rex out. Rex blocked most of the blows, but each one came faster and more painful than the last. Two fists to the side of her head sent her reeling. Alelta was good. She was better than Rex had anticipated. Rex knew she couldn't stay on the defensive and survive. But she also knew that Alelta, driven by demons as she was, would not give her any opening. A rogue thought flashed into Rex's mind.

What would Rider do?

She had to think like Rider—outside the arena. The arena here was the platform and the shield grid. *What did Master Ekeli say about the boundaries?*

. . . above and to either side of this platform . . .

And then she had it.

Blocking a fist with her forearm, Rex put her foot into Alelta's stomach and hurled her away. She deactivated her shoes and plummeted to the glass below. It cracked loudly under her feet, but held together. Still, Rex knew, enough added force would shatter it entirely.

She couldn't explain it, but she knew Alelta was diving toward her, hoping to crush her with a final blow. She drew her gun. Aiming it downward, she fired.

The glass beneath her feet exploded into a thousand shards. Rex dropped like a stone, letting herself fall beneath the platform before she activated her boots. Angling her feet upward, she streaked directly into Alelta's flight path.

There was a huge thump, and Rex heard Alelta spin end over end from the impact of the kick. Then the other girl became very still. After several seconds, Master Ekeli's voice rang out.

"Finished!"

Rex's blindfold disengaged. She let it fall. Around her, the shield grid faded into nothing. Alelta floated some distance away, completely limp, blood seeping from her nose. Rex had a sudden jolt of fear that she might have broken one of Alelta's bones—or worse. She hovered hesitantly toward the other girl.

"Leave her," Master Ekeli called. "Doctor Haradth will examine her to ascertain whether there are any serious injuries. Then we will know who is alpha."

A sharp blade seemed to penetrate Rex's chest as she backed away and was led down to the floor below by Sergeant Bailey. Everything that she had worked for could be ruined if she had hit Alelta too hard.

At least I didn't hit her with my metal foot.

***

While Alelta was being examined, Rex was a spectator to the match between Roth and Jonas. Jonas was an Israeli boy that looked to be a good match for Roth's skills. Despite that fact, Rex's blood boiled that Rider wasn't the one competing. However, now would be the perfect time to ask him questions. She peered through the crowd of other spectators to see where he might be. She caught sight of him some distance away, closer to the back. He didn't look happy. Rex was just moving toward him when a message appeared in her optical display.

027, report to medical bay.

Rex wasted no time. She raced down all three flights of stairs, out the door, and across the compound to where she knew the answer to her status lay. Rider could wait.

"No bones were broken," Leah reported. "She has a mild concussion, but nothing that some good sleep and water won't fix."

Rex let out a huge breath she had been holding despite having just run across the compound. "So . . . I'm alpha?"

Leah checked her wrist-screen and smiled. "According to Ekeli as of now . . . yes."

Rex stood, entirely still. She looked around the room, feeling that this couldn't be real, that it had to be a dream. Yet it was real.

Her father.

She would know what had happened. How he had died. If he had died.

Father . . .

She put one hand on a table and slowly beat her fist against its white surface.

She had won.

A few minutes later, Jonas was brought into the medical bay. Rex heard the tramp of feet as competitors—no, now pack members—returned to the barracks for long-delayed sleep. But she was still waiting for one thing.

Finally, Master Ekeli stepped through the door.

He wore an uncharacteristic smile on his face.

"Zero-Twenty-Seven. Congratulations. You are the female alpha for the Airborne Elite."

Rex took a deep breath to steady her shaking voice. "You said I could get whatever information I wanted."

"What do you wish to know?"

"I want to know what happened to my father. How did he die? Did. . . did he. . ."

Master Ekeli gestured to Leah. "Doctor Haradth, set up the briefing room." To Rex, he said, "Follow."

He took her down several hallways, past guards and the boy's barracks, and halted outside a door. He turned to Rex.

"In this room, you will find the answers you seek, but know that the truth will be painful. Center yourself on your goal, your desire for knowledge, and the pain will become bearable. Do not lose yourself." He checked his wrist-screen. "It is prepared and unlocked. Now, step into wisdom's halls."

Trembling and breathless, Rex opened the door.

ALPHA

Part 2

021

The room was dark at first, with three glowing symbols hovering in the center.

דַּעַת

Rex moved toward it. It was the Hebrew word for "knowledge." Pausing in front of it, she reached out her hand.

The symbols exploded into hundreds more that surrounded her, then fell into row upon row. Her eyes raced over the words as her heart pounded in her chest.

"*Captain Jerich Hai, Division 1223, Covert Operations.*"

A picture of her father—dark eyes, strong aquiline nose, serious face—fell into place beside the words.

"*Successfully completed thirty-four missions in Iraq, Afghanistan, and other undisclosed locations. Led the covert STRIKE Team 03 in all thirty-four missions. Awarded stripes for tactical excellence, bravery, and leadership.*"

"*2113 AD. Captain Hai's bloodline, marriage, and

achievements were examined by the military division of the United Intercontinental Alliance. He and his wife, Judith Bat'Fell, qualified to have their firstborn child drafted into the Stratotech Project."

"2115 AD. Captain Hai and his wife bore a daughter, Rexala. Captain Hai himself oversaw his daughter's training in her early years, until his thirty-fifth mission."

Rex stepped through the symbols before her, drawing her hand through them. They skittered away like gazelles before a lioness, then rearranged themselves after her passing. Rex turned around and around, gazing at the plethora of images and captions. There were pictures of her as a tiny girl with her father. In one, he knelt as she leapt at him, trying to topple him to the ground. Another depicted them both doing splits. But there was one that captivated her. It showed her father laughing—something she didn't remember him ever doing. He held her in the air above his head. She was laughing too, eyes squinted shut, and wriggling in his strong grasp. In the background, her mother worked with leather cord. Rex caught her breath. It was the necklace she had cherished for so many years. Tears prickled in her eyes and longing welled up in her chest. There was so much she had lost . . .

A light blinking farther toward the back of the room caught her attention. She passed by the picture and stood before the light. It was poised at the corner of another wall of words. As she paused, it stopped blinking.

Captain Hai's thirty-fifth mission was conducted in 2121 from a classified location in Iraq. His objective: shut down a branch of the State-allied terrorist organization Shat al-Shed. Time frame: 48 hours. The captain led his team on a flash attack on the terrorists. It did not succeed. Shat al-Shed was waiting with IEDs and a full force to meet them. Captain Hai's team was destroyed except for the captain himself, who was captured, and one survivor, Corporal Judah Thuraj, who escaped. Footage captured by Drone 13.

Rex reached out with bated breath and touched the blurry photo of her father in combat. Suddenly, she was drawn in. It was as if the picture had brought her into that moment itself. Her head was thrown back and her eyes stared upward, gripped by the unfolding scene, captivated and horrified at the same time.

Soldiers ran toward a desert fortress, carrying rifles. At a shouted signal, they fired at a line of defenders.

"Grenade!" someone shouted. They all dove for cover.

The bomb burst with a fountain of sand. As the soldiers coughed and brought their rifles up, the enemy took advantage of the dust and spread out from the armored doorway, circling behind the attacking force. Machine guns ripped bodies to shreds. Blood flew like rain. Rex gasped as she actually felt liquid spatter on her face. The rattle of the guns hurt her ears. The camera rocked crazily as a volley shattered the drone's camera. A heart-lurching pause;

then the footage resumed, this time from a different angle as another drone took up filming.

"Bullet formation!"

As soon as Rex heard the words, she knew it was her father. And then she saw him. Blood caked the dust on his face under the sweltering afternoon sun. His uniform was shredded almost to nothing on top, and a deep gash in his leg dripped blood as he stumbled to a shallow trench and knelt there, gesturing to his men to form up behind him. They rallied to him and gathered close in the military formation known as the bullet, then sent a thunderstorm of bullets outward at their adversaries.

But the terrorists had the advantage in numbers. One by one, the men in the trench fell to the earth, their blood coloring the sand black. Soon only her father and one other man were left. Rex's eye caught a small hand gesture her father made to his comrade. The man went flat, as if falling from a bullet wound, but Rex knew he was bluffing. The terrorists, however, were only interested in her father. Their leader called to him to surrender. He hesitated, pain and anger and blood coursing over his face. Then he slowly laid down his gun and raised his hands.

Watching him, Rex knew he wasn't surrendering out of weakness. He did it out of intelligence. Surrounded as he was, he would have been shot to scraps the minute he released another bullet.

He had been so intelligent.

And now he was gone.

Tears fell down Rex's face without her conscious thought. But they had only captured him. *Could it be . . . is he . . .*

As he was secured and led away into the fortress, a terrorist looked up, raised his gun, and shot the camera. Rex had been reaching out as if she could pull her father away from his captors when she felt the impact as the glass shattered and the screen went dark.

Another image of her father popped up to her left. She hurried over to it, wiping tears from her face, and tapped it, hoping for another screening. The image remained stationary. Words appeared below it.

Corporal Thuraj received a transmission in code from Captain Hai on July 1, 2133. The message stated that the captain was alive and being held for questioning. He believed he would remain in his current location as a POW until death.

Rex stared at the date contained in the message.

July 1, 2133.

Two weeks ago.

***

Sergeant Bailey was in her office with Master Ekeli when Rex burst in. She strode toward them, one purpose on her mind.

"My father is alive."

Sergeant Bailey nodded approvingly. "I see you made it out without a psychological breakdown. Ekeli thought you could."

Rex didn't have time for wit. "What can I do to get

him out?"

Ekeli raised an eyebrow. "You? Get him out? Remember, you are the alpha now. Where you go, your division must follow."

Rex stopped, full realization hitting her like a punch to the stomach. She struggled for a moment. Finally, the words came. "Are you telling me that you showed me all that and you won't let me do anything about it?"

"Not at all," Ekeli said mildly. "But there are certain steps that must be taken first. Today is only the beginning of the alpha phase. Training with your squadron, including a test mission, is required before any personal mission. In addition, my higher authorities must sanction any operation you wish to perform. They will see if it is a proper use of the Airborne Elite force and determine if it would further the overall campaign of the United Intercontinental Alliance."

"Basically, if your mission benefits the Israeli government's agenda, you can go," Sergeant Bailey put in. "But this is a highly specialized force. Your objective would have to be part of a larger plan."

As Rex drew breath to speak, Ekeli cut in, "If rescuing your father is what you want, we can put in a request to the authorities today. The Alliance does have a keen interest in the place he is being held. It is a research center that has been impossible to penetrate in the past. The terrorist group is called Shat al-Shed, which, in modern Egyptian, means 'The Evil One Saves.'"

Despite the sinister sound of the name, Rex didn't care what the group was called. "How long will that request take to process?"

Ekeli made an expansive gesture with both hands. "It varies. Regardless of the length of time, you must complete your alpha phase training first."

"If they say yes, chances are the permissions will be ready by the time you are." Sergeant Bailey ruffled some papers and shook them together, then placed them in a drawer in her desk. "I can type up a request while you sleep. All you'll have to do is sign it, and then I can send it to HQ."

"How do you send it?"

"We fax it, obviously," Sergeant Bailey drawled sarcastically. "That's classified. Any more questions? If not, I suggest you sleep."

"Not sure I can, Sergeant Ma'am."

Master Ekeli took a step toward her. "I'll have Doctor Haradth give you an injection."

Rex recoiled in alarm. "I'd rather not."

"It's either that or you miss part of your precious thirty hours of sleep," Sergeant Bailey remarked unsympathetically. Rex sighed. Having more needles stuck in her was not something she wanted, but it would be worse to lose more sleep than she already had. She followed Master Ekeli out of the room to the medical bay.

***

"Did she express interest?"

Leah stood against the glass wall of the exam room, arms folded gracefully as she queried Ekeli.

The arts master nodded.

"Yes. Intensely."

"And the papers are ready?"

"We only need her signature."

Leah smiled slightly, gazing out the transparent walls to the glorious morning beyond. She did love the sunrise. "That should take care of our problem," she said.

022

Rex had never felt so much relief as when she woke up from her full thirty hours of sleep. Though every bone and muscle ached from Hell Week, she felt a hope and a direction for the first time in a long time. The birthing sun on this new day brought with it the full realization that she was alpha. She had discovered the secret about her father, and there was a course of action that she could finally take.

As she had the thought, the sergeant's bark brought the pack members up from their beds.

"Come on, you lot! Your thirty hours are up, and you should be too. Shimmy those backsides! I want to see you in uniform and running in three minutes!"

Rex smiled as she shrugged on her tank top and stuffed her feet into her boots. The hard part was over. After the ridiculously difficult training the week before, morning exercises were like picking off people in laser tag. The thought brought Rider into her mind once again. She had questions, and she hoped he had answers. She would have to talk to him at breakfast.

***

It was harder than she thought it would be to get to Rider in the mess hall. Her old teammates and many of the other pack members crowded around her where she sat to congratulate her, or to check out what sort of a person their new female alpha was. At first, Rex felt trapped and overwhelmed, but she gradually began to enjoy the respect, admiration, and—most of all—the feeling of not being so lonely anymore. These were all good fighters who had made it through Hell Week with her. They were also the people who could help her rescue her father. Now that she wasn't competing with them, she would be able to properly assess them, respect them, and lead them.

Only Alelta and Ilianayah looked downcast at her success. As Alelta crossed by Rex's table, a tray in hand, she turned sullen grey eyes toward Rex. Her face was badly bruised, and there were several cuts on her skin from where shattered glass had found its mark. Rex gazed back, keeping her expression neutral. Alelta had fought well, and there was no need to antagonize her further.

"I didn't really care about being alpha."

Bridget's words caused Rex to forget all about Alelta. "What?"

Bridget smiled. "My daddy died when I was three. I never understood why, but I knew he was in heaven, so I didn't care how it happened. My family is very religious. I was going to tell ya and Zyanya about it that day when we talked about sharing our trials as a team. But we never got the time again."

Zyanya spoke. "I'm glad you are telling us now. And it's good that you have found peace."

Rex frowned. "You didn't want to know, even just a little bit?"

Bridget shrugged. "I did—I do—but I didn't want to hurt people over it."

"Well, it was kind of a killed or be killed scenario, except we weren't being killed." Rider plopped down beside her, a smile on his face. Rex's heart gave a small surge of emotion against her will. His eyes found hers. She could see something behind them—something Rider wanted to explain but felt he couldn't.

Rangorazi's voice interrupted their conversation. "Group training! Get to the toilet, clean up, and report to the training ground in five minutes! I don't want to hear anyone whining about a bathroom break out there," he warned.

There was only one thing Rex had to do before she reported for training. She caught Rider's attention.

"Hey. I need to talk to you the next time we have a break."

Rider cocked his head. "This wouldn't have something to do with me calling you captain the other day, would it? Because I can stop doing it if it bothers you."

"No. It's about something else. I . . . want to make sure everything is out in the open. And that we're good."

Rider nodded. "Okay, we should have some free

time out on the Ledge now that it's not Hell Week anymore. But they could switch it up. You never know."

Rex gave a final nod. "Good. I'll see you there."

"See ya."

***

The alpha phase of training began with an introduction of the alphas to the rest of the pack members, which Rex felt was rather unnecessary. Next came the announcement of everyone's positions in the pack. Rex stood beside Roth, twitching her forefinger as she waited for the litany of names to end. Finally, Sergeant Bailey came to something important—the roles each of the groups of the pack were expected to perform.

"Alphas, you're leaders. Your job is to make tactical decisions, and you'll be responsible for the hard calls in the field. You should be thinking outside the arena. That's why you've made it this far."

Rex snorted quietly. Roth wasn't exactly a creative thinker. *More of a person who threatens people into obedience.*

"In the days of ancient Rome, Italy was ruled by a republic. There were two alphas, known as consuls. They each controlled half of Rome's armies and could veto each other's propositions if necessary. But they worked best when they worked together. Build understanding with each other. When it comes to your other pack members, if someone has a question that you have time and are able to answer, answer it. But if you're in a time pinch, your pack members need to obey you instantly. However, your authority does not extend into personal matters. Anything that doesn't directly relate to keeping order and fulfilling the task at hand, let it go. Just because you have power over tactics doesn't mean you have power over every other aspect of your squad's lives. Do build rapport. Do boost morale. As a leader, it's just as important to be encouraging as it is to be demanding. Do your job well, and you'll keep a cohesive team. Am I understood?"

"Yes, Sergeant Ma'am!" Rex and Roth responded together with a salute. Somehow, Rex knew that the things Sergeant Bailey had stipulated were not in Roth's plans.

The sergeant went on, "Betas! Your job is to help the alphas keep the others fit and otherwise capable. Act as drill sergeants and keep the others in line. Two of you, whom the alphas will choose, will act as leaders in the alphas' absence. Deltas! You're all scouts. You perform reconnaissance in enemy territory and relay messages to other divisions. Last but not least, omegas. Your job is to simply follow orders. On missions, you'll perform camp chores and sentry duties. You'll also receive specialized medical training so you can take care of any wounded in the field. Any questions?"

"No, Sergeant Ma'am!" came the unanimous reply.

"Good! There aren't any assessments today, just a drill. Each lower pack member will be assigned a position on a squadron. Squadron One will be led by the male alpha. Squadron Two, the female alpha."

The sergeant began calling out the names of those who would be in Squadron One, under Roth's command. Fortunately, Rider was not one of them. When it came to Squadron Two, however, both Ilianayah and Alelta fell under Rex's command. Rex sighed. This was going to be interesting.

The drill was to practice dive bombing. Rex had to lead her squad of twenty up one thousand feet above the compound, get them into a cohesive battle formation, and have them dive directly downward at top speed, stopping just short of the training ground. Even having been airborne for the past six weeks, the dive was a new kind of terrifying for Rex. There was something about the sensation of falling for an extended period that reminded her of the tension she had felt with her stepfather. There was the same helpless feeling, knowing it wouldn't end right away, feeling her heart leap out of her chest and her body tense but not being able to do a damn thing about it. As she hurtled down toward the compound for the third time, Rex desperately swallowed the panic that threatened to overwhelm her. She could not let her squad see her that way.

"Three . . . two . . . one . . . pull up!" she called. Her stomach lurched as she pulled up. Beside her, she heard several gasps as others had the same reaction. Rex panted for breath, not trusting her voice to work. She was on solid ground, unmoving once more, but she couldn't breathe.

"Well, glad that's over," Rider said cheerily.

"What's next?"

Rex felt a surge of gratitude to Rider for breaking the tension. She found her voice. "Let's rest a moment and then take a water break. I'll ask Sergeant Ma'am and see if we can get some time out on the Ledge." She glanced at Rider, who gave her an imperceptible nod and the hint of a smile.

Sergeant Bailey approved, but called Rex to her office for "urgent business." When Rex arrived, she wasted no time.

"Sign here and here." The sergeant indicated two lines on two different sheets of paper. Rex picked up a pen lying on the desk and scratched out her name, grimacing at the result. Her handwriting had never been good, and the cybernetics only made it worse, for all the added touch sensitivity she might have. The words looked like they had been written by a blind man forced to print left-handed. Sergeant Bailey didn't seem to notice.

"That takes care of the request form. I'll send it over straightaway. Dismissed, Alpha Zero-Twenty-Seven."

With a smile on her face and a spring in her step, Rex opened the door and headed out to meet Rider.

023

Rex found Rider leaning against the railing, close to one wall of the training building. She sidled through the others gathered in the open space and came to stand casually beside him. She nodded as if expressing only a cursory interest in his presence, but her words cut right to the point.

"So, you're not alpha, and he is. Why didn't you take my way out? You gave me every indication that you were on board with it."

Rider gestured to the horizon as if pointing out something in the scenery. "I couldn't risk it."

"You take every risk. It's who you are. What made this any different?" She could see that Rider was uncomfortable from the way he stood a little taller than usual.

"Maybe I'm getting smarter. I don't know," he said.

She could also tell he was lying.

"Rider," she said softly, then waited for him to meet her gaze. When his eyes came up, she asked, "What's he doing to you?"

Rider ground his teeth together and let out a low, menacing sigh. "He's hit me at my weak point. For years, it's all I've wanted to do, for my sister, and now someone else. And of course he figured it out. He always does."

Rex frowned in utter confusion. She could normally understand Rider's logic perfectly, riddled with humor as it was. None of these words made any sense. "What?"

Rider turned away to appear disinterested, but his eyes still held hers. "He said he'd hurt you if I didn't do it."

Rex stared at him, speechless. She felt her mouth move, but no sound came from her throat. Finally, she blurted, "I could have protected myself. And why didn't you say anything to Tanner?"

Rider gave her a mirthless half-smile. "Roth finds ways. Believe me. The fewer people involved in his things, the better. Well, it's done now. Nothing more I have to do. For now."

"You carried through with the bribe?"

Rider nodded.

"So . . . you were . . . protecting me?"

The half-smile became a bit brighter, and Rex saw something unfamiliar in Rider's eyes. It was . . . gentle. Soft.

"You did that for me?" she repeated.

He didn't answer, but just kept looking at her. For the first time in her life, she looked away first. Something unfamiliar tingled in her stomach, and her breath came a little faster. A silence grew between them. She wondered if she should say something, but couldn't think of anything that would be appropriate. Rider solved the problem for her.

"Do you want to hang out later? There's this great place I know of where we can watch the sunset."

Rex cocked her head, unsure of what to say. "Where? The dusty training ground?"

"No. It's a bit better than that, Captain. Oh, sorry, you don't like it when I do that," he said.

"I don't mind."

"Oh." Rider grinned in that lopsided way, showing beautiful canines. Rex shook herself. *Why am I admiring his teeth?*

"Good to see that we're good on that. Okay, good. I've got a good place to meet that's good."

Rex couldn't stop a smile from breaking free. "Where?"

A small group wandered toward them, laughing. Rider edged past her and murmured out of the side of his mouth, a roguish twinkle in his eye.

"I'll tell you the good place later," he said.

***

Alelta angled through the crowd toward Roth as everyone was let on break. She came to a stop directly in front of him, quivering with rage.

"You promised me. And I paid you."

Roth considered her, one eyebrow raised in an infuriatingly disinterested expression. "It wasn't a promise as much as a good gamble. You lost."

"I paid you twice as much as Rider to make sure that didn't happen." She kept her voice low, but no less intense.

"Ekeli took the money for you, but he had plans

for Rex to be alpha. At least that's what I got from the way he was acting. I was in his plans, Rex was in his plans, you weren't. This whole alpha thing isn't just about skill. It's also about agenda. Of course, it only helped him that Rex won anyway. But I think he would have intervened if she was about to lose."

Alelta clenched her hands into fists. "It was *my* position. It was my money. He had no right to take it if he wouldn't give me what I paid for. Why is my money any less important than yours or Rider's?"

Roth shrugged. "Sometimes money can't sway those with an agenda, especially when they have power. Or something better. They take your money and still cheat you."

"That's not fair."

"Life's not fair. Try telling that to the master. I'm sure he'll enjoy explaining all his plans to a little beta like you."

Alelta gave Roth the most withering, hate-filled look she could possibly conjure. "If you're an alpha, it's only because he likes people just as full of themselves and domineering as he is." With that, she stalked off, closing her ears to any reply Roth might send after her.

***

Sekhmet, her splayed fingers pressed against the glass, watched her asset in its training confinement. Two guards with long electrical poles circled it—or so her victim thought. It was actually a mirage created by silent drones. Sekhmet could see them hovering, changing positions as the creature moved, crouched on feet and fingertips like a cornered wolverine. As it leapt a full six feet in the air, a drone zapped it with an electrical pulse. Sekhmet giggled and began singing to herself.

"My little toy, my little toy
Writhe and wriggle like a fish
You won't escape, you won't escape
But there's a star, so make your wish.
I like to play, I like to play
Without my mommy's watching eye
My little fish, my little fish
I know you made the wish to die."

The asset whirled and lashed out at the other drone. Despite the electrical shocks, it grabbed hold of the drone and dug its fingers into a weak point between metal plating, ripping out pieces of wire and hardware. With a crackle of electricity, the drone died, imparting a shock that catapulted the asset to the ground. It lay there, breathing heavily, sides rising and falling as it gasped in huge lungfuls of air.

"Enough!" Sekhmet called, and the remaining drone disengaged. The simulation disappeared. She satisfied the scanner with a quick fingerprint and retinal identification and went into the cell, heedless of the fact that there were no guards. She was transformed. She could match her creation's fighting if the need came.

"But first, I'll try honey," she said in a sweet, smooth voice. Her foreclaw went under the asset's chin, tracing its strong jawline and tilting its eyes up to meet hers. There was pain in them—a wild hypervigilance that she knew well. She smiled, baring her long white teeth, and licked her lips.

"How would you like to meet your special prey? She's coming, coming soon."

024

Rex snuck out of the dining hall during free time after supper. Her heart thumped in a mixture of apprehension at leaving the hall and anticipation in seeing Rider. He had told her where to go in an aside earlier that afternoon. She rationalized her behavior with the thought that it was free time, anyway. She wasn't disobeying orders directly. Besides, she was alpha. Confident that she would not be severely penalized, her heart became lighter as she crossed the training ground toward the south edge of the compound.

She found Rider perched on the railing—the very edge that overlooked the sky.

"Come up here, the view's great," he called, patting the steel railing. As she stepped onto it, he held out a hand hastily. "Watch the force field!"

Rex stopped herself from swinging over the edge and hitting the invisible barrier. "Thanks." Trying to avoid thinking about the miles of space below her, she looked out at the sky.

The view was more than great. It was breathtaking. Blue the color of a brilliant jewel surrounded them. Ahead and to the right, the sun glowed like an ember plucked from the fires of a Jewish temple. Puffs of cloud, tinted pink and purple and gold, meandered by on the ever-shifting wind. The wind itself was stronger here. Rex had to brush hair out of her face and into her elastic.

"It's amazing," she breathed. "It's been a while since I've stopped and really looked at anything."

Rider pulled one side of his mouth up in a toothy smile. "Yeah, it's pretty awesome what you can notice when you slow down and smell the roses."

"Slow down? That's not a term I normally associate with you."

"What do you associate with me?"

"Not slow."

Rider laughed. It was a deep chuckling noise. For a moment, Rex was at a loss for what to say. Feelings welled up to the surface inside her that she had previously dismissed. She wasn't sure what was going on. She asked the first question that came to mind to break the silence.

"Is this a date?"

Instead of laughing or scoffing at the simplistic question, Rider gave her a soft look. "Yes, if that's alright with you."

A smile broke out on Rex's face. It was the biggest grin she had had in years. "Yes."

Rider looked around. "For our next one, I can take you flying. Out there," he said, gesturing to the open sky.

"You're the person who literally just reminded me that we have a force field barrier," Rex pointed out.

"Well, see, I can shut down the whole field so we can go anywhere we want. I memorized the code." Rider grinned evilly.

Rex raised her eyebrows. "How in precious burning Gehenna did you manage that?"

Rider made a large dismissive gesture. "Never mind about that. All that matters is that the code is *2374890242*." He rattled off the numbers so quickly Rex could barely distinguish them.

"What?"

"2374890242," Rider repeated, a little more slowly, the wicked smile still on his face.

Rex shook her head and gave a sigh. She knew she'd never get the numbers out of her head now, though she didn't want to get in trouble for it.

They sat in silence for another moment, watching the brilliant sun begin to go dim. Then they both spoke at once.

"I have to—"

"What did you—"

They both laughed. Rider gestured for her to go ahead. Rex cleared her throat.

"I . . . I found out what happened to my father."

"Oh. That's great!"

Rex held up a hand loosely to forestall his excitement. "He's a prisoner of war. Being held by terrorists. But he was able to send a coded message to one of his old soldiers. I think Sergeant Bailey has a general location."

"So is she doing anything about it?"

Rex sighed. "I have to complete the alpha phase, and my request has to be approved by headquarters before I can launch a rescue mission."

"Rescue mission? At a terrorist hideout? That sounds fun. I'll make sure to bring my guns. Both sets."

Rex laughed out loud. "You don't have guns," she reminded him, although this time, she was playful. "Except for the actual ones that can lock into your hands."

Rider held out his hands. "You wanna check them out?"

Rex glanced over the wristbands and wire cordage that disappeared into Rider's arms. "It's kind of disturbing," she said with a chuckle. Gingerly, she reached out and touched the cybernetics. Her fingers traced his hand and the new steel supports that ran all the way to his elbows. As her touch went farther up his arm, she felt his gaze on her. His hand closed over hers, and her breath came faster as her heart thumped. Slowly, she raised her eyes to meet his. They were warm and dark, set above angular cheekbones and a strong—though not too large—nose. There was that gentle look to them that she had seen before. Suddenly, she became aware that he was strong, very strong, and he could take advantage of her if she let down her guard. But something also told her that he would never do that.

Rider's other hand came up to her face. He brushed his fingers along her cheekbone.

"I've always thought your face showed more

strength than a mountain," he said with a grin, his voice carrying a slight husky softness. It fell to a whisper. "You're beautiful, Rexala." He leaned in closer.

Two sides of Rex's brain warred with each other. On one side was her years of mistrust, and on the other was her knowledge of who Rider had always been: caring, loyal, respectful—though a little irreverent. He had called her by her full name. Not "Captain" or "Rex," but the name her father had always used. Her lips tingled, and her heart burned in her chest, screaming at her to close the distance between herself and Rider. She wanted, more than anything, to trust—enough to let him hold her in his arms, enough to let go of her fear, enough to let him protect her. But the habits of years of protecting herself prevailed. She turned away.

"I can't."

From the corner of her eye, she saw the barely masked disappointment on Rider's face. "Why not? We've been friends since the first day of training. We've slogged through hell together. You've been my captain. We've outsmarted the system and come out on top. I protected you."

Rex shook herself. "It's not that, it's . . . I've been through . . ." How could he possibly understand? How could he grasp the pain, the horror, the anger that had shaped her entire existence? There was no way he could imagine the hell she walked through. She looked him directly in the eyes once again. "You protected me, but I don't think that can change what I've been through. You wouldn't want to love a broken piece of glass." With that, she swung her legs back over the rail and headed for the barracks, pushing down the pain and the longing from what had almost been her first kiss.

025

The next days brought with them a monotony of training, dealing with the difficult group dynamic that included Alelta and Ilianayah, and awkward interactions with Rider. Ilianayah had adopted Alelta into her gang, and while they couldn't directly disobey orders, they made life difficult for Rex by questioning her or scowling at every opportunity. Rider was a different edge of the knife blade altogether. There wasn't bad blood between them, but their interactions were surface level; respectful but not like comrades as before. Impatience also simmered in Rex's mind and dominated her thoughts. She wanted the alpha phase to be over so she could find her father, assuming the Alliance would let her. Everything else was just a waste of time.

"Eyes on me, Zero-Twenty-Seven!"

Sergeant Bailey's bark caused Rex to tense, ready for an attack of some kind. Realizing her mind had wandered, she gave the sergeant a respectful nod. "Yes, Sergeant Ma'am!"

Bailey nodded in turn. "I want all squad members trained in how to properly use a carrier. Start basic, with someone getting buckled in and carried around. When everyone's comfortable with that, grab training weapons and start shooting at each other. Have people take turns picking up a 'wounded' person and carrying them out of bullet range. I don't care how organized or disorganized it is; war's not organized. Just get some real-time shooting in there and give people the chance to pick each other up."

"Yes, Sergeant Ma'am!" Rex replied. Roth replied in kind, and Rex elected to pretend he didn't exist. She had enough problems with two *kelbas* in her squad.

The drill went smoothly enough. Most of the squad members had used a carrier before, and the ones who hadn't had good balance from their arts training, at least. Both squads quickly began open fire to simulate a war zone.

Rex started off by picking up a girl named Harley. She was American, with enough muscles to outmatch Rex in arm wrestling two times over. Despite the somewhat vulnerable position of being in the carrier, Harley took the drill in stride.

"I'll have to carry you next, Alpha," she said good-naturedly.

Rex shook her head, twisting to avoid a bullet as she gained altitude. "No, I don't think that'll be happening anytime soon," she replied. She was willing to set an example by carrying someone, to get in the action and encourage her squad, but being carried by someone else was not a point she was willing to stoop to just yet.

When Rex put Harley back down, the muscular girl was approached simultaneously by Tanner and another boy, both eager to carry her. Rex gave a start at the close resemblance between Tanner and the other boy. She had forgotten he had a twin.

"I'll take you, Harley," Tanner said, strapping the carrier on his back.

"Here, milady," the other boy said, stepping forward dramatically. "I have first-class seating for you."

A bullet grazed Harley's cheek. She stood, unfazed and mildly amused, as the boys reprimanded each other.

"You let her get hit! She's not safe with you."

"Well, you didn't exactly do anything about it, either. Here, Harley," Tanner's twin said, gesturing again to the carrier on his back. Rex decided to intervene before Harley got hit by a barrage.

"You! What's your name?" she barked at Tanner's twin.

"Cal."

Rex nodded. "Okay, Cal, you're going to carry her up to altitude before she gets blown to pieces by a machine gun," she said, gesturing to Cal. "This is a drill, not playtime. Now, move it!"

Cal grinned triumphantly and bent one knee so that Harley could climb in easier. As she adjusted herself in the carrier, he took hold of her legs to help her get settled and gave his brother a sly look. The look was wiped from his face as Harley slapped him across both hands. Looking suitably chastised, he took off.

Rex couldn't help a smirk from breaking out on her face at the display. Beside her, Tanner sighed.

"One of these days he'll learn."

A hail of plastic bullets hit them both where they stood. Rex fell to a crouch, firing back at the figures around her who had sent the barrage. They fell away. Tanner laughed aloud. In spite of herself, Rex joined.

"Look at me, talking about learning, and I'm standing in the middle of a war zone! I'm going to shoot some people. Want to come with me, Alpha?"

Rex brushed a stray hair from her face, shouldering her gun. She was about to say yes when, in her periphery, she caught sight of Leah stepping closer to Master Ekeli. She hadn't seen either of them appear at the training ground before now.

"No, I've got some stuff to do. But it's good to talk to you again, Tanner." Rex realized that she and the tall boy had never had a real conversation. She would have to remedy that.

"Thanks, Alpha!" Tanner took off in pursuit of a pair of Roth's squad, who were having a little too much fun gunning people down.

As soon as he was gone, Rex strained her ears to pick up on what Ekeli and Leah were saying. The sound of their voices, though faint, was audible.

". . . he's got it," Leah was saying. "I've just confirmed the chemical balance."

Ekeli nodded thoughtfully. "I assume it is a prototype."

"Of course. But even so, it has to be a trap. No one

would send a *mitnakesh* with that much evidence on him."

Leah's eyes swept over the group and Rex glanced away, but she kept her ears open wide. A sudden realization flashed like arena lights in her mind. They were talking about the assassin she had captured. She had been so busy that he had only crossed her mind briefly. The chemicals must have been in the flat, garbage-like package she found in his uniform.

"Decoys," Ekeli mused. "It—"

"Not here," Leah murmured. She turned and strode off. Rex looked around as if checking over her squad members, but her mind was whirling. Ekeli and Leah knew who had sent the assassin, or at least knew which group he belonged to.

An Egyptian assassin.

Shat al-Shed was Egyptian, and they were holding her father.

Could the assassin be connected with her father's captors?

None of her superiors would tell her, but there was one way to find out. Her mind warred inside. Rider would do it. Despite their tenuous current relationship, she knew she wanted to take the same kind of risks he would.

She would just have to wait for free time.

026

Rex knew the Stratotech prison had to be near the interrogation room. She crept down the hall from Sergeant Bailey's office, then shivered and rolled her shoulders to bring warmth to her arms. The hall was cold, even for her hyper-heated veins.

Close to the end of the hall, past the interrogation room, was the room where she had received information about her father. Past it was a row of other doors. She scanned the doors in the wall and strained her ears. Nothing was in the information room—she was standing right next to it and couldn't hear anything. The room directly across the hall was probably a storage room of some kind. That was where the cold air was flooding from. *Wait.* She heard a sigh. One second, then another. She trained her eyes on the door. A display popped up on her retinal screen.

Abnormal heat signature: 97.2 degrees.

"Got you," she murmured, allowing a smile to form on her lips.

A retinal and fingerprint scan were required to enter the room. Rex considered simply hammering the control panel and forcing the door open, but knew that would probably set off a hundred alarms. She tried placing her finger on the scanner. To her surprise, a green light blinked and the retinal scanner lit up. After a few moments of stillness and bated breath as her eye was scanned, the door shot open.

The interior was lit by white lights that glared harshly in the surrounding darkness. Rex squinted hard, tears coming to her eyes. Chills swept over her body. It felt like the desert at midnight in a windstorm. She clenched her teeth together to keep them from chattering as she moved farther into the room.

The assassin was in the back, strapped to a heavy chair with metal restraints. The chair was tilted forward, and the floor lights shone directly into his face, probably as a discomfort tactic. She approached him warily.

"Back for more, pretty?"

Despite having steeled herself for the encounter, Rex's stomach twisted at the eerie sound of the assassin's voice. She swallowed as inconspicuously as she could. This man might have vital information about how she could rescue her father. She was alpha. She would act like it. She strode up to the chair and set her hand against it.

"Captain Jerich Hai, imprisoned where? Cairo? Sinai? Taba?" She rattled off the words like she did in the card game, searching his face for a sign of recognition. The assassin stared back, his green eyes glowing, even in the harsh floor light. He was unreadable. His training was impeccable.

He has to have a weakness. She just had to probe until she struck it. She set her jaw.

"Your eyes, your claws, your tattoo. How were you programmed? Who did it?"

A corner of the assassin's mouth came up in a leering grin. "You want to know a lot of things. But you're asking the wrong questions, pretty."

"Don't call me that."

The man chuckled. It sounded as if he had sand stuck in his throat. "You want to know? Do you? Because it could give you such nightmares. Rooms as black as the darkest caves. Not a soul, not a soul can be found by any of your senses. Pain like you've never felt."

Rex growled. "You have no idea what I've felt."

The smile remained on his face. "Oh, but I do. I know you fear walls and darkness and the unknown arrival of a tormentor. . ."

Rex slammed her hand against the chair. "You'll answer my questions! Where is my father?"

"Oh, you'd love to know, wouldn't you?" The assassin leaned forward as far as he could against his restraints. "He's in one of those black rooms, wasting away, brought out for another test every few weeks. You wouldn't recognize him if he looked you in the eye."

Rex quivered with fury as unwanted memories, grief, and trauma swept over her. She had to find out. She had to. She brought her face so close to the assassin's that their noses almost touched. "Where. Is. He? Or I swear by all the hounds of Gehenna, I'll kill you right now."

The assassin lifted a finger. "But you need me. You need me desperately, or you wouldn't have broken into a classified room to get to me."

A flicker of doubt came into Rex's mind, followed by the sudden realization that she had probably triggered an alarm by her entrance. But she wasn't finished.

"I don't need you. I'm going to find out one way or another. It'll only take me a few more weeks."

"When they file paperwork and go through the motions, yes," the assassin put in.

Rex didn't bother to ask him how he knew that. She was running out of time. From down the hall, she could hear someone entering Sergeant Bailey's office.

"If you want to live, tell me."

"He's in the playroom of Sekhmet, past the flowers of escape."

"Give me a location! What area? Who is Sekhmet?" Rex could hear footsteps getting closer. By the smooth, even gait, she could tell it was Leah.

"The location is a death warrant."

Rex hissed in frustration. Leah was at the door. "I'm not done with you," she breathed. Then she threw herself into a crouch and whirled into place behind a crate just as the door flew open.

027

Rex breathed deeply to silence any excess noise as Leah entered the room. The doctor paced to the assassin's chair.

"Where is she?"

Her voice was not loud, but it was commanding. Rex peered through the grill of the crate and focused her eye on the assassin, who had a leering grin on his face. He spoke in a mock chivalrous tone.

"Who do you mean, madame? You're the only female I've seen at this compound. Lovely body, too, I must say."

Rex frowned. Why was the assassin covering for her?

"Keep your eyes to yourself or I'll bore them out of your head," Leah spat. Her eyes searched the room. Rex froze as the woman's gaze passed over her. Leah turned abruptly and strode out of Rex's line of vision. Craning her neck, Rex tried to see where she had gone. Cautiously, she moved to one side of the crate, in the opposite direction of where Leah had gone.

"There you are, Rex."

Leah stepped out directly in front of her. Rex

tensed, meeting the woman's gaze warily, but with determination. She was not going to show fear. She was not sorry. The assassin's words burned in her brain—he'd given her a clue to find her father, vague though it might be. She thrust her chin forward.

"I will surrender myself for discipline."

To her surprise, Leah shrugged one shoulder. "You're curious. A good alpha is curious, especially when she needs to be. You and I are the only ones who need to know about this."

Rex blinked several times, then finally found words. "You're not going to report me?"

Leah glanced about and stepped a little closer. "There are some things a doctor doesn't have to enforce. Discipline is one of them." Without another word, she spun about and strode out the door.

***

"Wolves! Briefing, on the field, five minutes!"

Sergeant Bailey's bark roused Rex from a fitful sleep the next morning. When they got to the compound, however, she came fully awake at the sergeant's briefing.

"The next part of the alpha phase involves a real mission. You've all been evaluated throughout the last two phases, and you're ready to complete the third." She tapped her wrist-screen. A light shot out from it, forming a projector wall with the image of a map. Rex didn't recognize the area.

"Your objective is here." She zoomed in on a portion of the map. "This building is just outside of a town along the Jordan River. We've had issues with this town before. The locals turn a blind eye to the illegal things that go on in the town, including the capture and ransom of government officials. The objective of this mission is to retrieve two such officials."

Rex's heart sank. This wasn't her mission. For a moment, she had hoped they wouldn't make her wait until the alpha phase was over. Evidently, she had been wrong.

"One of the captives is fairly good in a fight." Bailey pulled up a screen with photos of the hostages. "He's a young guy, in his twenties. The other man is older, not in his prime. He's the younger guy's father. Don't leave them alone. Since you're more skilled than them—clearly—defending them and getting them out should be your priority. Once they're clear of the building, you'll follow these coordinates to a drop-off point up the river where a ground force will pick them up. It's fairly straightforward. The people you're dealing with are more interested in making a long-term profit than in holding onto two hostages they've got right now. They'll most likely scatter when you get there so they can shift their camp somewhere else nearby and resume business once our scuffle with them blows over. The dirty rats," she muttered to herself. "Anyway, it's a clean job. Get in, get out. As soon as you've dropped them off, head back here. No sense in letting more people identify you than necessary. Suit up and get going, wolves!"

***

The flight to the town took less than two hours.

As they came close to it, the Jordan stretched out below them like a shimmering sidewinder snake, both beautiful and sinister at the same time. The town itself was nothing more than a cluster of hovels by the waterfront, interspersed with a few whitewashed structures that must have once been official buildings before all the lawmen moved to the cities. Being half a mile out from the town, Rex decided it was time to go to ground.

"Squadron Two, descend," she called softly. Roth gave a similar command to his squad, and the whole force angled toward the ground. Their trajectory would put them directly on the roof of the target building.

A lone man, shouldering a gun that had seen better days, lounged in the sun against the wall of the building. Though they descended quietly, Rex could hardly prevent her squadron from casting a flurry of shadows across the man's upper body. She was just about to ask Rider to shoot him with a tranquilizer when he yawned, rubbed his face, then looked up in alarm at the group descending toward him.

"Demons! Soldiers! Under attack!" he yelled frantically in a broken mix of Hebrew and modern Egyptian. It was obvious he had no idea what was going on, but despite his confusion, he managed to run around the other side of the building before anyone could shoot him, hollering and causing a general commotion. A bell started ringing somewhere. Rex heard doors opening and shutting as people came out of their houses to see what was going on.

"We've got to get in there, quick!" Roth said. "Squad One, get me explosives at the door!"

Rex elected to let Roth's team blast their way in. The old door was solidly built, but its locking mechanism was easily short-circuited by the explosives. In less than a minute, the door shot open.

Shots greeted them as they marched in. Rex took the lead, not giving Roth the chance to go in first. She raised her giant machine gun and trained it on the nearest group of defenders. In the dark hallway, she ignored accuracy and simply swept the gun in vicious arcs around the room. Men screamed, running down any exits they could find. A few hid and returned fire. She moved past them, electing to let those behind her take care of them.

She passed several small doorways and came to a larger room with multiple open passages leading away from it. Along the walls were rows of crates and other assorted flotsam.

"Delta hounds!" she called. Zyanya and a small, wiry boy made their way to the front. Going ahead of the others, they took slow, measured steps past the crates. Zyanya fell into a crouch, cocking her head this way and that as she sniffed the air. Rex felt a twinge of respect for the other girl. She had become a delta hound to use her enhanced scent receptors to sniff out explosives, but based on her scoring, she could have been a beta.

"All clear," Zyanya called softly.

Rex motioned the others forward. Without hesitation, she took the hallway to the right. A group of yelling defenders rounded the bend, guns blazing. Rex dropped to a crouch.

"Bullet formation!"

The others grouped in around her. Just then, another commotion caught Rex's attention. It was Roth, pushing his way past her squad.

"Make way, Alpha coming through!"

His gun rattled, and a group of soldiers fell dead in front of them. Rex ducked a bullet as she craned her neck to try and understand what Roth was up to.

"What are you doing?" she hissed.

Roth smiled pleasantly at her. "Securing the mission. You stay here and fight off the guards. We'll meet you back here."

"You're what?" Rex straightened, let off a volley, and fell back to a crouch. "That wasn't the plan!"

Roth shrugged, picking off a soldier coolly. "Well, it is now, so get used to it. You might be the alpha, but I'm the alpha male. I outrank you."

Rex heard someone cry out in pain. She turned to see Bridget fall to her knees, clutching an arm.

"Abbi!"

The medic ran to Bridget's side, unlocking her zip-on backpack as she did. Rex turned back to Roth, grabbing his arm with her metal hand as he tried to move away. She squeezed viciously.

"Next time you tell me that I'm lower than you, you'll get this in the face, you *khatikhat kharah*."

To her gratification, she saw Roth wince ever so slightly. He wrenched his arm free.

"I'll tell you whatever I like," he snarled. Then,

without further discussion, he shot down the last defender and led his group down the hall.

Rex smoldered with barely controlled rage. She spat at the ground and turned to where Abbi was wrapping Bridget's arm.

"How bad is it?"

The medic looked up. "Not too bad. The bullet was lodged in the skin, but I pulled it out without causing too much blood loss."

"That quickly?" Rex was surprised.

Abbi smiled modestly. "Well, it was a surface wound. Besides, we don't really have much time. I'm sure more soldiers will be coming soon."

As Abbi said it, Rex caught sight of a figure hurrying across an adjoining hallway. She raised her gun casually and blasted a barrage at him. He crumpled to the ground.

"Form a circle facing outward," she called to her team. "This room is good because we have several escape avenues, but that also means they can come at us from those directions if they decide to. Get ready to defend."

"Funny you should say that, since we're the attackers," Bridget said with a faint smile. Rex could tell she was in pain, but trying not to show it.

"Well, once that *ben-zonna* named Roth gets back, we'll have to get out of here before anyone decides to whip together a real resistance force."

It turned out to be only a matter of seconds before Roth's squad returned. They came running like a herd of goats being chased by a desert lion.

"We ran into the head man; he's right on our heels! Move it!" Roth yelled.

Despite her anger, Rex gestured to her squad and they took off. Twisting her belt buckle, she motioned for the others to do the same.

"Alelta! Lead on!"

Alelta's sullen grey eyes turned up to meet hers. She obeyed with bad grace, pushing past the others to take the lead. Rex fell back to where Roth was still running. The two hostages were keeping pace, though the older man was stumbling from time to time.

"You have to get airborne!" she yelled.

"Not yet," Roth replied.

Rex grunted in frustration. Coming to a decision, she swooped down and heaved the older man bodily into the air. He yelped with fright.

"No need for alarm, sir," she said in the most reassuring tone she could manage between gritted teeth. "I'll keep you safe."

"Th-th-thank you," he gasped.

They were halfway to the front door when a row of defenders streamed out from a side hall, blocking their path. Rex cursed under her breath.

"Sorry sir, I'll just be a minute." She set him down roughly on the ground. "Abbi, guard him!" She swung her gun off her back and took to the air again. Nigel and Tanner joined her, along with several other boys who belonged to Roth's squad. In the close, dark space, it was hard to see a clear target. This stale, dusty building probably hadn't had this much activity in decades.

"Alpha!"

It was Harley. She had the younger hostage on her back. Beside her, one of Roth's team carried the older man. Rex sighed in frustration. She hadn't given the order to ascend yet, but she supposed there was no stopping it now.

"Let's get out of here!" she called. They pressed forward, scattering or picking off the remaining defenders, and flooded out into the sunlight once more. Rex gave a piercing whistle as they passed over Rider and the others who had stayed outside to watch the entrance. Rider soon caught up and flew into formation beside her.

"I heard a lot of yelling. How did it go?"

Rex sighed. "Well enough. We secured the hostages, as you can see."

Rider nodded. "And how are you?"

Rex gave him a thin smile. "I'll be a lot better once we get back home."

Home. Suddenly, she missed her mother's hands on her hair and day-old challah bread.

028

The older man had to be injected with a sleep drug and supplied with an oxygen mask. The younger man was able to stay alert and breathe as they glided at nine thousand feet up.

"Thank you," he said, looking intently at Rex from where he had his arms clasped around Harley's shoulders to help her bear his weight.

"It's my job," Rex replied brusquely.

The young man tried again to engage her in conversation, speaking loudly so he could hear his own voice above the wind. "What's your name?"

Rex hesitated. She was fairly certain that she wasn't supposed to identify herself to anyone she didn't have to. "I can't tell you. I'm sorry," she added, as his face fell. But he nodded.

"I understand. Your name can be the difference between life and death, depending on who knows it. But it's difficult, not knowing who I should thank."

"It wasn't just me. It was my squad." Rex tried to keep her voice loud enough for the young man to hear. Having been in the stratosphere with her ear implants activated for over two months now, it was hard for her to gauge what volume a normal person needed her voice to be.

"Of course. I always try to pay my respects to the leader, however." He paused. "My name is Seth. My father and I are indebted to you. He's getting older, and as he does, he makes more enemies. I'm not sure what those men planned to do, but it didn't look like we would be set free."

Rex frowned. "So, no one was interested in paying ransom for you?"

Seth sighed and unclasped one of his hands to run it through his long hair. "That is the problem with having mixed parentage and an unpopular father. You see, I'm not entirely Israeli, so I'm not allowed in politics. My father is full Israeli, but he's become less favorable to the people in our city."

"Which city?" Rex asked.

"Jerusalem."

Rex tried to control her involuntary surprise at the knowledge that this young man—he was barely more than a boy—could live within a few miles of her home, and she might have never known it. Seth must have seen the reaction on her face because he nodded. "You live there?"

"I used to. Well, not exactly."

"In one of the fading edge towns, then? Ah, I apologize, you can't tell me." He shook his head. "But if there's something I can do to thank you ... if I can't do it for you, would you let me do it for your town, perhaps?"

Rex hesitated, but she realized he would never know her name, and telling him where she had once come from would probably have no bearing on anyone identifying her. The populations in fading edge towns changed constantly as people died off or sought to move farther into the city and improve their livelihoods. "Ben-Valta," she said.

"Ben-Valta . . . I've heard the name, but I don't know much about it. What would you say it needs the most? As a politician's son, even a minor, unpopular one, I have some sway in the decisions our district makes."

"Ben-Valta needs a Domestic Violence Initiative," Rex said, her voice tight.

Seth's face lit up. "Really? Then I know I can help you! I am personally involved in two charity initiatives in Jerusalem, and one of them is for domestic violence. I had no idea Ben-Valta needed our help. Of course, all the fading edge towns struggle with poverty, but as you know, there's only so much we can do, with so many poor on the city streets as well. But in domestic issues I could make a real difference."

Tears stung Rex's eyes as she pictured her mother finally free of her stepfather's abuse. It hurt to speak. "Thank you," she managed.

Seth bowed his head slightly. "Of course."

Within the hour, they reached the drop-off point for the rescues. A small military ground force waited at attention outside an armored car. As the soldiers helped the older man into the car, Seth turned and clasped Rex's hand, placing a hand on her forearm in the sign of respect shown by Israeli officials.

"You have my gratitude. My father . . . he is all I

have left."

"I know." Rex couldn't say more, but she understood the anxiety Seth must feel.

"I hope to see you again, perhaps under a better sun. *B'hatzlacha*." He smiled, then turned and leapt up into the car. Rex looked after him as the car pulled away.

"*B'hatzlacha*," she murmured. And she meant it.

***

The next morning, after exercises, Sergeant Bailey called Rex to her office.

"Your mission has been approved."

Rex had been standing still, her entire body tensed. At the sergeant's words, she relaxed and shook both fists in triumph and relief.

"When can I go?"

"Next week."

"What? Why so late?"

The sergeant gave her a wry smile. "It's only four days. You can lead your squad out on Monday."

Rex sighed in frustration. Every day was agony. Her father could be killed in that time, or horribly tortured. Or the terrorists could somehow get wind of what was happening and decide to move him elsewhere. "There's no way to do it faster?"

Sergeant Bailey spread her palms. "Leah's our intel woman right now. She says the place is less guarded at a specific time on Monday nights. Doesn't make a lot of sense to me either, but in the army, you've got to go with the intel experts. We learned that the hard way at Pearl Harbor."

"Fine," Rex grunted. "Do you have a specific location?"

"We know where the base is, within a ten-mile radius, anyway. I'll give you the location on Monday when we brief your squad. I've got to warn you, though, you'll be going into one of the most heavily armed terrorist bases in Israel; it's where they do biotechnological research."

"I'll go."

The sergeant shrugged. "Alright then. You're dismissed. Go enjoy your four days of relative free time."

***

As she walked outside onto the compound, feeling the sun and the ever-present wind on her face, Rex heard someone calling her name. She turned to see Rider jogging up from the training field, breathing lightly.

"What's up?"

"We are, technically," he said with a grin. Rex raised her eyebrows.

"Very clever."

They strode together in silence for a moment, keeping to the edge of the railing that overlooked the open sky. Just when Rex was wondering if she should talk about her mission, Rider turned to her. His face was red, and he stood very straight.

"Look, Rex. I know you've got trust issues. But I really care about you, okay? Like, I've never felt this way about anyone before. You know, in my old town, I could get all the girls to swoon when I did one-handed pull-ups. But you made me realize that I had to earn your respect. I want to protect you."

"So you think I need to be protected?" Rex wasn't sure why she felt angry. She had a suspicion that she liked what Rider was saying, but anger was easier to feel.

"No!" Rider stammered. His face turned even redder and he swallowed hard. Then he sighed, and the color faded. "No, Rex. You're the strongest person I know. You're tough as nails. You're fearless—except in the one area I'm afraid of, too."

"What?" Rex didn't know what to make of that.

Rider motioned her to sit up on the rail, then hopped up himself. When they were settled, his voice became soft. "I was twelve when my little sister started being stalked. She was six. She said she thought someone was following her home from school. Said a man would appear at the corner of Fifth and Stellar Street and just watch her every day as she boarded the bus. I didn't think much of it at first. She was only six, you know. But after a while, I could tell she was getting more and more scared. There was no way she was telling stories. So I got on her bus one day to meet her when she got out of school. She didn't show up. I waited for about five minutes, after everyone else had gotten on, then I jumped off to go find her. She was in a back alley, being roughed up by two guys. I yelled to distract them. She tried to run, but one of them grabbed her and..."

His voice broke and he shut his eyes against the

memory. Rex waited, concern bubbling up in her chest. Finally, he spoke again. "He cracked her head open on the pavement. There was nothing I could do. Then they punched the lights out of me and ran for it. When I woke up, I just held her broken head in my hands. Her blood was the price I paid for not listening to her sooner." His voice broke again, then his face hardened. "To this day, I don't know what those guys were really up to. Every day I look back and wish I could have done better. It's my biggest regret—the whole thing. I wish I would have listened to her sooner. I wish I had done what I was supposed to do and ridden with her to school, or asked if she could stay home. But there's nothing. I'm helpless. It doesn't matter what I do or think now; I'm not able to protect her."

Rider's words were an exact mirror of the internal battle Rex had fought her whole life—wanting to protect herself, to protect her mother, to make things right.

"From then on, I knew I had to protect anyone else I cared about, or they could be taken from me."

Rex screwed up her face, confused. "Wait. When you first told me you were protecting me, you said something about your sister. How you had wanted to protect her for years, and that Roth figured it out. Did he... was he one of those guys who hurt her?"

Rider shook his head. "No. I trained with Roth for a couple of weeks at my arts school. He was transferred several times, probably because he was so problematic. Me and him and some of the other boys went drinking one night after arts practice. Of course, like the stupid kids we were, we didn't know when to stop. Somewhere between nighttime and early morning, after too many shots, my story came out. I didn't think anyone would remember it; we were so drunk. But Roth did. He knows that I have to protect the people that I care about—that I'm compelled to do so more than the average person. Because for me, it's not just about being there for someone. It's about keeping them alive. So when Roth threatened you, I had to go along. And even then, he hurt you. You could have died."

"How did he. . ." Realization flashed across Rex's mind.

The bullet in Roth's gun.

Roth's words to Rider afterward. *I told you this would happen.*

Rider twisted his jaw back and forth. "When you got shot, I swear, I almost died. But the only thing I could do was go along with Roth's plan, or he'd do something worse to you. I couldn't tell Tanner because I'm sure Roth would have come after him, too. Tanner's a very capable guy, but he doesn't always see how mercenary people can be. He's got integrity, and he looks for it in other people. Basically, he's too good for his own good. I didn't see another way out." Rider laid his head in his hands and heaved a sigh. "So you see why I want to protect you."

"Yeah." Rex shook her head, dazed.

"So." Rider's eyes met hers. "What are you fighting for? Why are you broken?"

Rex hesitated. Did she trust Rider? It was the question that had plagued her mind every time he got close. But she knew, in her mind and in her heart, that he cared for her. Her voice shook as she began her story. She told him everything, starting from when her father disappeared and her mother remarried. When she was finished, Rider gazed at her with a deep concern.

"I know that was very difficult for you to tell me. But I'm glad you did."

Rex's eyes stung. "It hurts." Her voice broke. The tears came spilling out, and her body shook with sobs. She felt Rider move closer, felt his arms tight around her, comforting her, holding her. He cradled her head on his shoulder.

"Shh. It's okay." He smoothed his fingers through her hair, and she felt his lips as he placed a soft kiss on the top of her head.

"Will you keep it safe? What I told you?"

"Of course."

And they sat together in the brilliant light of the morning sun, their feet dangling over forty thousand feet of nowhere.

***

"Rexala."

Master Ekeli's voice reached Rex's ears as she scraped the scraps from her lunch plate. She had told Rider her secret pain two days ago, and since then her heart had felt as though it could beat freely in her chest once more. She gave Master Ekeli a smile as she walked over. "Yes, Master?"

"Come with me. We need to talk."

"Yes, sir." Rex followed him out of the dining hall and to the hallways behind Sergeant Bailey's office, where she had visited the assassin.

"In here."

Ekeli opened the door to a room Rex had never entered before. It was dark inside, only lit by tiny bulbs from within a glass box. The box was taller than her and wide enough to fit several people.

"Get in," he told her.

Rex immediately became suspicious, but she had always been taught to trust and obey her arts master. She stepped into the box. Ekeli shut the door.

"Two days from now, you will be briefed on what to expect when you go to rescue your father." Ekeli's voice carried clearly through the glass to Rex. "We have received information that the enemy base has unusual security measures. One of these is the use of the drug helethetamine that will be released as a gas if any entrance is breached. It is strong enough to penetrate the gas masks we currently have, and it causes hallucinations. From what we know, however, the effects are lessened by previous exposure."

"Like a vaccine." Leah appeared beside Ekeli. "Your squad will all be inoculated before we send you off." She strode to a control panel on the wall. Tapping at her wrist-screen, she called out stats. "Temperature: sixty-five point two degrees. Time: thirteen twenty-eight hours." Coming to the box, she opened the door and held out a hand with several electrodes in it. "Let me put these on you."

"Wait." Rex swallowed anxiously. "What will I see? How long will the hallucinations last?"

Leah tilted her head. "That depends. They'll wear off after an hour." She pressed electrodes to each of Rex's temples and wrists, one on her throat, and one over her heart.

"An hour?" Rex's voice cracked. If she saw her stepfather, she wasn't sure she could last an hour. Even having mostly overcome her fear of tight spaces, the box was small, and there were other memories she didn't want to see ever again.

Leah stepped out and shut the door. "Commencing helethetamine desensitization."

Green, noxious clouds billowed down from the ceiling of the box. Rex placed her palm against the glass, fingers spread and shaking as she tried to focus on the freedom just outside. Then Master Ekeli and Leah disappeared from view as the clouds enveloped her.

029

Rex coughed and choked as the gas went up her nostrils. Her throat burned and her eyes watered. She sank to the floor, trying to find a space where she could breathe.

Suddenly, the room changed. Rex sat straight up, staring at the landscape around her. It was filled with trees clustered around a pool of water. Beyond were more pools, stretching into the distance. People milled about, going to and from the water into open verandas with tiled roofs. Others lounged on couches made from exotic carved wood with cushions of silk. Laughter and the buzz of happy conversation surrounded Rex. The scent of cedarwood and burning incense from nearby braziers wafted on the cool wind that sighed across her face.

"Rexie!"

Her mother appeared, carrying two goblets, a smile on her beautiful face. Rex caught her breath.

"Mother. It's been so long."

Judith Bat'Fell smiled even wider. "Yes! Here, take this." She held out a goblet.

Rex took it and sipped. Her eyes widened. It was a mild, sweet wine, some of the finest she had ever tasted. It had not been watered down.

"Come, sit!" Rex's mother took her hand and led her to a couch. She hailed a passing servant, who stopped to offer Rex a selection of plump grapes.

"Your father will be here soon."

"Father?" Rex adjusted her seat on the couch, her hand hovering over the tray of grapes. She pulled off a generous handful from the vine. "It's so soon. We still have two days left." She wasn't sure why there were two days left. If her mother said her father was coming, that should be good enough.

"Don't you worry about time, dear. Drink!"

Rex took a large mouthful of the wine. Suddenly, she felt very happy. Her mother was here. Her father was coming soon. She had every need attended to. *And this wine . . .* She gulped down the rest from her goblet and held it out for more.

After several glasses, she and her mother were laughing together over old stories when a flash hit Rex.

"Where's Rider?"

Her mother refilled her goblet from a bottle the servants had brought. "Who, dear?"

"Rider. My . . ." Rex didn't want to say "boyfriend." She wasn't sure that's what they were yet. Her life was so complicated; nothing they had done together was normal. She struggled to remember where exactly she had come from. They had fought together . . . for some reason.

She had a sudden feeling that something was wrong. She began twisting and turning on the couch, searching the crowd for some sign of him. "Rider!" she yelled.

"Calm down, dear. Rider isn't alive anymore."

"What?" Rex looked around frantically, taking another large gulp from her goblet. She grimaced at the taste and looked down.

The wine had turned black, and it tasted of blood.

Her blood was the price I paid for not listening to her sooner.

Rider had said that, about his sister.

Rex felt a jolt through her body as she landed on her feet on hard pavement. A small girl lay on the ground, her head caved in on one side, her light hair turned dark and wet and matted. The stench of blood was all Rex could smell. In horror, she looked at her own hand, which held a wrench. More blood dripped from it.

"You killed her."

She whirled around. Twelve-year-old Rider stood, shaking, fury and grief on his face.

"It's your fault she's dead! You said you wanted to protect the people you care about." His dark eyes accused Rex.

"I do! I didn't . . . I couldn't have . . ." Had Rex killed her? Rider was right. All she wanted to do was protect people. But she was holding the wrench. And Rider's sister was dead.

From behind, Rider's hands clamped around her arms, dragging her backward. She yelled and thrashed, but his grip had become like manacles, binding her down. As she had the thought, steel shackles appeared around her wrists, and she was yanked down into a chair. The shackles locked onto the chair arms with an ugly click.

"Well, pretty. Seems we've changed places."

Two glowing green orbs floated just out of Rex's reach—that is, if her hands had been free. They came closer. She could vaguely make out the shape of the assassin's face. A blinding light flicked on, and she squinted furiously, trying to escape the extreme discomfort.

"These are the flowers of escape I told you about." A hand appeared, its clawlike fingers grasping an overflowing bouquet of red-and-black-spotted flowers. As Rex watched, the petals turned into writhing snakes. The assassin stepped closer. "Want a taste, pretty?"

"Get away!" Rex tried not to let her voice break, but she was close to tears. She grunted, rocking back and forth in the chair, seeking some means of escape as the horrible flowers came closer.

"Oh." The assassin's face twisted in a leer of mock pity. "You want to live? Then he dies."

Another light flicked on in the distance. Rex could make out Rider, his mouth gagged, bound to a chair as she was. The assassin stepped slowly, inexorably toward him. With each step, it was as if Rex was walking closer to Rider. She could make out the horror on his face as the assassin brought the flowers close.

"Rider!" Rex screamed, just as one of the snakes struck.

The world spun. Suddenly, Rex lay on the ground. A weight was on her back, crushing her. Rain spattered on the pavement and into a red puddle. More blood.

Only this time, it was her father's blood.

He sat, his neck twisted at a horrible angle, eyes wide open. His hand quivered and reached up, then fell limp as his heart stopped.

"You came too late."

The voice was unfamiliar. More weight pressed on Rex's back, and she knew her captor was holding her down with a foot.

"No! I have to save him! He can't die! Not after I just found out he was alive!" Rex struggled to tear herself free, to go to her father, to pump life back into his heart. She screamed as her captor grabbed her arm and twisted savagely.

"You came too late."

The voice hissed in Rex's ear, and she sobbed uncontrollably, hearing her heart thump in her chest.

Boom. Boom. Boom.

Her eyes shot open. She was back in the glass box, staring at the ceiling, her eyes streaming and her heart pounding.

030

Rex stood at the head of her squad on Monday morning, her fingers clasping and unclasping as she listened to Sergeant Bailey's briefing. Though she knew the details were important—no, vital—to the success of the mission, she couldn't help but wish that she was already at the enemy base.

"This building is in the middle of nowhere, and that nowhere is in enemy territory," Sergeant Bailey was saying, demonstrating with the hologram from her wrist-screen. "It's hidden from most aerial surveillance drones by digital camouflage, but your visual implants should be able to pick it up. There will likely be snipers outside the base; our guess is four, one for each major corner of the building. Your best chance of avoiding them is to focus in on the base visually when you're about a mile out. Pick five of your wolves as snipers—four to take out enemy snipers, and one for backup. We have long-range sniper guns in the weapons room."

Rex caught Rider's eye and nodded.

"So far, we only know of one exit to this place, and it's the same as the entrance. How many guards are there on the inside? We don't know. Are there any other security measures within? Don't know that, either. Based on the structure of the building"—she adjusted the view of the photo on her wrist-screen—"we think that Captain Hai is in a prison underground on the south side of the building. So basically, you'll be going in blind with only a rough idea of where your target is, no clue how many guards there will be, and no idea if they have traps waiting for you. But this is your job. You've all been trained to be as tough as nails. We had Hell Week for a reason." She paused, then continued in an uncharacteristically lower tone. "There's nothing about this mission that I think you can't do." With that, she stomped her foot twice.

All the wolves clapped their fists over their chests in salute.

***

The wind at forty thousand feet above ground was stronger than usual out in the open sky. Rex gloried in the surge of fear and anticipation that filled her body. Now, she only had a matter of miles between herself and her goal, and she was leading the deadliest elite squad on this side of the world to save the one person whose absence had destroyed her life.

That morning, she and her wolves had put on war paint. The others wore blue; she wore dark red. She recalled the feeling of dipping her fingertips into the paint and spreading it around her eyes and dotting it along her cheekbones, forehead, and chin. It served a double purpose—as proof of their graduation from training and as camouflage on the exposed parts of their faces. It made her feel powerful, as if destiny was finally calling her to put on her war paint and seek her father. She also couldn't help but notice that it looked like blood.

What she saw in her hallucination had frightened her, and she had barely slept the past two nights, worrying that she would be too late to save her father. Finally, after years of longing for his return, after knowing it was impossible, getting him back was within her grasp. He just had to be alive when she got there. Ekeli's words from that morning echoed in her mind.

Bring back whatever you find, whether he is a man or a shadow of one.

It was a long, long shot that he would be who she had always known him to be. After years spent in captivity and torture, who knew if he would even remember his little girl? She pushed the thought away.

And Rider . . . Rex realized that she must care about him more than she had thought. For him to be the focus of three of her hallucinations . . .

Her retinal display beeped and a notification popped up. *1.2 miles from destination.* Apprehension burned in her stomach. She blinked hard several times, and her retinal display began counting down the distance. The last mile seemed to creep away. She could almost envision grains of sand dropping one at a time through an hourglass.

"Hey, Captain." Rider came into her peripheral vision, his voice breaking into her thoughts. "I know

now isn't the greatest time, but I wanted to let you know that I've got you," he said softly. And she understood everything he meant.

She responded with a command. "Snipers, prepare for takeout."

"Yes, Alpha." Their replies reached her ears faintly. She heard Roth call out to the snipers in his squad. After a moment, their guns clicked in preparation.

"Target Two, in my sights," came Rider's voice first.

"Target One, in my sights."

"Target Three."

"Target Four."

Four shots fired in unison, muffled by the silencers on the guns.

"Look! Flowers!" Bridget's awed whisper caused all heads to turn downward. Miles below lay a field of desert flowers. Rex remembered the assassin's words.

He's in the playroom of Sekhmet, past the flowers of escape.

At least they looked nothing like the ones in her hallucination. Then she remembered what the assassin had said about the place.

The location is a death warrant.

She heard the drones before she saw them.

"Armed drones!"

The rattle of bullets on metal shrieked in her ears as she swooped downward. Yells echoed around her; she wasn't sure if they were in pain or just alarm.

"Nigel! See if you can get us a shield! The rest of you, spread out so we're not an easy target, and shoot those drones down!" Rex slung her machine gun off her shoulder and took aim at three drones clustered together. They scurried apart. Swinging the gun, she tried to pick off several individual drones. A bullet bounced off her helmet and another was stopped by the reinforced Kevlar on her chest. Every barrage she let off seemed to find the spaces between the drones.

"They're highly motion sensitive. Great. Okay, new plan." She flew backward, calling to her wolves. "Rider, Tanner, Cal! Cover our rear. Wolves, get ready to dive!"

"They're shooting at us from the ground!" someone yelled. Rex thought it might be Ilianayah, but she wasn't sure. Sure enough, bullets streaked upward at them. Rex winced as one bounced off her helmet right next to her eye.

"Deltas! Come up front with me. Betas! Get ready to throw some high-alt grenades!"

The wolves moved into formation behind her. Then she angled downward in a direct dive. The display in her retina counted down the altitude as she descended.

39,000 ft, 38,000...

They sped downward. The hail of bullets increased. Rex brought both arms up to shield her face, grunting against the danger whistling by. She wasn't even sure where the building was.

Then she saw it—a massive stretch of buildings,

camouflaged to blend with the sand. There was a line of guns on the roof, firing at them. The place was huge. Had she unknowingly stumbled upon a giant terrorist base?

More yells—someone was definitely hurt.

"One of you omegas, get ready to administer first aid as soon as we land. Betas! Are those grenades ready?"

"Yes, Alpha!" they barked.

"Aim for the guns! Let fly in three . . . two . . . one . . ."

As one, the betas let their grenades fall. A heartbeat of stillness—then a low boom and a crack. Smoke billowed up. Rex squinted against it, fighting the urge to cringe as memories of the hallucinogenic smoke filled her mind. The hail of bullets lessened abruptly.

"This is our chance!" Zyanya called. Rex knew she was right.

"Wolves, straight to the front door! Nigel, intercept the door code!"

"Kind of hard to do when I'm about to bloody die!" he yelled back. But he pulled up the display embedded in his hand sensors.

The feeling of falling without restraint was both terrifying and exhilarating. Training was nothing compared to this. The ground rushed toward Rex, miles of golden sand opening up to envelop her. She heard more gunfire as the smoke from the grenades cleared enough for the defenders to see them.

The ground—and the front door—came closer.

20,000...15,000...

"Nigel! Get that door open before we all hit it!"

"Workin' on it..."

10,000...5,000...1,000...

"We're going to die," Rex muttered.

031

With a scuttling noise, the door opened. Rex shot through the small opening and twisted her belt buckle just in time to prevent herself from meeting a high-impact death. She had no time to think as bullets pinged off the metal all around her. Whirling aside, she shouted more orders to her squad.

"Snipers! Guard the entrance. Squadron Two, follow me!"

It was a mess of darkness, swirling smoke, and yelling from all sides. Rex fired down into the mass of soldiers below, unsure if she was actually hitting anyone.

"Delta hounds! Seek!"

The hounds went ahead to search for explosives and map out the fortress. Rex caught sight of a tangle of pipes above them and made for it.

"Wolves, take cover up here!"

"Captain!"

Rex turned to where Rider had wedged himself behind a pipe. He rose up, fired several shots into the seething mass of enemies below, and went back into cover as bullets deformed the pipes all around him.

"When the Delta hounds get back, you go find

your father! I'll take over here."

Rex leapt out from her hiding place, squeezing the trigger as she soared across to where Rider was, and fell back into cover. "Not an option! You're coming with me."

"Rex, you know I'm a better shot than you. I can go through these guys easy."

Zyanya appeared around a bend in the hallway. "Rex, I've found a way to what I think is the prison level!"

Rex hesitated. She didn't want to leave Rider. *If something happens to him . . .* She gripped his sleeve. "I . . ."

Rider gave her an encouraging grin. "Go get what you came for."

Rex bit her lip and nodded, then turned away to follow Zyanya as Rider covered her back.

They pushed forward into the fortress at a much slower pace than Rex would have liked. Halls led into halls like the passages in a termite hill, and in each one a swarm of defenders would appear. Rex yelled with effort as her machine gun rattled nonstop. Around her, several members of her squad—people whose names she couldn't recall—held the enemy at bay. Beside her, Tanner and Cal swung their guns in an outward circle to cover their flanks, but every time someone went down, another person took his place.

"There's a lot of them!" Cal called.

"You're telling me?" Tanner replied, his gun rocking wildly with constant recoil.

Rex had taken to the ceiling to avoid presenting herself as a direct target. "Zyanya! How much farther?"

"I think just to the next hall! I can smell a change in the air there."

Rex swooped down and smashed her foot directly into the nearest defender's face. His gun angled skyward, and she felt more than one bullet clatter off her cybernetic leg. A few inches to the right, and it would have been her torso. Despite it being reinforced, it was not an area she wanted to risk getting a bullet in.

More defenders poured in, but Rex had had enough. She was here for her father, and no one was going to stop her from getting to him. With a roar, she smashed, hammered, and mowed her way through the defenders, ignoring the blood on her face and ignoring the stinging pain as a bullet grazed directly across her chin. She burst into the single hall beyond.

It was entirely empty, and led to a larger room that she couldn't see much of. Zyanya held up one hand to stop the squad's advance. She listened closely, sniffing the air.

"Something's not right. There's no one here. I'll seek ahead."

"Okay, take Tanner with you. If you see anyone, don't engage. Come back here and we'll make a plan for how to move through the next room."

Zyanya nodded and moved ahead, followed by Tanner.

Rex, Cal, and the five or so other squad members waited in silence for several agonizing moments. Rex could hear the quick breaths from several people as they remained alert, expecting danger to come at any moment.

Then the screaming began.

"Come on!" Rex yelled. She flew down the hall, following the sounds. Coming upon an open room, she saw Zyanya and Tanner in combat with a huge group of armed men. Rex howled a war cry and flew into the melee. Firing indiscriminately while punching and kicking, she carved a path toward the two delta hounds.

Someone's hand came down hard on her shoulder, swinging her around. Glowing green eyes stared at her. This time, she was not unnerved. With a yell, she hammered her metal fist into the man's jaw and was rewarded with an ugly cracking noise. The hand fell from her shoulder as the man dropped like a stone. More fists landed blows on her body. Her gun was too large to be used in such close quarters, so she threw it directly into the face of an attacker. Baring her teeth, she deflected multiple fists at once—right, left, backward, forward. Someone caught her on the cheek. With a growl, she brought her knee up into the figure's stomach.

"Alpha!" It was Cal. He held a lariat with several objects hanging from it in his hand. "I've found what I think is the key!"

Rex brought her elbow crashing into the side of a man's neck. She gasped as someone drove a blow into her ribs. "Coming!" Leaping up, she spun in the air and brought her cybernetic foot around in a whirlwind kick. Two men went down. It bought her just enough time to get higher.

"Cal, throw it!"

Cal hurled the lariat into the air. Rex caught it just as a hand reached up to pull her down. Clamping the precious keychain between her teeth, she wrenched her leg free and kicked the attacker. Past the crowd, a sliding door led to what she knew must be a vertical transit. The prison level had to be lower down. If she could just get to that door . . .

Zyanya's howl echoed across the room. Rex's heart sank. She knew that sound was not made out of fear. She ground her teeth together, feeling the lariat rope that held the key to her father's escape. But she couldn't leave Zyanya. With a roar, she leapt up and soared over the crowd, landing just shy of where the other girl lay, kicking feebly at an attacker who had fired a volley directly into her chest. Rex seized the man's shoulder. Yanking him backward, she grabbed his head in both hands and twisted his neck as hard as she could. With a sickening crunch, the man fell limp to the ground.

"Zyanya!" Rex knelt beside her friend. Blood coursed from the bullets that had torn open the other girl's flesh. Rex looked away from the mangled spectacle.

The Native American girl gripped Rex's arm. "Find . . . your father."

Rex shook her head doggedly. "We're going to get

you help. Come on, don't die on me now."

Zyanya managed a smile despite the pain. "You sound like Rider. He's a . . . good one . . . He loves you a lot." She fell into a fit of coughing. Blood spattered onto Rex's face. Zyanya's grip on Rex's arm tightened. "Share your trials with your warriors. It is strength."

"No. No." Rex grabbed hold of Zyanya and lifted her head, willing her to stay alive. "You can't leave me now. I need you."

"I'm going to die." Zyanya set her jaw. Her dark eyes pierced Rex with their determination. "Share your trials. Find . . . your father. Then I won't have done this for nothing." She fell back against Rex's hand, shutting her eyes, and brought both fists up over her torn chest in a final salute. A deep breath . . . then, nothing.

Rex bowed her head, grief overwhelming her. Then, with another savage roar, she hurled herself toward the remaining enemy soldiers. She shoved aside everyone in her path with a devastating blow.

"Wolves! We're getting to the prison level right now!"

"There's too many of them!" Tanner called. "I'll take over here. You go, we'll hold them off!"

Rex drove a punch into someone's stomach and risked a glance at Tanner. There was confidence in his eyes. He gave her a nod.

"Go."

She turned and ran for the doorway.

032

Rex swiped the key over the scanner in the doorway. The door shot open, and she leapt inside just as bullets spattered the metal around her. She slammed her fist against the first button she saw—the lowest level.

She gasped as the transit shot down at lightning speed. This was worse than free-falling; so much worse. She couldn't see where she was or where she would end up. Her breath turned to a single, drawn-out yell as she descended. Lights flashed around her. Each level that flew past brought with it increasing darkness. Then she hit bottom. Her entire body lurched, and she had to tighten her stomach to avoid vomiting.

She knew she had reached the prison the moment she saw it through the door. Rows of steel-barred cells stretched down a long hallway, like some animal containment facility. She fumbled with the keychain. Several cards were on it, and she couldn't be sure which one was the right one. She swiped each card across the scanner in quick succession. After the third swipe, the door creaked open.

Rex floated cautiously into the hallway. A thick

paw shot out and grabbed her shoulder. She grunted as the creature's claws stung her skin. Letting it pull her in close to the bars, she gave a kick to the first vulnerable spot she saw—a beady yellow eye. With a rumble, the creature released its hold on her.

"You've met Stenh, apparently."

Rex whirled around. A girl—or was it a woman?—stood in a corner between the stairwell and the first cell. She leaned on the edge of the bars, one leg tucked under her thigh-length skirt, a smile parting the red-purple lips on her face. Pigtails bobbed on each side of her head. Her eyes glowed luminescent green, like those of the assassin Rex had captured.

"Who are you?" Rex was in no mood for delays.

The girl's—woman's—smile grew wider. "I just run the experiments on these beautiful subjects."

"Where is Captain Jerich Hai?"

The green eyes widened. "Ohhh, so you're the captain's little girl. I've got a surprise for you."

"If it involves locking me in a room as dark as a cave with pain like I've supposedly never felt, like your assassin said, you'll have a hard time getting me through the door."

"Oh dear, I'm so terrified. Lucky for me, I've got all these wonderful experiments to do the work."

Rex had a surge of panic as she realized she had just voluntarily walked into the middle of an angry mob of prisoners. She tightened her jaw, determined not to show fear. "Try what you will. You won't lock me up. I'm here for my father, and a half-sized twelve-year-old like you isn't going to stop me from bringing him out." She realized that it vaguely sounded like something Rider would say.

The figure laughed, her head tilting back to reveal long fangs like a vampire's. "Oh, don't worry about bringing him out." She clapped her hands. "I think we've had enough pleasant conversation for now. Time for your surprise." Before Rex could move to stop her, the girl brought up a screen out of nowhere and pressed her palm to the scanner. "Sekhmet," she vocally identified herself to the scanner.

Rex turned as she heard a door open at the end of the hall. At first, nothing happened. Then a figure crawled out of the cell.

"I'll be watching to see how you do with him." Sekhmet giggled and jumped backward. A glass door closed, separating Sekhmet from Rex and the prison. Another closed off the door to the transit.

Rex turned to face the figure. He stood to full height, hands raised, ready to fight. Unlike the other creatures in this prison, he was human. His dark hair hung long and tangled about his hard features, and his eyes glowed amber rather than green. Rex's heart hammered in her chest, and she zoomed in on his face, assessing every detail that might tell her she had, after so many years, found her father. His nose was straight, his chin too small . . . his brows were similar, but too angry.

It was not him.

"You liar! What have you done with him? Where is my father?" Rex yelled. Her raised voice seemed to anger the man, who strode forward more quickly.

Sekhmet's voice carried through the glass. "Did I tell you your father was here? No, I don't recall saying that. You see, I'm no liar. I just let you hear what you wanted to believe. It was your own imagination."

Rex ground her teeth together. Sekhmet was right. And she had fallen for it. "But you knew who I was when I came in, and you know where he is. Where?"

The man stopped, his amber eyes assessing her. Rex raised her fists slowly, trying not to let Sekhmet distract her.

"Oh dear. I'm afraid he's dead. He was long before I got here."

The man sprang. Rex had no time to think as his fingers sought her throat, scrabbling over her shoulders. He grabbed hold of her hair and yanked hard. Rex yelped as she felt a handful being torn loose from her braid. She brought a solid punch to the man's jaw. He staggered back—but only a step. Then he was reaching for her throat again.

Fear caught at Rex's heart. That punch should have knocked him senseless, or at least brought him to the ground. She was forced to give ground as he leapt at her again. His limbs were everywhere—a punch to her arm, an elbow to her shoulder, and a knee driving the breath from her stomach. Desperate, she blocked his more severe blows. She had never seen so much raw, wild ferocity. She grabbed hold of his arm with her cybernetic hand, squeezing hard in a pressure point grip around his wrist. Pain came into the man's amber eyes, but it did not stop him. His other hand shot out, knocked her guard arm aside, and closed around her throat. He lifted her up. Rex felt herself falling as he pushed her toward the ground. She brought her knee up to his groin twice. He only grunted and shoved her onto the cement. Straddling her, he wrenched his other arm free from her grasp and squeezed her throat with both hands.

Stars burst in Rex's vision at the strength of the man's grip. There had to be a way out of this. Suddenly, she was furious. She had trained for weeks, survived Hell Week, fought off arrogant blackmailers like Roth, and come all this way—only to be told that her father was dead. She would not let it end like this.

She grabbed hold of the man's left arm, bucking her hips up violently. The man toppled sideways. He scrabbled desperately to regain his dominant position, but Rex held tight to his arm to keep him from regaining control. As he fell, she scooted backward, freeing her legs from his weight. Keeping hold of his arm, she pulled it between her legs and shoved his head down. He struggled and thrashed as she aligned his thumb upward and pressed her hips up.

There was a loud crack, and the man screamed as his elbow joint dislocated. Rex seized her advantage. She mounted the man and, as he tried to turn and get up, took control of his back. Wrapping her arms around his neck in a choke hold, her heels tucked into his thighs, she pulled back to cut off the blood flow to his head. The man thrashed, but Rex clung on and increased the pressure on his neck, knowing this was her only chance. The man fell still. Rex held her position for a few more seconds to make sure he wasn't bluffing. Then she stood, letting his limp, unconscious body slump to the floor.

"Sekhmet!" she yelled. The girl's face appeared at the window.

"What fun!" she giggled. Rex quivered with fury.

"When did my father die? And who killed him?"

A long, clawlike finger tapped against the girl's bright lip. "Hmm, it must have been at least seven years ago, because that's when I came. And the master must have killed him. Or at least ordered his execution."

"The master? Who is he?" Rex did not seriously expect Sekhmet to answer. To her surprise, the girl elaborated on her previous statement.

"He's someone who sees talent and potential and then cultivates it. I happen to be his most important experimentist."

Rex frowned at the unfamiliar word. "You mean scientist?"

"No, science is only part of the work I do. Most of it is psychological experimentation."

"Using torture, I assume." Rex decided it would be beneficial to keep Sekhmet talking while she figured out a plan to get out of the prison.

"Yes, of course! You understand torture. You've experienced a lot of it from your stepfather."

"How do you know about me?" Rex demanded.

"We've known things about most of the assets since your masters initiated Crisis Protocol. It made it easier for us to know what you feared most, based on what you lost. For instance, you lost your father and you lost his protection, so naturally you feared not being protected, or others not being so."

"How do you know that? What's Crisis Protocol?"

Sekhmet laughed. "When they gave you your tragedy."

"What?" Rex's head spun. "But . . . that . . ." Dread crept over her. If the Alliance had *given* her a tragedy . . .

They had let her father be killed.

Sekhmet continued gleefully, "You didn't really think the Alliance had simply learned about a convenient personal tragedy, then milked it to get their future prized asset to do what they wanted?"

Rex shook her head furiously. "No. They couldn't have . . ."

"Of course they did. They led your father to his death so they could play on your fears for the rest of your life. The Alliance is no different than we are, than my master is. The only difference is that they manipulate you secretly. We do it using pain."

The assassin's words echoed in Rex's mind. *No mind of your own, pretty . . . These people are not who you think . . .*

Why hadn't she seen it before now?

"Stupid, stupid," she muttered. She had known she couldn't trust the Alliance. But she had stopped listening to herself when she was recruited. She clenched and unclenched her fists as rage boiled inside her.

"You know why they call me Sekhmet?" The girl scratched idly at something on her claw. Rex watched her warily. Sekhmet continued without waiting for an answer, "In our old mythology, Sekhmet was a goddess of war and destruction. The fear of war, the fear of death . . . it's a powerful thing. Everyone hates leaving their life behind—the people they love, their accumulated wealth, the bodily pleasures. For some people, they have the additional fear of meeting a final judgement with whatever god or goddess they believe in. For others, they would rather die themselves than let it happen to someone they love. So you see, it can be used as a powerful weapon. I simply specialize in making people fear their deaths in a unique way."

While Sekhmet spoke, Rex's eyes darted around the room. She still had the keys. If she could just buy enough time to open the door to the elevator...

Bring back whatever you find, whether he is a man or a shadow of one.

That was what Master Ekeli had said. Had her master known who she would really find here? He had known her father was dead. He may have even led him to his death himself.

She should have seen this coming, but she had been too blinded by her desperate need to save her father. Maybe there was an explanation. She would return and demand the truth.

The man at her feet stirred. Rex bent down and

delivered two heavy punches to his jaw.

"What's your goal? Why are you telling me this?" Rex made as if to come face to face with Sekhmet, but used the movement to gain a bit of ground toward the vertical transit.

"I'm revealing the truth. Shat al-Shed and the Alliance are hardly different."

The door to the transit was only a few feet away. The scanner blinked steadily, waiting for the key to command it to open the door. Sekhmet seemed to guess Rex's intention.

"Don't bother trying to get out. It's locked. Those keys are useless. The only reason you got in was because I wanted you to."

Rex's heart sank. She set her jaw. Maybe she could crack the glass with her metal hand . . .

"Well, it's been lovely chatting. I'll leave you to my pets. They should take care of you, even though you incapacitated my favorite asset." She eyed the man on the floor. Then, with a laugh, Sekhmet swiped her palm over a scanner on her side of the door.

Every cell door in the hallway slid open.

033

Rex wished she had her gun. The creatures that crawled out of the cells were like something from a nightmare. Twisted, grotesque faces stared at her, each with blistered or scaly skin, and some with multiple sets of limbs. They shook themselves, peering around at their newfound freedom. Then all eyes, large and small, turned simultaneously on Rex.

With nothing but her fists and her arts training, Rex stood squarely as the creatures rushed toward her. The first, a piglike hunk with wickedly crooked tusks, galloped from the middle of the hall. Rex blocked its charge with her cybernetic leg. The boar squealed as she kicked its face. It charged again, its tusks seeking to tear her flesh open. From the left, a one-eyed dog the size of a German shepherd snarled and snapped. The creature Sekhmet had called Stenh grabbed Rex's hair and heaved her bodily from the ground. Rex yelled with pain as her entire weight was suspended from her single braid. She lashed out at Stenh. In response, the giant bearlike creature seized her shoulder and began crushing it.

More creatures piled in, each one scrabbling for a hold on her. Rex lashed out at anything that came within reach of her legs—snouts, claws, eyes. She was rewarded by several yelps of pain. But each time a creature fell back, another took its place. Claws scored a dozen scratches on Rex's body. She could feel blood trickling down her skin.

But she was not finished yet. With a supreme effort and a howling war cry, she grabbed hold of Stenh's arm and swung her feet up to hit his face. One, two, three times she kicked. As the bear-thing staggered back, Rex wrenched herself free from his grasp.

"Come and get me! Come on, just try!" She panted, fists raised, as the dog came at her again. Two humanoid figures circled behind her. She landed a staggering punch to the dog's open, slavering jaw and whipped around just in time to catch a fist aimed at the back of her neck. She threw the arm to one side and hammered her other fist into the attacker's face. Blood spattered on her hand. She blocked or caught or deflected every attack in a series of motions faster than she could draw breath. Her years of hypervigilance had made her alert to every sudden movement and possible threat, and she used that now to full advantage. Right, left, right, forward, left, backward . . . she held off every blow that sought to tear her limbs or break her bones.

Eventually, the sheer number of attackers began to exhaust her. She activated her shoes, trying to buy some space, but half the creatures could reach to the low ceiling and the other half could still bite at her feet. The dog sank its teeth into her ankle—

her heavy boots could only give so much protection—and jerked backward, throwing her to the ground. She kicked to free herself, but then the other creatures were piling atop her, crushing her with their weight.

So this is how I die. At least they can say it took twenty of them to bring me down.

Teeth and claws raked across Rex's body. She struggled ferociously, determined that she would not die without costing her attackers as much as possible.

"Alpha!"

Tanner's shout broke through the pack of snarling creatures. Rex heard two shots and the shatter of glass as the window in the elevator door was broken. Tanner hit the pack like a madman, howling and whooping as he blasted with his pistols. More blood spattered over Rex's face. Roars and groans echoed off the walls as the creatures scattered. Cal joined Tanner, hefting his AR-15.

Rex gasped as a creature tore its claws from her ribs and ran down the hall. Tanner knelt beside her.

"Come on, let's get you out of here," he said. He and Cal each seized one of her arms and lifted her to her feet. Rex moaned and gritted her teeth.

"Him . . . we have to bring him."

"Who?" Cal asked.

Rex raised a shaking finger and pointed to the man. He crouched in a corner, peering up at them with a sullen gaze.

"Why?" was the twins' immediate question.

Rex breathed deeply. It hurt to speak. "The master wants him. Quick! But whatever you do, restrain him before you put him in the carrier."

"Okay." Cal pulled out a small tranquilizer and fired two shots at the figure. As the man slumped, obviously weakened, Cal grabbed rope from his belt and secured the man's hands—though not without a struggle.

"Hurry. There'll be reinforcements coming from the south end of the building soon. I heard someone calling for it over a radio," Tanner said.

The other squad members were still in the transit, trying unsuccessfully to open the door properly. Rex, Cal, and Tanner had to squeeze into the elevator through the broken window one at a time. Tanner went first and helped Rex through. Next Cal prodded the man until he complied and allowed them to shove him through. Finally, Cal followed up the rear, firing a last shot at a braver—or more stupid—creature who tried to follow.

The transit shot upward. Rex had hoped it would be less difficult going back up, but she was wrong. The force of the ascent pushed her to her knees beside her squad members. Tanner let out a grunt, trying bravely to keep a supporting arm out for Rex to hold on to. Finally, the transit lurched to a halt and the doors opened.

From there, Rex let the twins lead the way. Cal had strapped the man to his back in preparation for flight, but that didn't stop him from going through any attackers with comparative ease. He called directions to the other squad members as they moved forward. Rex followed, blood and sweat blurring her vision. She shook with pain and found it difficult to fly in a straight line, especially with the tangle of attackers running around them and firing at them. But she pressed on, knowing that she had to keep going.

As they passed through the open room leading from the stairwell, Rex's eyes filled with tears. Zyanya lay, eyes closed, not twenty feet away. Rex wanted to go and say a last goodbye to the brave, loyal girl who had given her life so Rex could find her father.

She had given her life for nothing.

Near her lay Rex's machine gun, and Rex sped over and seized it, casting a quick look at Zyanya's still face. Then she turned to catch up with her squad members as a group of defenders pressed hard on their heels.

Out in the opening hallway, Rider and the rest of Rex's squad had taken control of the entrance and were holding up valiantly against the group of soldiers facing them. Roth's squad had blocked one of the main adjoining halls. Judging by the constant bark of Roth's voice, he had that hallway under control. Rex pushed to the head of her group and looked to where Rider, his face contorted with effort, blasted left and right at the swarms of soldiers coming at him. With a huge breath against the pain she was about to feel, Rex whispered an order. She hefted her machine gun and fired at the soldiers' exposed backs.

The surprise attack, though only manned by a small group, had an enormous effect. The enemy soldiers, suddenly attacked from behind, milled about in confusion like ants from a scattered anthill. Rex gritted her teeth and let out a low roar as the recoil from her machine gun sent waves of pain through her torn body. But the soldiers fell in front of her. She and her group quickly cleared a path to where Rider and the others had constructed a makeshift barrier of crates.

"Wolves, let's fly!" she yelled hoarsely. Just as they shot out the front door, Rex heard the thunder of hundreds of feet coming after them. Reinforcements. "We've got to make altitude as fast as we can!"

Bullets fired up at them as the reinforcements rushed out of the door. Rex pushed it to double speed to lead her squad to safety. She blinked hard. Her head jerked, and her flight path faltered. She was falling...

"Alpha!" Tanner caught Rex from behind. "We need a medic!" he shouted into the group. Rex's lips moved, but only a breath came. She tried again.

"No... time... do it when we get out of range."

Tanner hesitated, then nodded as a hail of bullets whistled by. "I'll get you on my back."

"No." Rider's voice cut in. It was not harsh, but it was firm. "I'm taking her."

Tears of pain and exhaustion squeezed out of Rex's eyes as Rider secured her to his back with a harness. "Thank you," she managed.

Rider's hand reached back and touched hers. "You're safe now. Let's get you home."

034

Rex woke up, once again, in the medical bay with glass walls surrounding her. Her eyes darted back and forth, and her breath came quickly as she tried to assess if she was in immediate danger.

"Hey." Rider's soft voice came to her ears like a breath of wind. She turned her neck—it was the only thing she could move without pain—and looked up into his face. He was sitting on a low rolling chair, which meant that his head was not much farther up than the bed.

"Rider. What happened? Did everyone make it out alright?"

Rider shook his head. "We've got at least ten people who are bedridden, and a dozen others who'll have to take it easy for a couple of days. We had one casualty. It was—"

"Zyanya," Rex finished. Tears spilled over her cheeks, and she let them come. "I couldn't get to her fast enough."

"Hey." Rider's fingers slipped into hers. "It's not your fault. Things like that happen in war. Thank God you didn't die, too."

"But she died for nothing. The man we brought

back—he isn't my father."

"What?" Rider frowned. "Then who is he?"

Rex ground her teeth in frustration. "I don't know! Some experiment of Sekhmet's. My father's been dead for years."

"Wait, who's Sekhmet? And your father is dead? But you got word only like a week ago that he wasn't."

"They lied to me." Rex grunted and heaved herself upright on the bed. "I have to go ask them what's really going on."

"Whoa whoa . . ." Rider gently tried to push her back down. Rex resisted. "You've got gashes on you that look like they were made by chopping knives. You need to rest."

Rex scoffed, acting tougher than she felt. Every breath certainly felt like a knife stabbing into her. "I'm sure they're not that bad."

"Rex, I bandaged you myself. Well, with Abbi's help. Don't go anywhere."

Rex stared into his eyes. "I have to," she said. Biting back a scream as her feet hit the floor, she pushed past him to the door.

Rex found Ekeli, Leah, and Bailey in the sergeant's office. Though she was limping, Rex managed to stand upright as she confronted her superiors by slapping a hand on the desk.

"You sent me in there believing a lie. You knew my father was dead. Because you let him die. Why?"

Ekeli exchanged a glance with Leah. "His death was for a greater good."

"What greater good?" Rex demanded. "Just like the death of Rider's little sister was for the greater good? Just like every other tragedy you've inflicted on each of the soldiers here?"

"What?" Rider's voice came from behind her, where he had followed her into the office.

"Yes, they've lied to your face, too, Rider," she said without looking. "They either let your sister die or they sent someone to kill her."

Leah stepped forward. "You don't understand. You were chosen for this project at birth. With that came insurance. We did what had to be done in order to motivate you."

"So 'motivation' was worth killing someone? You killed Zyanya's *whole tribe.* Yeah, Zyanya—that warrior who just died for your precious mission, who you probably know as Zero-Thirty-Eight—she lost everyone when she was a child. And that snarling animal I rescued was more important to you than my father? Really?"

Leah crossed her arms. "That 'snarling animal' is a very valuable experiment that must be studied. It was a weapon for Shat al-Shed. We hope to prevent more terrorist attacks by running tests on it so we can neutralize others like it."

"You even call him an it. That's how little you care."

Leah's eyes hardened. "You were the one that called it an animal."

Ekeli placed a hand on Leah's arm to calm her. "Rexala," he said in a reasonable tone, "the missions we have planned for you are all of such importance, it was necessary that we make them personal so you would complete your training and lead a squad into some of the deadliest places on Earth. After the war, we knew we had to build harder soldiers to help us survive. The Alliance needs your services more than you know. We have tried several of these missions—including the one you just completed successfully—with other forces, to no avail. There are other problems we have needed to address for a long time, and each recruit was given a tragedy that would qualify them to complete a certain type of mission. But, over time, Shat al-Shed became our top concern as we realized the scope of their project. Your tragedy was unique—and none of the other recruits had the drive to complete this particular mission at the heart of Shat al-Shed's experimentation base. It was our hope that we would not have to tell you that your father was dead."

Rex laughed bitterly. "How did you expect me not to know? The minute I looked at his face, I knew it wasn't him."

Ekeli sighed. "We had hoped . . . since you were a child at the time . . . that you would not remember him."

"So you were just going to fake that he was actually my father. Incredible." Rex looked around, searching for some explanation for such blatant dishonesty.

Sergeant Bailey, who had been silent up till now, spoke up. "I agree, Rex. It's a completely stupid and irresponsible way to motivate someone." She ignored the looks of annoyance from Ekeli and Leah. "But they didn't have a choice."

"Who's 'they?' Ekeli and Leah? Or some other Alliance official?"

Sergeant Bailey raised her eyebrows. "That's classified. Just know that your father's death caused more remorse for the Alliance than you realize."

Rex nodded sarcastically. "Hah! So much remorse that they had the audacity to film him being led to his death. Please, do let me know, what is so important about the man I brought back that it was worth killing my father and sentencing me and my mother to a life of torture?"

"You do not understand the danger of Shat al-Shed's experimentation," Ekeli said.

Leah cut in, "If their plan works, it'll launch China's one-world government."

"How so?" Rex challenged. "Sure, their experiments are horrible and vicious. They could probably kill a couple hundred people. But a handful of those isn't going to make a country like Russia submit to China."

"That's classified, Rex. I understand you're angry, and you have every right to be." Sergeant Bailey folded her hands across her desk. "But there's some information that you'll just have to do without for now. I can file a request to my superiors to see if I can give you anything else."

Rex clenched her fists. She nodded once. "Just like when you filed a 'request' for me to go save some psychopathic experiment I believed was my father."

"You're dismissed, Zero-Twenty-Seven," Sergeant Bailey said with an edge in her voice.

Rex turned, fists balled, breathing heavily, and strode out the door. Rider trotted to catch up with her.

"How did you know all that?" he asked.

"I talked to Sekhmet."

Rider sighed in frustration. "You never told me who that person was!"

"She's the experimentist for Shat al-Shed. She was the one who set all those experiments on me in the prison. I'm sure Tanner told you about that, since it ended with me covered in cuts that looked like someone attacked me with a chopping knife."

"Yes he did, but he didn't mention this . . . Sekhmet. Look, Rex, I'm just as shocked as you are. But you have to go back to the medical bay. We'll talk about this in a bit, when you're resting again." He caught her arm. "Please, Rexala."

Rex sighed. "Why did you have to call me that?" She felt her body giving in to exhaustion.

"Because I don't want to watch you die, covered in blood, too. Come on." He put his hand on her back and gently led her toward the medical bay.

***

Late that night, Rex lay on the flat mattress, her sleepless eyes staring up at the ceiling. She had gone over the events of the past day—along with the events of most of her life—repeatedly, trying to wrap her mind around the horrible duplicity of it all. Her father was really dead. After all these years, they had dangled her deepest hope in front of her like bait, telling her he might be alive. And like an ignorant fish, she had taken the bait. Through it all, she had ignored her intuition, what she had always known—that the Alliance couldn't be trusted. She should have known when they had captured the assassin. She should have known that it was too convenient that everyone here had a tragedy that was hidden. The Alliance had *caused* the tragedies. *Crisis Protocol.* Who knew what else they had done? What lengths were they still willing to go to in order to accomplish their goals?

After that, she had debated what to do next, now that she knew the truth about her father's death and the truth—or most of it—about the Alliance and the Stratotech Project.

She had a plan. She just had to wait for the guards in the hall to switch shifts, and for her body to gain enough strength.

The moment came. Rex pushed herself up from the bed, stifling a groan as her torn flesh burned from the movement. She took her necklace from the table beside the bed and slipped it around her neck. Her boots and belt were on the floor. She slid them on as quietly as she could. Twisting the belt buckle, she floated silently through the door and into the hall.

The guard's back was to her as he strode in the opposite direction. In a few seconds, his replacement would come. She had only moments to get into the dining hall. Airborne as she was, she managed it easily. From there, after she filled her water pack, it was a straight shot out the back door onto the compound —though she knew that door triggered an alarm at night.

She stopped by the weapons room. Though it was locked, her palm scan gave her access. She slung her machine gun onto her back. Going to a control panel she had seen Leah use to disable the barrier grid, she typed in the code that Rider had told her on their first date: *2374890242*. She selected the option to disable only the east side of the grid, by the training field, rather than shutting down the entire grid and leaving the other wolves vulnerable to another attack. On her way out, she grabbed a pair of fingerless gloves. Everything else she left behind.

"Halt! Identify yourself!"

A group, accompanied by Sergeant Bailey, was marching from the barracks toward her. Rex turned to face them, her eyes searching for only one person.

"Rex!"

There he was. Rider stood, half-dressed, a look of confusion on his face. Rex's heart throbbed. She wouldn't see him for a long time.

"Goodbye, Rider," she murmured. She knew he could hear.

Then she turned away and shot out into the open sky. Behind her, she heard Sergeant Bailey calling orders and wolves launching into the air in pursuit. She just had to get away. She had to clear her head and reassess where her loyalties lay. She knew it was not here at Stratotech.

"Shoot out her thrusters!" she heard someone call.

"Don't hurt her!" That was Sergeant Bailey. Rex felt a rush of respect for her sergeant. She, unlike Ekeli and Leah, actually cared about her soldiers.

Shots began firing. Rex swerved to avoid them, spinning in the air, diving, then swooping up. If she could just gain enough distance, she could lose them in the darkness . . .

Or if she went closer to the ground.

A shot hit her left boot. Smoke drafted up from it, and she heard it powering down. She had to get away before they shot her other one. Grabbing a smoke bomb from her belt, she activated it and hurled it as hard as she could into the torso of one of her pursuers. As his companions paused, confused, she switched off her boots and tightened her stomach against the dive.

The cold night wind rushed through her loose hair as she descended. She fell through clouds and licked their moisture from her lips. Rival wind currents sought to take control of her, but she kept her dive straight and true, never faltering. Behind her, she knew from the receding exclamations of surprise that she had lost her pursuers.

When she was only eight hundred feet up, she activated her boots again. Her descent slowed. Just as she reached the ground, with a puttering sound, her left boot died.

Feeling the familiar desert sand under her feet

once again, with the glorious freedom of nothing in sight—and no clear direction to take—Rex set off into the night.

035

Rider waited, kicking at the dust outside Sergeant Bailey's office. Bridget came out, running ahead of the group to meet him.

"What's the plan?" he asked.

"Roth's taking a team to go find her. She's a top priority."

"And why was I not allowed in? Can I go?"

Bridget clacked her teeth anxiously. "The sergeant—well, not really her, it was Ekeli and Leah—said that you're too emotionally attached to go. Ye'll have to stay here."

Rider pulled his hands through his hair with a groan, his mind racing as he and Bridget walked back toward the barracks. If Roth found her... well, he was certain that Roth wouldn't be able to drag Rex back to Stratotech without permanently damaging her.

They reached the dining hall. As Bridget was about to step up to the door for the customary pull-ups, Rider put out a hand to block her path. He drew her some distance from the door and spoke in a low tone, glancing around to make sure no one could hear. "I'm going after her."

Bridget's mouth formed into a small *O*. "Without permission?"

Rider nodded decisively. "Yes."

A smile lit Bridget's face. "I'm comin' with ya."

ACTION

Hey there! The name's Rideout Terrault Griffin; Rider for short. How you doing? Gotta be awesome after that book, huh?

Listen, I've got a super sweet deal for you. If you liked this book and wanna see more of me and Rex, you can get behind-the-scenes advance access to parts of our story before the rest of the world does! You'll also get extra content from the Stratotech world, like epic high-tech battles, assassin stories, genetic experimentation, mystery, a little romance...you know, the works. You might even get some of my well-guarded tragic backstory. Come on, you can't resist getting to know the big heart behind this bad boy!

But you know what the best part is? You could have a direct connection with the person who wrote this book! (I won't say author; I'm the author of my own story. She just summarizes the amazing things *I* choose to do.) And you could be part of the production of her next book! Not only would you get to help launch a potentially bestselling novel, but Mariel can connect you with her contacts in the author world and give you resources to get started writing your own bestseller!

Wanna read new quality science fiction content every week? Wanna be friends with a real author and get exclusive tips that'll boost you on the path to success?

Well, my awesome admirer, I've got the keycard to unlock all these benefits. Guess what? It's absolutely free! Just go to the homepage at www.thecybersoldierlink.com, enter your best email address in the subscription form so you won't miss any important updates, and *presto!* You'll get complete access to everything I just mentioned.

Now, once you're done with that, just leave a review on Amazon and tell other book-lovers all the things you love about me (and the book). I'm a pretty cool guy, but I can only do so much, so I need you to promote me, and reviews are the number-one way you can support me. Thanks, comrade!

Well, see you in the next installment of the Stratotech series! Over and out.

ACKNOWLEDGEMENT

Thank you so much to all the people who made this novel possible! First, to my Creator, who gave me a passion for creativity. To my mom and my younger brother. In honor of the broken parts of myself that I wrote this book to heal. To my editor, Courtney Andersson, who pushed my limits and made this book a thousand times better, and to Natalia Junquiera, my patient cover designer. To Teresa and Nick, my writing buddies. You guys got me out of so many rough spots with your suggestions! To the people at Self Publishing School who helped me make my book a success, especially Barbara, my one-on-one coach. To all the friends who supported me and joined my launch team. This is the first novel of a lifetime of writing, so get ready for many more! I might even write one of my future novels on a getaway in Rome…stay tuned!

Have an awesome 2021!

ABOUT THE AUTHOR

M. T. Lancet

Mariel Teresa Lancet is a young author with a passion for all things dramatic and creative. Fast-paced stories with plot twists, internal conflict, and compelling themes are her favorites. Her debut novel, Stratotech 027, is the first of a science fiction series in an apocalyptic world. She loves to travel and also enjoys art, bold fashion, and hip-hop dancing. Mariel lives in the Woodlands, Texas.

Made in the USA
Coppell, TX
22 March 2022

75358105R10184